A RAMAZ DONADZE THRILLER

NO HARM DONE

AJ LIDDLE

Disclaimer:
This is a work of fiction. All characters, locations, and businesses are purely products of the author's imagination and are entirely fictitious. Any resemblance to actual people, living or dead, or to businesses, places, or events is completely coincidental.

ISBN: 978-1-8381911-0-8

For Jacqui and for Mum

Every rose will fade and wither, no matter though it once was fair.
The dry rose falls within the garden, a new rose arises there.

—Shota Rustaveli, The Knight in the Panther's Skin

ONE

It was four in the morning and Donadze lay sweating in the narrow bed, listening to the arthritic whir of Tamuna's air conditioning losing its unequal battle with the August city heat. Forty degrees yesterday and something similar threatened today. *God, I really hate summer,* he thought. The heat and humidity made sane people go crazy and he'd had no option but to endure the drunken carousing and alcohol-fuelled protestations of love and courage bellowed in the streets below. The partying had been tailing off by two and he'd fallen asleep, only to be woken shortly after by fireworks set off by a senseless fool, the flashes and bangs lighting up apartment bedrooms and rattling windows but winning appreciative cheers from the remaining drunks still out enjoying their cigarettes and the dregs from their bottles.

The heat and the noise didn't seem to bother Tamuna. She'd left the apartment an hour ago. He'd kept his eyes closed, feigning sleep, still smarting from their row. He'd convinced himself that she had been at fault but now, lying alone, he'd rewound their argument in his head and realised that his words had been chosen to wound. He groaned in self-despair, only now anxious to be given an opportunity to apologise, to make amends.

He picked up the note she'd scribbled, *'Been called into Casualty—multiple car crash west of the city.'* Georgian roads were always dangerous, but especially so in the summer when city dwellers dashed to and from the Black Sea coast, too many with a relaxed attitude towards the country's strict but casually enforced drink-driving laws.

Sane people gone crazy, he thought again. He re-read the note, trying to decide if it was deliberately abrupt. With no signature and no expression of affection, he concluded it was.

It was almost a relief when his phone rang. 'Donadze.'

'*Gamarjoba*, Lieutenant. Mtatsminda Station here. Patrol's fished a girl out of the river. Looks like she was helped in. Right bank near the dry-stone bridge. Duty detective required.'

'Thirty minutes.'

Donadze washed and dressed, picked up his ID, pistol, phone and wallet and was out of the apartment in ten. It had been nearly impossible to find parking close by and he was freely sweating in the damp, still air by the time he reached his ageing BMW. He started the engine and cranked up the air conditioning. *Thank God for German engineering.*

2

'What happened to this girl?'

She looked young. The uniformed officers had dragged her out of the Kura and there she lay on the river bank, landed like a fish, eyes drying out and milky, skin purple, lips ghostly white, dyed blond hair matted and rank with river water, straggling what might have once been a beautiful face.

Metreveli was the medical examiner. He pulled back the plastic sheet covering the near naked body. 'Well, Lieutenant, I'll be able to give you better information after I get her back to the morgue, but she was strangled and probably dead before she went in the water.' He used a pencil to point to the corpse's lower neck. 'She was most likely killed by a thin rope. Not been in the water very long, maybe six or eight hours. Dead maybe a few hours before that. As you know, external signs are often absent in victims of strangulation. We're lucky that *our* victim is exhibiting red linear marks and bruising to her neck, both of which are consistent with strangling by ligature.'

Just another stiff to you, Donadze thought. 'Not my idea of luck, Doctor,' he said.

Metreveli winced and exchanged a look with the officer opposite, *Donadze the hard ass*. 'I think you know what I meant, Lieutenant.'

'Who was she?'

The officer had been enjoying the exchange between Donadze and Metreveli but now fumbled for his notebook. 'Her name was Nino Adamia. We've seen her at the Dream Casino. Call girl in Kaldani's stable. Top of the range—two thousand *lari* a pop, I heard.'

He was referring to Dato Kaldani, head of the family crime business which had known interests in drugs, gambling, prostitution and most other categories of felony and misdemeanour.

'Kaldani's *stable*? Does she look like a horse to you?'

'No, sorry Lieutenant.'

Kaldani had inherited the family business from his old man, Zaza. A low-level gangster from Shida Kartli, the breakaway region known internationally as South Ossetia, Zaza had exploited the anarchy arising during and after the civil war and the endemic corruption that had followed under President Shevardnadze. The Rose Revolution in 2003 and subsequent clean up by President Saakashvili had driven many of his competitors out of business but Zaza had seen that day coming and had burned time and money, making political connections and buying influence. He managed to survive several assassination attempts by jealous challengers, but his son was already in charge by the time he succumbed to his three packs a day habit.

The Kaldani family flourished as Dato consolidated power in Tbilisi and eastern Georgia as well as making connections in Armenia, Azerbaijan and Russia. Donadze had investigated many crimes committed by the family, most with limited success as Dato was generous and ruthless in equal measure. Loyalty and silence provided a good living. Betrayal guaranteed a slow and painful death.

He gazed at the girl's body. *I'm sorry this has happened to you, Nino. But I will find who did it,* he silently promised. He shook his head and looked away. He had made the same promise to all his murder victims but had let down several and failed to achieve justice for his own sister. He turned to the uniform. 'Next of kin?'

'Mother's in Rustavi. We were going to let the locals notify her.'

'Too close to shift change for you? Don't worry, I'll speak to her myself.'

The medical examiner was fidgeting—his work at the crime scene was complete and he wanted to go home.

Donadze turned to climb the bank. 'Let me know when you're ready to start the autopsy.'

Rustavi depressed him. A Stalinist monument to central planning, it was constructed to provide accommodation for the workers employed at the huge steel plant, Soviet Georgia's largest industrial complex. The plant was now defunct and stood rotting in apocalyptic silhouette, the twelve thousand jobs it had supported now gone.

Multiple lines of low-rise Soviet era apartment blocks reached out in regimented symmetry from the town's main thoroughfare. Most apartment balconies had been walled up with brick, block or timber to create a little more living space than central planners had thought necessary. Laundry was cranked out on pulleys to dry in the hot humid air and side streets were littered with potholes and smashed lights. The sickly grey concrete facades of some blocks had been painted to soften the brutalist impact of unaccountable urban planning and political dogma's victory over humanity, but the overall impact was oppressive and alien.

Adamia's mother carried an air of defeat, despair and inevitability as she opened her apartment door. 'You've come about Nino,' she said softly, holding onto the door for support.

Donadze recited his standard consolation as she set about preparing food and drink for her guest, as tradition required. He put her age at about forty, but she could have been sixty. She was thin and dressed carelessly in skirt, leggings, and a faded blouse. Her skin was an unhealthy grey and she moved stiffly about the tiny apartment.

Donadze looked at the few photographs on the dresser which dominated the living area. One was of a young woman and man in formal wedding pose and two others were of a pretty girl of about fourteen and later at about eighteen. The young teenager looked care-free and innocent, but the older girl seemed more aware and knowing.

'Mr. Adamia?' Donadze asked.

'Died five years ago, cancer, this place probably.'

'I'm sorry. May I ask you some questions about Nino?'

Donadze politely nibbled a small slice of cold greasy *khachapuri* as Mrs. Adamia recounted Nino's short life story. She was a bright girl, very spirited and a head-turner from an early age. It was obvious that Rustavi and the local boys wouldn't hold her, and she had left to go to Tbilisi when she was eighteen. Her looks helped and she had found work in the bars and the international hotels which were springing up as Georgia became established on the global tourist map. Tbilisi was less than one hour away by bus and Nino had, at first, visited her mother on a weekly basis.

'I'm not stupid. I could tell she couldn't afford the

clothes and jewellery or the cash she gave me from hotel work. I didn't like it, but I can't say that she had a worse life than me. She was still my daughter, but we lived in different worlds. It's been two months since I last saw her—and now I have no one.' She blinked back her first tears and looked at Donadze searchingly. 'A girl like Nino, she's not going to be a priority for you, is she?'

Donadze rubbed his fingers together to remove the cheese grease and stood to place a hand on the woman's shoulder. 'We all try to make the best choices in life we can, Mrs Adamia. It doesn't matter to me what choices Nino made or why she made them. Someone took your daughter from you and it's my job to find them. And I will do that, I promise you.'

TWO

Donadze pulled into the Mtatsminda Police Station car park after stopping to buy some corn bread, a favourite from his childhood in Abkhazia. He had a desk in the detectives' bureau, an open-plan area within the station where he and his colleagues could do their paperwork, most of it now essentially digital. He strolled to the kitchen area to make a coffee. Misha Arziani was already there. 'Hey, Ramaz, I heard you picked up the Kura job last night,' he said, pouring boiling water into Donadze's mug.

Arziani had spent three years in uniform before joining the Crime Police as a detective. He was in his late twenties and kept in good shape by playing rugby and basketball. He was a smart dresser, with thick expensively groomed hair and tightly controlled stubble. Unusually for Georgian men, he neither drank nor smoked. That and his speedy promotion to sergeant meant he was viewed with suspicion by some of his older colleagues. He and Donadze had worked a few cases together and Donadze had found him to be both smart and conscientious.

'Yeah, real shame, wasted life,' Donadze said.

'Well, let me know if I can help.'

Donadze knew that Arziani was ambitious and would have liked the Adamia case for himself. 'Thanks, Misha, will do,' he said, returning to his desk.

He logged on to the Crime Police system, took a sip from his mug and sat back in his chair to gather his thoughts. He glanced up to see the station commanding officer, Captain Dima Bukia, motioning to him through the glass of his small office at the top end of the bureau.

Bukia was in his mid-fifties and hoped to retire within a few years. He had survived the mass sackings initiated by Saakashvili after the 2004 presidential elections, not by merit of efficiency nor integrity but because Saakashvili had prioritised clearing out the inept and inherently corrupt Traffic Patrol, the uniformed branch most despised by the citizens of Georgia.

Bukia's office stank of stale cigarette smoke and poor hygiene. He eased himself into the chair behind his desk, wheezing from the effort, his shirt buttons straining against a belly bloated by too much stodgy food, wine and lack of exercise. He attempted a smile as he motioned for Donadze to sit opposite. 'Tell me about the Adamia case, Ramaz.'

The Captain's seemingly friendly manner and use of his first name made Donadze uneasy as he recounted the limited information he had gathered to date.

Bukia nodded distractedly. 'So, Lieutenant, what are your thoughts? Sounds to me like your girl picked up the wrong client. Maybe he got angry after she tried to rip him off? Maybe a sex game gone wrong? We've both seen this kind of thing before. How much time are you going to need to close this case?'

'Not really *my* girl Captain. And it's difficult to say at this stage how much time I'll need. I want to know who Nino had seen recently. She might have kept a diary or maybe she had something on her phone. I'll be visiting her apartment in Vake and see what I can find there. I also want to speak to Kaldani and see what he knows.'

'You're saying Kaldani is involved in this?'

'It's possible. We know that Nino was working for Kaldani and making him good money. If he had nothing to do with the murder, he'll at least be pissed that one of his best girls is out of the picture. But maybe he was involved? Maybe Nino wanted out and he was sending a message to his other girls? I'll get a feel for that after I speak to him.'

'I'm not so sure about that, Donadze. You're obsessed with that man. He's not the only gangster in Georgia, is he? Kaldani might have been running *your* girl and it's even possible he might have had something to do with her murder. But at this stage you have no evidence. Whether you like it or not, Kaldani has friends and I don't need calls from HQ or the Prime Minister's office complaining that one of my officers is harassing a prominent citizen.'

So, there it is, Donadze thought. *This is about more than protecting your pension. How long have you been on Kaldani's payroll, Captain?*

'Have I made myself clear, Lieutenant?' Bukia snapped.

'Crystal, Captain. I'll enter a file note to record your instruction.'

'Don't be a smart ass, Donadze. I have advised you, as your senior officer, how I expect you to conduct this case. I have not given you specific instructions in your dealings with Dato Kaldani or anyone else for that matter. Is *that* clear?'

'Crystal, Captain,' said Donadze, standing to leave.

Donadze returned to his desk. He thought about calling Tamuna to apologise for the row earlier that morning but sent a cowardly text instead. *'Still good for dinner this evening?'*

He started a new file on Nino Adamia, recording the information obtained to date and setting out his draft investigation plan. His first objective was to track down her most recent movements and determine who she had been in contact with.

He drove to the fashionable district of Vake in the west of Tbilisi. Vake was popular with foreign business and embassy people and the limited number of Georgians who could afford the high-end apartment leases. *Out of my league*, Donadze thought as he left Chavchavadze Avenue and entered the warren of narrow and congested side streets. He passed several restaurants, bars and coffee shops, most with French, Italian and other international names and aspirations as he searched for Nino's apartment block on Abashidze Street. A forensic examiner's van and a marked police car were parked on the road ahead, telling him that he had found the correct location. Donadze got out his car, leaving a laminated sheet printed with "Official Police Business" on the dash.

The modern apartment block nestled comfortably with the faded genteel nineteenth century architecture which characterised this district. The contrast with the Soviet era block where the murdered woman had been brought up was stark. *Quite a change for you, Nino*, Donadze thought.

The elevator was quiet and took Donadze smoothly to the seventh level. He walked a few metres to the apartment entrance. A uniformed cop was leaning against the corridor wall, drawing deeply on a cigarette, the patterned sole of his shoe resting against the white painted wall.

Donadze glanced at the half dozen or so cigarette stubs ground onto the marbled floor. '*Gamarjoba.*' He showed his ID.

'*Gamarjoba.* Are you here to investigate the whore's murder?'

'I am here to investigate the murder of the occupant of this apartment, a twenty-year-old female called Nino Adamia. What are you doing here?'

The officer straightened. 'I have been instructed to secure Miss Adamia's apartment and only let authorised personnel enter, Lieutenant.'

'Very good, and am I authorised to enter?'

'Of course,' the officer said, stepping to one side.

'Thanks. I'm sure you will want to brush up your cigarette stubs and clear your shoe prints off the wall before you leave.'

Pushing the yellow crime scene tape aside, Donadze

entered the apartment. It was pleasantly cool. A wood lined corridor led off to several rooms with open doors, through which he could see two bedrooms, a shower room, toilet and large storage cupboards. A spacious balcony fronted the equally spacious lounge which was tastefully decorated with ornaments and art pieces set on dark wooden cabinets. Limited edition prints and water colours were arranged on the walls with spotlights presenting them to best effect. Donadze thought the seating would be described as contemporary but, to him, just looked uncomfortable. The kitchen was equipped with marble work surfaces, a barn-doored American fridge freezer and top-end German appliances. Utensils and pots and pans, which looked unused, hung off stainless steel rails.

Natia Gagua was the forensic examiner assigned to the case. She was middle-aged and wore fashion normally designed for women at least twenty years younger. Donadze admired her apparent disdain for approval. An introvert by nature, he also felt slightly intimidated by her exuberant personality.

She had put on protective clothing to enter the crime scene. Donadze watched as she bent to sprinkle black magnetic fingerprint powder onto a television controller. Several items had already been bagged, sealed and labelled, ready to be taken to the lab for DNA analysis.

'Hey, Ramaz,' she said, without looking around.

'Hey, Natia, good to see we have the A-Team on the job.' They had worked several successful cases together. Her professionalism and calm demeanour under hostile cross-examining meant her trial testimony was rarely undermined.

'What have you got?'

She turned and took her mask off. 'Flattery could get you everywhere, Donadze,' she smiled broadly. 'Well, we haven't finished here yet but, so far, we've not found any evidence to suggest that Adamia was killed in this apartment. That's not to say it *didn't* happen here though. She was strangled, I believe, and that could have been achieved without too much of a struggle, especially if she had been drugged beforehand.'

'Any signs of that?'

'Only recreational substances found. There was a small bag of coke in the bedroom and some traces on the bedroom units. Probably got snorted there. Maybe by her or maybe it was a service offered to clients—I'm told it boosts sexual performance,' she said, winking suggestively at Donadze.

He chose to ignore her teasing. 'Any digital evidence?'

'We've bagged her laptop and iPad. No sign of a mobile phone but it was probably synced with the iPad and the cloud so we should get most of her images, contacts and mail once we've cracked the passwords. Shouldn't be too difficult.'

'Notebooks, diary?'

'Thought you'd never ask.' Gagua held up a clear plastic evidence bag containing a small book. 'This seems to be her diary. Take a look.'

Donadze put on the latex gloves she offered. Holding the notebook by its edges he flicked through the pages. He recognised the names of a few prominent people, including some foreigners, but most were unfamiliar. 'Can you get this to me as soon as possible?'

'Of course. Have I made you happy, Donadze?'

'You've no idea. All right to look around?'

'Feel free.'

Donadze carefully went room to room. The apartment had a melancholy feel to it. The kitchen had only a little food, but the fridge was well stocked with champagne, white wine and European beer. Bottles of French vodka were stacked in a freezer drawer. One bedroom held a king-size bed, the cabinets containing branded clothing, some still in their store wrapping. He opened bedside drawers and saw lingerie and sex toys.

The other room held a single bed with a long nightdress folded under the pillows and a battered teddy bear standing guard on the pillow top. A single picture of her mother and the wedding picture Donadze had seen in Rustavi sat on the bedside cabinet. *I know where you preferred to be,* he thought.

His phone buzzed a curt text from Tamuna. '*Okay, King David at 8.*'

Should have called her, you idiot, he told himself again.

Donadze made a point of arriving at the King David on time. Built into old brick cellars on the bank of the Kura River, it was their favourite Old Town restaurant. He ordered a bottle of *Tsinandali* and, feeling nervous after their row, was two glasses in by the time Tamuna arrived. She walked through the restaurant, attracting attention from the male customers and frowning when she caught him glancing at his watch.

He sometimes found it difficult to believe that she was with him. Definitely *punching above my weight*, he thought. Tamuna was thirty, two years younger than Donadze, but looked about twenty five. She was average height, slim with long dark hair, which Donadze liked loose on her shoulders, but which she often wore tied back, especially when working. She used little makeup and had an understated but effective fashion sense. Dressed in denims and a white cotton blouse with a scarf tied loosely around her neck, she looked beautiful, Donadze thought.

Tamuna's family was from a small village in west Georgia, twenty kilometres inland from the Black Sea coast. Her father had died two years previously. A physicist, he had been unable to find work in his discipline after the collapse of the USSR and had stayed home, tending a small number of animals and growing fruit and vegetables in the hectare of land surrounding the house his family had owned for four generations. His efforts meant that the family was self-sufficient in food and could generate a small income selling produce at the village market and by the side of the road which ran past their house. Her mother was a retired teacher, still living in their family home with income from a small state pension and the garden produce she continued to sell.

Her parents had instilled the value of education in Tamuna and her brother, Erekle. She had left home to study medicine in Tbilisi and was now an orthopaedic surgeon at the Medifirst Clinic. The Clinic operated a casualty department and Tamuna was periodically on-call for major incidents in addition to holding a routine orthopaedic surgery. Donadze had met her when he was checking on a detective who had broken his arm during a pursuit.

He stood to kiss her, but thought she was a little reserved, probably because of their row the previous night. 'Tough day?' he asked.

'Most days are but, yes, it was pretty bad last night. Two fatalities from the crash, one a young girl. Several life-changing injuries as well—all very avoidable, unfortunately. It was mid-morning before all the survivors were stabilised and then I had to see some urgent cases at my surgery after that. How about you?'

'You must be exhausted after all that—but I'm really pleased that you could still meet me. I'm okay, working on a new case—a murdered call girl with connections to a gangster called Dato Kaldani.'

'I've heard of him. Is he dangerous?'

'Not as dangerous as me,' he joked. Getting no response, he continued, 'Listen Tamuna, about—'

'Have you chosen what you would like to eat?' the waiter interrupted.

Neither was very hungry and the waiter hovered as they chose a few dishes to share.

Donadze tried and failed to fill the awkward silence with small talk, then gave up.

'Tamuna, I'm sorry about this morning. I was in a foul mood and you got the brunt of it.'

'Yes, I did, and not for the first time. What's bothering you Ramaz?'

'Nothing...well maybe the heat and maybe the job. I don't know, it's in my nature I guess.'

'Well, this is not going to work if—'

'Another bottle?' the waiter interrupted again.

'No!' Donadze snapped.

'Just a glass for me, please. *Tsinandali* is fine.'

Donadze frowned at the implied reproach. 'I said I was sorry.'

'And you've said it before and probably meant it then as well. Listen Ramaz, it's late and I'm too tired to eat. You stay and have your meal. But I think you should go to your own apartment tonight. Call me tomorrow.'

'I really am sorry.'

She examined him closely for a minute, gave a slight shake of her head before putting her napkin on the table and standing to leave.

Donadze watched her walk to the door. 'At least my aircon works,' he said quietly to her back, trying for and failing to find, consolation.

THREE

Donadze didn't sleep well in his Kandelaki Street apartment. The drunks were out again but his mind was racing, and he wouldn't have slept anyway. He eventually got up and watched television. TV1 news had a short piece on a body being recovered from the Kura River—the Police categorising the death as murder.

He still felt numb from his disastrous dinner with Tamuna. He thought about calling her or sending flowers but did neither, instead recovering his car from the apartment block's underground parking and heading to Mtatsminda Station.

Donadze wasn't surprised that Captain Bukia hadn't made it in yet and there was only one other detective in the bureau. His desk phone was flashing, and he picked it up and listened to a bright voice mail from Natia Gagua.

'Hey Donadze, it's your favourite forensic examiner.

Good news, we cracked Nino's laptop and iPad. Same password on both, mother's maiden name, would you believe? I'm getting them sent over to you. I had a quick look myself and there aren't many contacts, looks like she didn't have a lot of friends. She's got a Facebook account of course, who hasn't? As for the diary—you'll recognise some of these names. I'll take copies and email them over. Hope you're still happy! Take care, Ramaz.'

There were no messages from the medical examiner which probably meant that Metreveli hadn't started the autopsy yet. Either that or he was making Donadze sweat for the results. It didn't matter. There was no doubt that Nino had been murdered and Donadze knew that the best chance of finding any killer is when evidence and witness' memories are fresh.

Feeling tired, he made a strong coffee with plenty of sugar and logged onto his Police account to find Gagua had already emailed copies of Nino's diary. His phone buzzed. 'Please come to my office, Lieutenant.' He looked up, Bukia had arrived at the station and was staring at him through his office glass.

'Right away.' Donadze pointedly took a few minutes to finish his coffee and shut down his computer before getting up.

Bukia's desk was littered with stray documents and stodgy food. His face was red and sweaty as he nodded to Donadze to sit opposite. 'I warned you yesterday, Lieutenant, this Adamia case is attracting a lot of attention. What new information do you have?'

'Attention, Captain? May I ask from whom?'

'That's not relevant to your investigation, just answer my question.'

'It's still very early days. I'm trying to build a picture of who Nino knew and who she had seen shortly before being killed. Gagua has her diary but I've not seen it yet,' he lied. 'I'll obviously want to speak to her last clients and friends as well as Kaldani. One of these people might have been the last to see her alive.'

Bukia shook his head impatiently. 'We talked about Kaldani and I hope you remember my guidance on how to proceed. The same goes for anyone listed in that book. Subtlety isn't your strong point, Donadze. Watch how you go. I wouldn't want to have to take you off this case.'

'Thank you, Captain, I appreciate your support. Will that be all?'

Bukia stared at Donadze for a long moment. Donadze, face neutral, stared back.

'Get back to work,' the Captain said, reaching for his breakfast.

The autopsy was well advanced by the time Donadze arrived at the morgue—Metreveli and his technician had a reputation for efficiency.

He looked at the corpse laid out on the aluminium table—cold, pale and grotesquely violated. A rubber block had been placed under the chest to raise it and allow easy access for the medical examiner's tools.

Metreveli eyed him through his protective visor. 'Here

to check up on Tariel and me?' he said, nodding at the technician who was chasing bloody body fluids into the table drains with a water jet.

'Not exactly, but I would appreciate an update.'

'Always happy to help the Crime Police! Well, as I told you at the riverbank, this woman was strangled. The abrasions and contusions to the neck are classic indicators. I suspect the murder weapon was a thin rope, possibly about ten millimetres in diameter, nylon or another synthetic material.'

'Time of death?'

'Difficult to be sure of the exact time, as you know. However, I would estimate eight to twelve hours before she was found. That would put the murder at between twelve and four the previous afternoon.'

'When will you have completed your sample analysis?' Donadze said, referring to the examination of stomach contents and organ tissue.

'We'll be finished at the table in about an hour. Tariel will put everything back together and stitch her up while I get my microscope out. We'll be done by mid-afternoon.'

Donadze turned to the technician. 'Make sure you return this girl to her mother the way she remembers her,' he said.

There had been a thunderstorm a couple of hours previously and the air was cool and fresh as Donadze parked his car and took the elevator to his fourth-level apartment. He poured a glass of *Mukuzani* and sat in the quiet of his lounge, considering his next move.

He was almost pleased that Dato Kaldani was part of the investigation but recognised how perverse that was. Bukia had accused him of being obsessed with Kaldani and he knew that to be true. He didn't know why he was so fixated. Perhaps because he and Kaldani were both in their early thirties and both were born and raised in Georgia's separatist regions. If circumstances had been different, might he have followed a similar path?

Donadze had studied the man and learned much about him. Legend had it that Kaldani had killed for the first time at age eleven—a gangland execution, the pistol handed to him by his father.

Violence in all its forms seemed to fascinate Kaldani and he became expert in the use of personal weapons, particularly guns and knives. He was also a gifted kickboxer, later graduating to mixed martial arts where he competed in amateur events.

Donadze had attended one of these events, staying in the shadows. Kaldani seemed to have no fear and showed no mercy, attacking his opponent ferociously, even after the referee had attempted to stop the fight.

It seemed to Donadze that defeat for Kaldani wouldn't have been smart for his opponent or for the referee, but he couldn't deny that he had talent.

He kept himself in good shape and dressed well. With carefully styled hair and three-day designer stubble, he could be mistaken for an Italian footballer in the twilight of his career. He owned several exotic sports cars and SUVs. His good looks, apparently glamorous lifestyle and easy access to cocaine and other drugs meant he had no problem attracting beautiful girls. But Donadze had heard he liked his sex rough and the girls didn't stay long.

Kaldani wasn't the only crime boss that Donadze had dealings with but there was something dark and malevolent about the man that chilled his blood. There was no doubting his intelligence or strategic instincts. His father had done a fine job grooming him to take over the family business, but Kaldani had extended his reach across Georgia and into neighbouring countries in ways that Zaza could not have imagined.

He worked hard on his public image, donating cash and volunteering to work on community projects across the country. Not quite Robin Hood, but it made him popular with the gullible. He also extended the family's influence with politicians, judges and the media. He recognised that it was easier for powerful people to associate with him if he could demonstrate a pretence of respectability. Some of his businesses were indeed legitimate, albeit useful money laundering conduits.

The two men had crossed paths many times over the years. Kaldani had even provided information on rivals. They'd talked off the record and Donadze had been struck by how he was able to justify himself. It was possibly an exercise in self-delusion but Kaldani could argue, quite persuasively, that crime was a human condition, that what he did was no different from what governments did, only on a smaller scale, that he was providing employment and that ordinary citizens had nothing to fear from him.

He even managed to strike a patriotic note, claiming that, if his family was not controlling the different markets: drugs, gambling and prostitution, then the vacuum could be filled by the Russian or Chechen mafia, both of whom were, of course, foreign and possibly even more ruthless than himself. Such was his argument and, at some level, Donadze could understand his logic.

Tamuna had been alarmed on hearing that Kaldani was part of the investigation. She knew he was dangerous and, although he had tried to laugh it off, Donadze understood her concern better than anyone. He knew his badge wouldn't protect him if Kaldani felt threatened and that there were many ways he could strike back. He knew he couldn't expect Bukia to watch his back and he resolved to treat Kaldani with the respect an adversary of his calibre deserved. *But I'm still coming for you Dato*, he thought.

Kaldani kept an office on Rustaveli Avenue, close to the Parliament building. *Convenient if you're shopping for politicians*, Donadze thought.

He had made an appointment for one and arrived on time. A middle-aged woman occupied a desk which guarded the door to Kaldani's inner office. She was conservatively dressed in a dark grey trouser suit with short stylishly cut hair, the name plate on her desk indicating that she was Kaldani's personal assistant.

Donadze showed his ID. 'I have an appointment.'

She offered a professional smile. 'Of course, Lieutenant.

Please take a seat. Mr. Kaldani is finishing a call with an associate. He'll see you soon.'

Donadze scanned his surroundings. The clean lines, wall hangings, deep carpets and soft lighting suggested a legitimate and prosperous business, which was clearly the intention, he thought. He assumed that the office had hidden CCTV and he took out his phone and made a show of casually reading email while he waited, feeling alone in a dangerous environment.

As expected, Kaldani kept Donadze waiting long enough to be irritating but stood and walked loosely round his over-sized desk to greet him when he was eventually invited through. He was dressed stylishly in a light blue suit, complementary blue silk shirt with no tie and loafers which showed off fashionably bare ankles. His tan looked expensive but could have come from a bottle or lamp, Donadze thought.

'*Gamarjoba,* Lieutenant. Please take a seat,' Kaldani said, offering his hand and indicating a small conference table with four chairs. 'I've asked my attorney, Mr. Melua, to join us, I hope that's okay?'

'Your choice.'

Donadze declined coffee and brought out his notebook, 'Let's talk about Nino Adamia.'

'Of course, very sad, a lovely girl. Do you have any idea who did this terrible thing?'

'I'm following up on a number of leads—which is why I want to talk to you.'

Kaldani smiled. 'Well, I'm not sure I'll be able to help, but please go ahead.'

'Nino was your employee.'

'Of course, she was a hostess at my casino.'

'What did that entail?'

Kaldani looked puzzled by the question. 'Quite simple really. She was there to look good, to greet guests and to bring drinks to the tables. Most of my guests are men and men like to have beautiful women around while they're gambling.'

'Did she have any other duties?'

'Other duties? What do you mean?' Kaldani said, frowning.

'She was a prostitute. She had sex with men for money. And she met some of these men at your casino.'

'Lieutenant, are you making a specific allegation against Mr. Kaldani?' Melua said.

'It's okay, Petre,' Kaldani said evenly, looking directly at Donadze. 'I didn't know this girl well and I didn't know she was a whore. If I had known she was using my casino to pick up men I would have had her fired. But I'm not surprised. She was poor, had nothing when she came to the city. Working at the casino, she met some rich guys. Maybe one or more of them made her an offer and she fell into the life.'

'I thought you didn't know her well?'

'I didn't, it's a typical story for girls like her.'

'Girls like her?' Donadze put a sheet of paper on the desk, 'Do you know a Giorgi Licheli?'

Melua took the paper. 'What is this, Lieutenant?'

'A name from a notebook, a date, time and location. Licheli was with Nino two days before she was murdered.'

Melua passed the sheet to Kaldani. 'It's a common enough name—but I have an employee at the casino called Licheli. My security manager.' He turned to Melua. 'I must be paying him too much,' he joked.

'I want to speak to him. Do you know a Robert Morton?' Donadze demanded.

'I don't think so, American, English?'

'American, General Manager for United Energy, Georgia.'

'The pipeline operator?'

'Yes. Where were you between twelve and four on Sunday afternoon?'

'You don't have to answer that, Dato,' Melua said.

'That's fine. I believe I was here,' Kaldani said, his smile stretched.

'I'll need proof of that. I also need to see employment records for Adamia and Licheli.'

'Lieutenant, Mr. Kaldani agreed to meet—'

'I'll get them to you,' Kaldani interrupted. 'Anything else I can help you with Lieutenant?'

'Not at this time. We'll speak again.'

Kaldani rose smoothly. 'Well thanks for coming to see me. Good luck with your investigation. And please give my best to Captain Bukia and your lovely lady friend— Tamuna isn't it?' he said, his smile not quite reaching his eyes.

FOUR

Donadze left Kaldani's office and called United Energy from his car. Robert Morton's personal assistant said her boss would not be available until the following day as his schedule was, 'totally jammed.' Donadze insisted on a meeting that day and, after being kept on muzak-hold for a couple of minutes, agreed that 4:00 p.m. would be acceptable.

He had put off calling Tamuna but dialled her now.

'Ramaz...' she answered after a few rings.

'Hi Tamuna, are you okay to talk?' Donadze said, knowing she would be holding her surgery.

'I thought you were going to call yesterday?'

'I know, sorry.'

'What happened?'

'I think the reason I didn't call yesterday was because I was a bit nervous, you know, the way you stormed out of—'

'Stormed out? I don't think so!'

'No, I didn't mean it that way. I'll say it again—sorry.'

Tamuna paused, 'Okay, apology accepted, but you're not the only one with a tough job and I'm no punch bag, Ramaz.'

'Understood. Can we meet this evening?'

'Probably best give it a bit longer. I'll call you in a couple of days.'

'Well... okay, but please, don't give up on me yet.'

'I wouldn't be calling you in a couple of days if I was, would I?'

'That's a relief! One other thing. You remember I told you that a gangster called Dato Kaldani might be connected to my case?'

'I remember—you said that you're more dangerous than him.'

'Comedy's not my strong point. Just wanted to check. Have you ever met Kaldani, maybe at work?'

'Not that I'm aware of, why?'

'It's nothing, just that I interviewed him yesterday and he mentioned you by name.'

'Mentioned *me,* what have I got to do with this?'

'Nothing. I was pressing him pretty hard and he probably just wanted to spook me. It wouldn't have been difficult for him to find out we're seeing each other. Nothing to worry about, but, you know, just be a little bit more careful than normal. The usual common-sense stuff. Keep your doors locked, watch where you park, avoid dark streets. Let me know if you think anything doesn't feel right. But don't worry, this is just me being paranoid. Kaldani knows better than—'

'Don't worry? Did you have to tell me all of that? And, for the record, I *am* worried now.'

'Please don't be. Call me soon.'

'Goodbye Ramaz,' she said, hanging up.

Handled that really well, he thought as he started the car's engine.

Donadze crossed the Kura River using the Galaktioni Bridge and drove into the old German neighbourhood of Marjanishvili. This was one of his favourite areas in Tbilisi with beautifully restored nineteenth century architecture sitting comfortably alongside redundant Soviet factories, one of which had been divided into bars, restaurants and funky art shops, a popular hangout for Tbilisi's hipster generation. He parked on Petersburg Street and walked two hundred metres to United Energy's office. The temperature was in the mid-thirties and he wiped his brow before stepping into the cool of the reception area.

He was fifteen minutes early for his meeting with Morton, but it took ten minutes to receive a visitor's pass and another ten minutes before Morton's personal assistant arrived to collect him.

'Welcome to UE, Lieutenant,' she said. 'We talked on the phone. Rob is in his office—he'll see you now.'

They walked up two flights of stairs and along a short corridor before Donadze, refusing a cold drink, was shown into an office with a name plate stating, 'Robert Morton, General Manager.'

Morton smiled, showing perfect, if unnaturally white, teeth. He took a couple of paces towards Donadze, looking up as he offered his hand. It was damp and withdrawn early, prolonged contact avoided. His thinning hair was carefully brushed to provide maximum coverage and was very dark, except for some strands at the back of his neck where the dye hadn't quite reached. An open necked white cotton shirt was tucked into khaki chinos which were belted around an expansive middle. Donadze guessed he was in his late forties.

'*Gamarjoba*,' said Morton in mangled Georgian. He continued in nasally English, 'Rob Morton, good to meet you. This is my security manager, Nik Botkoveli. I'm embarrassed to admit that my Georgian is almost non-existent and I've asked Nik to help with translation.'

'That's fine,' said Donadze. 'I believe my English is passable, but I'm happy for Mr. Botkoveli to stay.'

Morton indicated a small table with seats. 'How may I help you, Lieutenant?'

'I'm investigating a murder.'

'That sounds serious, please go ahead,' he said, flashing his near-perfect teeth again.

'Murder is always serious.' Donadze looked around the office which was decorated with pictures of Morton with his family and with mementos from job roles in different parts of the world. 'You seem to have travelled extensively,' he said.

'Well, UE is one of the biggest energy companies in the world. We're American, of course, with our HQ in Houston, Texas, but with operations all over the world—so there are plenty of opportunities.'

'What brings United Energy to Georgia? We have very little oil or gas of our own.'

'True, our production is from the Azerbaijani sector of the Caspian Sea. As you know, the Caspian is pretty much an inland lake and we use pipelines to transport oil and gas from Azerbaijan across Georgia to markets in Turkey and Europe. A bit like the old Silk Road. We also supply gas to Georgia. You're probably not aware but about thirty percent of the gas used in your kitchen comes from our pipeline.'

'Very kind of you to help our poor country in that way,' said Donadze, noting Botkoveli's discreet smile.

'We're happy to do so,' Morton flashed again, missing the sarcasm.

'I read an article about a project to expand your operations in this country.'

'Yes, well, that's certainly one possibility. We've committed to producing additional gas volumes from the Caspian but the existing pipeline is at capacity and we'll need a new export route.'

'So, a new pipeline in Georgia?'

Morton shrugged noncommittally. 'It's an option but it's also possible we'll tie into a different pipeline further north.'

'Further north, you mean Russia? I thought the EU was trying to reduce its dependence on Russian gas?'

'It is, ideally. But UE as a company has to consider all its options. I'll be providing my assessment on the viability of a new pipeline here in Georgia.'

'We're in good hands then. Let's get back to the investigation. Did you know a woman called Nino Adamia?'

Morton hesitated. 'I don't think so.... When you say "did" you know?'

'She was murdered three days ago.'

'Murdered?' Morton paused then looked across to the security manager. 'Nik, Lieutenant Donadze's English is as good as mine,' he said. 'We'll be fine, I'll let you get back to work, thanks.'

Morton fidgeted until his office door was closed. 'Um, Lieutenant, this is a little sensitive,' he said, his smile now tentative.

'How so?'

'Well, I did know that girl.'

'Then why did you lie?'

'It wasn't a lie, just a little sensitive as I said.'

'What was the nature of your relationship?'

'I think you know that already, don't you? I was seeing Nino.'

'When you say you were seeing her, do you mean you were paying her for sex?'

'If you put it like that.'

'Is there another way to put it?'

'Lieutenant, I understand that you'll do your best to find this woman's killer and I'll certainly help as much as I'm able—but I think your line of questioning could be more constructive.'

'Thanks for the advice but please let me decide what is and what is not constructive. You're married aren't you, Mr. Morton?'

'I am, but how can that be relevant? Lieutenant, you should understand that UE is one of the biggest investors and employers in Georgia. We have an extremely high political profile. I speak to your Prime Minister every month. Last week I had dinner with your President. I can tell that you are a very conscientious police officer and I wouldn't want to see your career being damaged unnecessarily.'

'Thanks again for the advice but please let me worry about my career. Where did you meet Miss Adamia and how many times did you pay her for sex?'

Morton sighed. 'Okay Lieutenant, if you want to take that line. I was introduced to her at a reception UE was hosting at the Tbilisi Grande Hotel, about a month ago. She was with an investor who was looking for ways to develop tourism in Georgia. She let me know she was selling it, although I'd already guessed that by then. Anyway, she was incredibly beautiful and, what with my wife being away and all...We got together a few times at her apartment. You know how it is...' he said, resurrecting a conspiratorial smile.

'No, I don't know. Tell me, does your company have a policy on senior managers cheating on their partners and paying prostitutes for sex?'

'Of course not. Listen, I made a mistake, I know that, but haven't you ever done something you regretted later?'

'I will want to speak to you again. Please do not to leave Georgia without consulting me first.' said Donadze, standing to leave.

Donadze left United Energy's office and walked back to his

car. Black storm clouds were crouched over the city and the first rain spattered onto the BMW's windscreen as he closed the door.

He sat immobile as the storm built. Within moments, fat drops of water were falling in dense sheets, exploding off the roads and pavements and sending torrents downhill. Thunder cracked over the distant hills and lightning released unimaginable energy through the violated skies. Thousands of years of civilisation were temporarily forgotten as men, women and children ran for cover, shouting, squealing and laughing but, in their primordial hearts, also cowed by nature and the power of the gods. He imagined the rain washing through the city and leaving it virtuous. If only it were that easy.

Donadze decided to wait out the storm. He pushed his chair back and listened to the rain bouncing off the car's bodywork, the squalls rocking the worn suspension. He thought about the events of the last few days. He had more of Nino's contacts to interview but was happy with the pace of the investigation so far. He had been deliberately provocative when questioning Kaldani and Morton. Kaldani had been clearly rattled and shown his teeth, implying threats against Tamuna. He took these threats seriously. Morton was undoubtedly terrified that his indiscretion could become known to his wife and to his company. Donadze didn't doubt the American's influence with Georgia's political leadership but thought that the threats made by him were clumsy and disproportionate. But he understood what he was up against. He had been threatened by two powerful men and knew his own power was limited to the authority he held as a police officer.

Donadze started his engine and looked out the window as the wind and the rain eased. He felt exposed and alone. *Why am I doing this?* he thought. *Does anyone really care?* He looked at the clock on his car's dash—just after six, not too late to drive out to Shindisi.

Donadze had served one year of compulsory service in the Army, including fighting in the 2008 war against Russia. Most conscripts resented losing a year to the military, but Donadze had decided to make the most of the opportunities available.

He was lean and, at one eighty, not particularly tall. He was, however, strong and agile with quick reflexes and good eye to hand coordination and had excelled at unarmed combat and weapons training. It was during a training session that an opponent's stray elbow had broken his nose. The Army medic had packed it in ice and painfully reset it, but it remained slightly crooked—an effect Donadze quite liked when he inspected his otherwise unremarkable features in the mirror. The only person ever to have declared him handsome was his mother.

Donadze had found purpose in military discipline and had looked for something similar when he had demobilised. Reforms instigated by Saakashvili had improbably shifted the Georgian Police from being one of the country's most despised institutions to one of its most respected and he had joined in 2009.

Transferring out of uniform at the earliest opportunity, he became a detective under the command of Major Levan Gloveli. Gloveli had retired two years ago and now lived a simple life in the village of Shindisi, high in the hills southwest of Tbilisi, where the air was cleaner and the pace of life slower. He had however retained an interest in Police work and had made it known to Donadze that he would remain available for advice. The two men became unlikely friends and continued to meet occasionally.

Donadze parked outside Gloveli's home. It was a simple structure of wood with corrugated plastic roofing, set in grounds extensive enough to grow all the fruit and vegetables the old policeman could eat. He rapped loudly on the front door.

'Come in, Ramaz.'

Gloveli was sitting in front of a small wooden table which held a bottle of clear liquid and two shot glasses. Donadze knew he was in his mid-sixties but had kept himself in good shape by tending his garden and walking in the hills. As a senior officer in the Crime Police, he had maintained a smart appearance, always wearing a suit, shirt and tie. He had required a similar discipline from the officers under his command, including Donadze, who had a more relaxed approach. Now retired, Gloveli sat in grubby work clothes, with unkempt hair and white stubble which looked about five days old. His wife had died in the same year he had retired and Donadze thought that probably explained his dishevelled appearance now.

'*Gamarjoba*, Major. How did you know it was me?'

'You're the only one who knocks before coming in. I

also heard you coming, your big end bearings are shot. I told you that last time you visited. I'm surprised you made it up the hill.' Gloveli poured the *chacha* into the two glasses and passed one to Donadze as he sat down. 'At least your timing's good. I've just made this batch. See what you think.'

'I think it'll kill you,' said Donadze putting the fierce grape vodka to his lips, before returning his glass to the table.

'Ah well, something's got to, that's for certain.' He took a sip and grimaced. 'Now that's good.' He put the glass down. 'What's on your mind Ramaz?'

'I was hoping to get your advice on a new case.' Donadze brought his old commander up to speed.

'Bukia's a lazy weasel. I should have sacked him when I had the opportunity. He's dangerous though, so watch your back. Assume anything you tell the good Captain will get straight back to Kaldani. And don't think your badge will protect you if you get anywhere close to taking Kaldani down. He has ways of burning over-enthusiastic Police officers, some subtle and some not so subtle. Another thing, it sounds like this Nino girl was top end. Her clients will have money and power and won't want you poking around in their affairs.' He paused. 'But you know all this already. What's really on your mind, Ramaz?'

Donadze played with the glass, rotating it between his fingers as he gathered his thoughts before speaking. 'I'm having some doubts, Major...Why am I doing this? My relationship with Tamuna is on the rocks. I'll burn hours of unpaid overtime trying to find someone who killed a girl I never knew. I'm up against dangerous men and I have a corrupt boss working against me. The system's burst—why should I be the one to fix it? Maybe I should learn from Bukia—arrive late, go home early, collect my pay and keep my head down?'

Gloveli shook his head. 'You're right, you should do that. But you won't and you know it. You need to be in the Police because you need to belong. Maybe that's because of where you came from, your family history—who knows. You can't be in the Police and not do your best for people like this girl, Nino. It's not in your nature. There's no doubt you're obsessive and it's surprising any woman would put up with you, but maybe Tamuna sees something in you that's worth holding on to? You can be a real prick, I know that better than anyone, but you care and that's what makes you a good detective.'

'That's quite a speech by your standards, Major. So, you're telling me not to back off?'

'Would it make any difference what I told you? Do what you have to do but be careful.'

It was late evening before Donadze returned to his apartment on Kandelaki Street. He was tired and decided to have a glass of wine on his balcony and an early night.

The open bottle of *Mukuzani* was cooler than it should have been—but still drinkable, he told himself. He threw a couple of cushions onto his cane chair and, glass in hand, settled back to gaze at the Tbilisi skyline and the few stars which were visible through the haze and light pollution.

He swirled the wine, held the glass to his nose and

inhaled the oaky wood aroma. His father had made the best wine in Abkhazia, at least that was what he had told his son. It was always drunk at the village *supras*, the men seated at the long tables, eating, smoking and toasting each other while the women and girls brought them endless plates of food and jugs of his wine. His mother and sister, Ana, had served these men—their friends and neighbours—constantly changing their plates, cutlery and ashtrays, seemingly accepting of what they saw as their place in a natural order.

The civil war and ethnic cleansing in 1992 had stopped the *supras* as the men who had sat around the tables no longer recognised their neighbours as friends. Ana was twenty-one when their front door had been broken down. Donadze and his father were beaten unconscious and his mother knocked to the ground and made to watch as her daughter was brutally raped then stabbed to death. They had fled to the safety of Tbilisi. Classed as internally displaced persons, his parents had assumed, beyond reason, that they would return to Abkhazia one day. That wouldn't happen for his father who had died eight years ago. It remained a fantasy for his mother and a nightmare scenario for Donadze, who now considered Tbilisi home.

He inhaled the woody aroma again. In reality, the *Mukuzani* was nothing like his father's wine and Ana would never get justice, her murder only one of thousands. *But maybe Nino will,* he thought.

The wine was soothing and Donadze was pouring the last of the bottle when his phone rang.

He glanced at the caller ID, his mother. *Shit!* He swiped to answer, '*Deda.'*

'I thought you were eating with me this evening, *Ramazi*?'

'I'm really sorry, *Deda*, I should have been. I got caught up in a new case and just forgot. It's not a good excuse, sorry.'

'Well, it's an excuse, but you're right, not a good one. How have you been?'

'All good with me. This new case, you know what I'm like, a bit single-minded.'

'Yes, well don't overdo it. How's Tamuna?'

'She's fine, very busy at the Clinic of course.'

'Don't take that girl for granted. Neither of you is getting any younger and she won't hang around waiting for you forever.'

'Neither of us is thinking about that just now.'

'Don't be too sure of that, *Ramazi*. You sound tired, I'll let you go. Come and see me when you can. '*Dzli nebisa*'

'*Dzli nebisa*,' said Donadze, feeling guilty.

FIVE

Donadze got up early to drive to Mtatsminda Station. He made himself a coffee, glad that Bukia hadn't made it in to work yet. He wanted to avoid him entirely if possible but had to review recent information from the autopsy and crime scene reports. He also had to update his case files, including the notes from his interviews with Kaldani and Morton. This was standard Police procedure and he didn't want to give Bukia any justification to criticise his work.

The autopsy report had nothing of significance. The examination of organ tissues and stomach contents had determined that Nino had been a cocaine user and that her last meal had been bread, cheese, salad and pork—standard fare. With the autopsy complete, the body would be returned to Nino's mother and Donadze made a mental note to ask when the funeral would be held.

Turning to the crime scene report, Donadze read that

DNA samples had been recovered from six different people, not including Nino herself. The only match on the DNA Index System, was for Giorgi Licheli, Kaldani's security manager.

Donadze brought his Licheli's record up on screen. He was thirty-eight, ex-army and had a string of convictions, most involving acts of violence, for which had had served three prison sentences. He had been employed at Kaldani's Dream Casino for the last two years.

Donadze reviewed the names obtained from Nino's diary, iPad and Facebook account and listed the people he intended interviewing next. Irakli Toreli was the government Economy Minister. The diary indicated that he had been with Nino five days before she had been killed and his name was added to the list.

Donadze realised that he knew very little about Nino's life in Tbilisi. She didn't seem to have many friends but did speak frequently with someone called Avto Sabauri. His Facebook page showed he was the same age as Nino and worked at the Dream Casino. Donadze shut down his computer, picked up his car keys and headed for the door. Almost ten thirty and Bukia hadn't made it in yet. *Useful having a lazy boss.*

The Dream Casino was open and preparing for the day and evening ahead when Donadze arrived. He went to the bar where shelves were being stacked with glasses, fridges were being replenished with bottled beer and spirits were being transferred from economy to premium brand bottles. The bar tender paled as Donadze showed his ID.

'Not really a fifteen-year-old single malt Scotch then?' Donadze said. 'But don't worry, I'm not here to drink whisky. I want to speak to Avto Sabauri.'

The bar tender smiled gratefully. 'Avto, the cleaner? I saw him earlier, probably vacuuming around the tables.'

Donadze walked to the gambling hall where the roulette, card and dice tables waited impatiently to prey on the hopeful. Slot machines were lined against the outer walls, lights flashing, eager to offer an improbable fortune in return for a tiny stake. Cleaners were buffing the highly polished wooden table surrounds, removing spill stains from the carpets and artificially freshening the air. Avto was bagging rubbish as Donadze produced his ID.

'I'd like to speak to you about Nino Adamia.'

Avto looked much younger than his twenty years. His slim build was accentuated by narrow denim jeans and a tight-fitting tee shirt. He was pale and had highlighted light-brown hair gelled back over his forehead. His eyebrows were shaped and both ears contained gold studs.

He replied hesitantly. 'Nino? All right, just let me tell my supervisor where I'm going.'

Avto took him to a poker table in a quiet corner of the hall.

'I'm sorry about Nino,' said Donadze, sitting down. 'I understand she was a friend.'

'Murdered...Couldn't believe it. Still can't.'

'How long did you know her?'

'A long time, maybe eight years. We went to the same

school in Rustavi—but we weren't friends then. I was working at the Dream for about six months before Nino arrived. She started in the bar but then went on to do hosting. Not surprising really, with her looks. Neither of us knew many people in Tbilisi and we just got along.'

'Was she your girlfriend, Avto?'

'No, nothing like that.'

'Did you know she was a prostitute?'

'Yeah, told me she hated it.'

'Did she want to get out?'

'Didn't say. Probably thought it wouldn't happen.'

'Why not?'

'What else did she have?'

'Did she meet any of her clients at this casino?'

Avto hesitated, 'I wouldn't know about that.'

'Why not? I thought she was your friend?'

'Well, she was, but I don't know where she met her...clients.'

'Would you say that the casino expected her to find men here? That it came with her job as hostess?'

'She served drinks at the tables and talked to the customers. That's all I know.'

'Do you know Giorgi Licheli?'

'Yes, he works here. Security Manager.'

'Was he seeing Nino outside the casino?'

'I wouldn't know about that either. Why don't you ask him?'

'I will. Do you have any idea who killed Nino?'

'No.'

'Why do I feel that you are holding out on me Avto? Is

there someone you're scared of? Someone at the casino perhaps?'

'I've told you all I know. Are we done?'

'For now.' Donadze put his business card on the table. 'Call me if you think of anything,' he said.

Donadze walked back to the bar where an attractive young woman had taken over bar duties and was smiling as she poured her first customer a drink.

Donadze produced his ID again. 'Is Giorgi Licheli in the casino? I'd like to speak to him.'

'He may be in the video surveillance room,' her smile was practiced and perfect. 'Let me call and see.' She picked up the phone, pressed buttons carefully to avoid damage to her manicured nails and spoke in a voice too quiet for Donadze to hear.

She replaced the receiver. 'Yes, Gio is there. He said he can't leave at the moment and asked if you could join him. She pointed to a flight of stairs. 'Up one flight and turn right, end of the corridor, you can't miss it.'

'Thanks.' Donadze turned to the customer. 'I'd avoid the Scotch if I were you.'

Licheli was sitting in a swivel chair in front of a bank of CCTV screens. He was slim with dark hair swept back off his forehead. His cheek bones were sharp under swarthy pock marked skin. He was smartly dressed in black trousers, tailored white shirt and narrow black tie, his suit jacket hanging from a coat stand in the corner of the room.

Donadze could see from the screens that the first customers of the day had taken their places at the tables and slots. The house cameras would keep them and the casino staff honest. *Honesty being a relative term*, he thought.

Two chairs, which Donadze assumed would both be occupied during peak operating times, were located in front of the screens. Licheli remained seated and pointed to the empty chair on his left. 'You're here to ask me about Nino Adamia,' he stated, his eyes not leaving the screens.

'That's correct, how did you know?'

'It's my job to know,' he replied distractedly, adjusting controls on the panel.

'Mr. Licheli, we can speak here or at the station, but I need your attention.'

Licheli made another adjustment then swivelled slowly away from the screens to face Donadze. 'All right,' he smiled. 'Ask me your questions.'

'You knew Nino Adamia?'

'Of course, I know everyone here.'

'When did you last see her?'

'Her last day at work, Saturday.'

'The day before she was killed.'

'If you say so.'

'Did you have a relationship with Nino?'

'Depends what you mean by relationship. I fucked her a few times,' he smiled again.

Donadze straightened in his chair. 'Nino was high class, *Gio.* How could a cheap enforcer like you afford her?'

'Touched a raw nerve, Lieutenant? Maybe we were in love? Or maybe she thought it was smart to keep on my good side. Anyway, I didn't pay a *tetri*.'

'Were you at her apartment on Friday?'

'You know I was, you've seen the security video, haven't you?'

'Where were you on Sunday afternoon between twelve and four?'

Licheli made a show of picking up his phone and consulting his schedule. 'Mr. Kaldani asked me to meet him at his office. We had a business matter to discuss.'

'On a Sunday?'

'Not a problem for me.'

Donadze stood and looked down on Licheli. 'That's it for now,' he paused. 'By the way, did you know that the Dream's licence is up for renewal at the end of the year?'

'Mr. Kaldani handles that side of the business, it's not something that concerns me.'

'Well, maybe it should. I think the Revenue Service will be interested to know that a convicted felon is working at the Dream. Might make licence renewal a bit difficult. Thanks for your time,' Donadze said, feeling the need for fresh air.

Driving through the congested streets to return to his apartment, Donadze realised that he had not eaten since early morning. He enjoyed Indian cuisine and decided to go to a restaurant near his apartment. He ordered food and had just taken a welcome sip from his cold lager when his phone rang.

'Tamuna, great to hear from you, how—'

'You'd better come to the Clinic. It's Levan, he's been attacked.'

'No! Is he badly hurt?'

'His injuries are serious. He was in a lot of pain and he's been given morphine. He wants to speak to you. Can you come right now?'

'Tell him I'm on my way,' he said, throwing money on the table and making for the door.

He used his blue light and was at the Medifirst Clinic within twenty minutes. He produced his ID and insisted on seeing Gloveli immediately. Tamuna was waiting outside the ward door and gave him a tight hug—Donadze hanging on a fraction longer than was necessary.

'How is he?'

'He's been badly beaten, multiple blows to the head and body, two broken ribs and middle fingers broken on both hands. I think he was attacked at home in Shindisi and a local ambulance took him here. He's been stabilised and he'll recover.' She fixed Donadze with a stare. 'Ramaz, has this got anything to do with your investigation?'

'Let me go in and speak to him. I'll find—'

'Is Dato Kaldani involved in this?'

'I don't know, Tamuna. I'll speak to Levan now, see what he can tell me.'

'Okay, but don't tire him out. Come and find me before you leave.'

Gloveli was in a private room off the main ward. He was dressed in a hospital gown, propped up on pillows, face and head bloated and coloured various shades of purple and blue, hands bandaged and resting on his chest, an intravenous line dripping liquid into a vein in his right wrist.

'I warned you about that *chacha*, didn't I, Major?'

'Very funny, Donadze,' he whispered. 'I'd laugh if my ribs were up to it.'

'Kaldani?'

'Not personally of course, but his men. Told me Dato said hello.'

'Could you identify them again?'

'Not from their faces, they were wearing masks. Probably a good thing—it meant they weren't going to kill me.'

'So, a warning then. To me, probably. I'm sorry Major, I—'

'Don't be,' he winced.

Despite the morphine, Gloveli was clearly in severe pain and Donadze bent close to catch his fading words.

'Listen Ramaz, Kaldani's crossed a line. Even his old man, Zaza, wouldn't have pulled this stunt. He's got no respect for you or anyone else. You need to change that.'

'What's your advice, Major?'

'You need to make him fear you,' Gloveli spoke through the pain. 'But you need to be focused and that means you can't be worrying about anyone else. I'll be all right. I know people in Shindisi, people Kaldani would be stupid to mess with. I'll be ready for these bastards if they come again. But Kaldani's done you a favour. I've still got friends in the Police and attacking a former officer won't go down well. I'll get Bukia off your back and get you some help. Speak to Bukia, tell him you want protection for Tamuna and your mother—you'll get it. The thing is, this is war—someone's got to win, and someone's got to lose. You'd better be sure you're up for it, Donadze.'

Gloveli's eyes fluttered as he drifted into medically induced stupor. 'And keep your 941 close...'

'Yes, Major,' Donadze replied to the broken man, patting his Jericho 941 pistol.

SIX

Donadze returned to the clinic's reception and asked to see Tamuna. She arrived ten minutes later, bursting through the double swing doors and stood over him, hands on hips, no hug offered this time. 'What's going on, Ramaz?'

She stepped back as Donadze reached out and tried to touch her. He glanced over to the desk where the receptionist was watching. 'Is there somewhere we can talk?'

'Come with me.'

Tamuna led the way to the doctors' coffee room and dropped onto one of the padded chairs, arms folded across her chest, not speaking.

He sat on the chair beside her. 'Tamuna, let me explain—'

'Did Dato Kaldani do that to Levan?' She uncrossed her arms and turned to face Donadze.

'Yes, but he—'

'And he did it as a warning to you. It's to do with the case you're working on,' she stated.

'I think so, but he—'

'And now you think he'll come after me!'

'I don't know, but it's possible.'

She pulled her arm away as Donadze reached out to touch her. 'So, next time it could be me lying on that bed, or maybe somewhere worse!'

'I won't let that happen, Tamuna,' he said.

'Like you didn't let it happen to Levan?' she snapped.

'Kaldani's laughing at the Police, he's laughing at me. He's arrogant and out of control. He's got be stopped. You've got to understand—this is my job.'

'Your job, not mine. How did I get involved in this?'

'I just want to keep the people I'm close to safe.'

'Just as well that's a short list then. How about your mother? Is she safe?'

'Yes, of course, but I—'

'So how *do* you intend keeping us safe, Ramaz?'

'You *are* safe—I promise. Kaldani made a mistake attacking Gloveli. This is high profile now and my bosses can't ignore it. I'm turning up the heat. But the first thing I'm going to do is have a patrol car stationed at your apartment. You'll be okay at the Clinic—Kaldani wouldn't try anything here.'

'So, you've worked it all out? Lieutenant Ramaz Donadze to the rescue. Should I faint and fall into your arms?'

He held up his hands in surrender. 'I don't understand, Tamuna, I just want to protect you.'

'I know you don't understand, that's the problem. Ramaz, try to understand *this*—I don't want you to protect me, I want you to be with me.'

'I'm with you now.'

'Are you? I don't think so.'

'I'm sorry, Tamuna, I know you're angry, but I don't know what else I can say.'

'What about your mother?'

'I was hoping she could stay with you for a while. I know that's a lot to ask. But it'd be better for her.'

'Pretty hard to say no when you put it like that. What about you?'

'I can look after myself,' he said, resisting an impulse to touch his pistol.

Tamuna leaned forward again, this time touching Donadze's arm. 'Ramaz, have you ever thought through your priorities? You say that Kaldani has got to be stopped— but what are you prepared to lose to make that happen? What's most important to you, us being together or you beating that man?'

Donadze put his hand over hers. 'You're the best thing in my life, Tamuna. But I can't step back from this case. It's gone too far now. Please try to understand.'

Tamuna stood, his hand falling off hers. 'I've got to get back to work,' she said.

Donadze slept badly and was up early to drive to Mtatsminda Station. He sat at his desk and called his mother, asking her to pack a bag and take a taxi to Tamuna's apartment. She was more concerned for him than for herself but went along with his suggestion with little resistance. Donadze knew that she and Tamuna got on well and his mother would enjoy her company.

He then went online and did some research on Irakli Toreli and his ministry. The Ministry of Economy and Sustainable Development covered wide ranging areas, but its overall remit was to facilitate a business environment which promoted national economic growth.

Donadze knew that Georgians were divided on their attitude to business and Western capitalism generally. Some, mainly living in rural areas, were nostalgic for the days when the Soviet planned economy ensured everyone had a job. Others, who tended to live in the cities, were Western leaning and fully supported Georgia's aspirations to join the EU and NATO.

Toreli had been in role for about eighteen months and was generally considered to have been successful. He was an ally of the current Prime Minister and seen as a likely future successor. His name was, however, in Nino's diary and Donadze intended interviewing him soon—while being fully aware that a politician of his seniority could be a challenging adversary and that he had to therefore plan his approach carefully.

Bukia arrived at the station at nine forty-five, carrying several greasy food bags and trailing a rank odour as he made his way past the detectives' desks to unlock his office door.

Donadze gave him time to collect his coffee before knocking on his door. 'May I give you an update on the

Nino Adamia case, Captain?'

'Give me ten minutes to get my feet under the desk,' he replied, his mouth full of *khachapuri*.

Donadze returned in twenty minutes.

'Okay, Donadze, what's been happening,' Bukia said, wiping his face with a handkerchief which had once been white.

'There have been some developments, Captain.' He summarised his investigation to date, including his interviews with Kaldani, Morton and Licheli. He decided not to mention his discussion with Nino's friend, Avto Sabauri.

'I've heard from United Energy already,' Bukia said. 'Mr. Morton didn't take kindly to your line of questioning. What did I tell you about being diplomatic?'

'Morton was one of Nino Adamia's clients—I had to speak to him.'

'How about Kaldani?'

'I was just coming to that.' Donadze looked directly at Bukia, 'Kaldani had our former commander, Major Gloveli, attacked in his home in Shindisi. He did it to try to make me back off this case. It hasn't worked. Kaldani made a mistake by attacking the Major. You'll be hearing from HQ today. You will be expected to fully support this investigation and give me all the resources I need. That includes protection for the people close to me.'

Sweat was beading on Bukia's forehead. 'Are you suggesting that I haven't been supportive?'

Donadze smiled at Bukia. 'I want Kaldani to know I'm coming after him.'

'How will he know that?'

Donadze smiled again. 'Thank you for your time, Captain. I appreciate your support. I'll pass on your order to send a car to Tamuna's apartment.'

Donadze returned to his desk and called to update Tamuna. She had been cool towards him, but he was relieved that she and his mother were now under Police protection. He was wondering how to set up a meeting with Minister Toreli when his mobile rang.

'Donadze.'

'Lieutenant. It's Avto. I need to speak to you.'

'Okay. Do you want me to come to the casino?'

'No, I've called in sick. Meet me in Rike Park. I'll be in the kids' play area. When can you get there?'

'Thirty minutes.'

He parked close to the Concert Hall, the futuristic worm like construction commissioned by President Saakashvili but spitefully prohibited from use by his successor.

Avto was sitting on a bench in the play area. Donadze sat beside him. 'What do you want to talk about?'

'Nino of course.'

'Okay, go ahead.'

'This has got to be between me and you. I'm dead if Kaldani finds out I've spoken to you.'

'He won't find out from me.'

Avto looked around nervously. 'I told you that Nino and I were friends— but we were more than that.'

'She was your girlfriend?' Donadze asked.

'No, I don't like girls, not in that way at least.' He smiled ruefully, 'That's why I came to Tbilisi. Got kicked out by my dad.'

'I'm sorry to hear that, Avto.'

'It's okay, it's not really his fault—it's just the way some people think—or get told to think anyway.'

'When you said that you and Nino were more than friends?' Donadze prompted.

'We were more like brother and sister, we told each other everything.'

'Go on.'

'She was scared. Kaldani had set up some scheme. He told Nino to sleep with some guys. Someone filmed it—blackmail she thought.'

'When did this happen?'

'Recently, in the last few weeks. Up to about when she was killed.'

'Did she know who these men were?'

'Yes, but she said it was better not to tell me.'

'Do you know where she met them?'

'Her apartment I think.'

'Why was she scared?'

'Kaldani's a very scary guy. You wouldn't want to be caught cheating at the tables when he's around.'

'What about Licheli, was he part of it?'

'I don't think so. He'd do anything Kaldani told him to do, but Nino didn't say he was involved.'

'Do you think she might have been protecting him? He told me they were in a relationship of sorts.'

'A relationship! It wasn't anything like that. She hated him and so do I...' Avto put his face in his hands, bent forward and wept silently. 'He was rough with her and liked to tell me about it. He knew we were close...'

Donadze laid a hand on the young man's shoulder. 'I'm sorry...'

Avto straightened and wiped tears off his face with the back of his hands. 'Thanks. It's just that it's so unfair...'

Donadze waited a moment while Avto composed himself. 'What will you do now?' he asked. 'Are you going back to work at the casino?'

'I'll have to, at least for a while. They'll get suspicious if I don't.'

'Then I need you to do something—for Nino.'

Avto looked at Donadze apprehensively. 'What?'

'Help me find her killer. Go back to the casino and keep your eyes open. Get back to me with anything you pick up. Who Licheli and Kaldani meet up with, any papers you come across. Really, just anything which looks a bit odd or—'

'Are you crazy? You've no idea what would happen to me if I get caught.'

'I won't let anything happen to you, Avto.'

'You can't guarantee that...'

'You're right, there is a risk, but you said Nino was like a sister, didn't you?'

'You're not any better than Kaldani and Licheli, are you?'

'You and I both want the same thing, Avto, you can help us get it.'

Avto paused for a long moment. 'Okay... but I'm doing it for her, not you.'

'Thank you. Be careful and try to stay out of their way. You have my number, keep in touch and call me if you need anything, anytime,' Donadze said.

Donadze returned to Mtatsminda Station. Bukia had just returned from lunch and was in his office, red faced and sweating freely. Dark stains were visible under his arms as he leaned forward, using two fingers to punch buttons on his keyboard.

'I need your advice, Captain.'

Bukia looked uneasy. 'You need my advice? You're usually the one with all the answers. Is this to do with the Adamia case?'

'Yes, as you know I have been interviewing Nino's most recent contacts and I want to speak to Irakli Toreli, Minister of—'

'The Economy! Please don't tell me he's a suspect!'

'Not a suspect at this stage—but his name was in Nino's diary. He was with her five days before she was killed.'

'Have you any idea what this could do to Toreli's career?'

'That's not my concern, Captain.'

'In that case, do you have any idea what this could do to *your* career? To *my* career?'

'I can't think of that. I just have to go where the evidence takes me.'

'Do you have anything on Toreli other than the diary?'

'Yes, there's CCTV video of the Minister entering and leaving Nino's apartment block.'

'Wonderful! Anything else?'

'I'm obliged to interview this man, Captain. I just need your advice on how to set it up.'

'I suppose I should be grateful you don't already have him in a cell... All right, I'll speak to HQ, see what the Colonel thinks.'

'Thank you. When will you get back to me?'

'I said I'll see what the Colonel thinks. Get back to work, I'll call you when I have something,' Bukia said, returning two fingers to his keyboard.

Donadze decided to drive to Tamuna's apartment and make sure the patrol car was in position. It was parked with two wheels on the pavement, its engine running, with two uniformed officers inside, one looking distractedly out the windscreen, the other head down over his mobile phone. Donadze knocked on the side window, a blast of cold air escaping the car as the officer wound it down. '*Gamarjoba*,' he said.

'Can we help you?'

'Is Tamuna Losava at home?'

'Who wants to know?'

'Merab Ninidze,' said Donadze, using the actor's name. 'I'm a friend.'

'She's not in, probably at work. There's an older woman in the apartment now.'

Donadze showed his ID. 'Lieutenant Donadze—that older woman is my mother. What are your orders?'

The other officer turned his phone face down and

answered. 'We've been told to maintain a presence outside this apartment block and screen visitors as they enter, Lieutenant.'

'Does that include playing games on your mobile phone and passing on information to people using fictitious names?'

'No, Lieutenant, sorry.'

'Okay, I know this is a tedious assignment, but it's important. I'll be visiting regularly so stay alert. Pass that on to the next shift,' Donadze said, walking into the apartment block.

There was no elevator and he was hot and breathless by the time he had climbed to the third level. He had a key to the apartment but rang the bell and waited until his mother came to the door. Donadze was pleased to see that she used the security chain before letting him in.

'How are you, *Deda*,' he said.

'Good, very good. Can you stay for dinner with Tamuna and me?'

'I can't, sorry. I'll have to get back to work.'

'Stay for ten minutes. Sit down, I'll get us some water.'

Donadze sat on the couch and waited while his mother brought two glasses of water and a small bowl of nuts. 'Are you sure you can't stay for dinner?' she asked.

'No, sorry. I just wanted to check that you're okay. Anyway, I'm not Tamuna's favourite person at the moment.'

'What do you mean?'

'She's angry with me because she thinks I've put you both in danger.'

'She's not really angry, *Ramazi*. And it's not because she

thinks we're in danger. She just doesn't know where she is with you. Girls her age need some certainty, it's nothing new.'

'She does know, I've told her.'

'I don't think so...' She looked closely at her son. 'You know, Ramaz, we hardly ever talk about the old days, we never talk about Ana.'

'I know, it's too painful. I don't want to upset you.'

'I'm not upset anymore. Yes, I miss her and pray for her every day. But I'm at peace with her memory. You must come to terms with what happened as well, Ramaz. The way Ana was killed by these people, it tortured your father until the day he died. But you've lived with it for too long. None of what happened was your fault. You couldn't save Ana, your father couldn't—and I couldn't either. Don't allow something as ugly as that to ruin what you have with Tamuna. She's there for you but she needs to know you're there for her as well.'

'I'll try *Deda*, I'll try,' Donadze said, blinking mist from his eyes.

'Stay for dinner, Ramaz.'

'I really can't, but I'll be back soon. Tell Tamuna I'll call later,' he said, opening the apartment door to leave.

Donadze was walking down the stairs when Bukia called. 'No one at HQ is happy with this but I've set up a meeting with Toreli tomorrow morning at eleven. Be at the station for nine for a briefing.'

'Thank you, Captain, where will we conduct the—'

'I said I'll brief you tomorrow,' Bukia said, ending the call.

SEVEN

Bukia was already in the station when Donadze arrived at seven forty-five. He was dressed in a fitted suit with white shirt and blue tie. His desk was clear of food for once and he was writing on a notepad as Donadze knocked on his door. '*Gamarjoba*, Captain, you're in early,' he said.

Bukia looked at his watch, 'Not particularly. What do you want, Donadze?'

'You said you would brief me on Minister Toreli's interview.'

'I said I'd do that at nine. But now that you're here...' he sighed, putting his pen down and lifting his notepad. 'As mentioned yesterday, I have discussed this matter with the Colonel. He wasn't convinced that we should interview the Minister at this stage. He was also concerned that you are designated lead investigator on this case—your reputation precedes you, I'm afraid. He did eventually agree to the interview but stipulated that I have to conduct it. You'll come with me but will only speak if the Minister or I invite you to. Liaison Department has been in touch and we will meet him at his office in Sanapiro Street at eleven. I have a car and driver organised for ten—make sure you are ready for then. Any questions?'

'What was Toreli told about the nature of the interview?'

'I believe that *Minister* Toreli was told that we have requested the interview in pursuit of a murder enquiry, I didn't speak to him directly.'

'Was Nino Adamia mentioned? We need him to tell us what contact he had with her.'

'Thanks, Donadze, but don't worry, I was doing this kind of Police work while you were still at the Academy. What new information do you have for me?'

'Just what we already discussed.'

'In that case, let me get back to work. Be ready at ten.'

Bukia and Donadze arrived at the Ministry head office in Sanapiro Street fifteen minutes early. They were met at Reception and taken to a large conference room which had about twenty chairs arranged around an elliptical table. Donadze poured water from a cooler into two plastic cups, placed one beside Bukia and sat down, leaving an empty chair between them.

Bukia struggled to his feet when Toreli and a second man entered the room at eleven twenty-five. They strode importantly to the opposite side of the table, reached over to shake hands, then sat down. Neither apologised for being late. Donadze recognised Toreli from his appearances on television. He was forty-six but looked younger, with a full head of stylishly cut hair. He was shorter than Donadze had realised but looked trim and fit in tailored suit trousers and a close-fitting white open-necked cotton shirt.

Toreli spoke first. 'Gentlemen, I'm not entirely sure why you wanted to meet me today. However, I understand there is an ongoing Police enquiry into the murder of a young woman, and I have therefore asked Mr. Jibuti, my legal counsel, to join us.'

Jibuti nodded in greeting and gave both detectives a business card but didn't speak. Donadze thought he was also in his mid-forties with soft, poorly defined features, wispy brown hair and a modest belly which his tailored dark blue suit couldn't quite disguise. He pulled back his jacket sleeve to expose an expensive looking watch, apparently eager to have the meeting started and concluded.

'Certainly, sir,' Bukia said. 'That's quite understandable.' He nodded in Donadze's direction. 'My Lieutenant is lead investigator on this case but, given possible sensitivities, I will conduct this interview.'

'I'm not clear why there should be any sensitivities,' Toreli said. 'But please proceed.'

'Thank you, sir.' He cleared his throat and looked at the Minister earnestly.

'Did you know a woman called Nino Adamia?'

'Yes, I read that she had been murdered. Incredibly sad.'

'What was the nature of your relationship?'

'The Minister will be glad to answer your questions, Captain,' Jibuti spoke for the first time. 'But before doing so, please confirm that any information you are given today will be treated as strictly confidential and will not be discussed outside of this room—unless relevant to your investigation of course.'

'We're not here to embarrass the Minister, Mr. Jibuti.'

'The Minister has nothing to be embarrassed about. I merely wish to establish the parameters of your enquiry and obtain your confirmation that information provided will remain private, unless pertinent to your investigation. There are only four of us in this room and it should be obvious where a leak originated, should that indeed occur,' Jibuti smiled.

Bukia's forehead was beading despite the efficient air conditioning. 'Of course.'

'I intend to help you as much as I can, gentlemen.' Toreli said. 'However, I do place great value on my privacy. Is that clearly understood, Captain?'

'Very clear, sir. If I may repeat my question? What was the nature of your relationship with Miss Adamia?'

'It was sexual.'

'Where did you meet?'

'We met at the Dream Casino, here in Tbilisi. I play poker now and again—I find it relaxing.'

'And she was working at the Dream?'

'I was playing in a private room. She brought me a drink and stayed with me. Brought me some luck—I won that night for a change.'

Bukia returned Toreli's smile. 'Can you recall when that happened?'

Toreli looked thoughtful. 'I can check my diary, but it was about six weeks ago.'

'Did your relationship with Miss Adamia start that day.'

'Yes. We left the casino and went to her apartment.'

'How long did your relationship continue?'

'It was ongoing. I was shocked when I heard she had been killed.'

Bukia closed his notebook and began extracting himself from his chair. 'Thank you for your co-operation, Minister, I think that is all we—'

'Are you aware that prostitution is a criminal offence in Georgia, Minister?' Donadze interrupted.

Jibuti looked at Bukia. 'I thought you were conducting this interview, Captain?'

'I am. Let's go Donadze. We've taken up enough of the Minister's—'

'Where were you on Sunday afternoon between twelve and four?'

Toreli put both hands on the table and leaned forward, fixing Donadze with a stare. 'Please sit down, Captain. It appears your Lieutenant has more questions to ask.'

'Are you aware that prostitution is a criminal offence in Georgia?' Donadze repeated.

'You're surely not thinking of charging Miss Adamia?' Toreli smiled, turning to Jibuti who smiled back.

'Do you think this is funny, Minister?'

'That's enough, Donadze, Bukia said. 'I warned you before—'

'No, I don't think it's funny, but I do think you are exceptionally insolent.' Toreli interrupted. 'Prostitution is illegal, paying for sex is not.'

'Then why worry about confidentiality? Maybe the

voting public wouldn't see that distinction? How embarrassed would you be if this got out?'

'No laws were broken by me. Ask your questions, Lieutenant, I have a meeting with the Prime Minister, and I won't be late.'

'Do you know Dato Kaldani?'

'The owner of the Dream Casino, yes.'

'How about Giorgi Licheli?'

'No.'

'And Robert Morton?'

'Yes, it's my job to know all our foreign investors.'

'Where were you on Sunday afternoon between twelve and four?'

'With my family. We visited church in the morning and spent the rest of the day at home.'

Donadze turned to Bukia. 'That's all I have for now.'

'I hope you enjoyed yourself, Lieutenant.' Toreli said coldly.

'Captain, Lieutenant, the Minister has been very generous with his time and has fully answered all of your questions. Please honour your commitment to maintain his privacy,' Jibuti said.

'Of course, sir. Thank you again for your time, Minister. I apologise for my Lieutenant's behaviour. Let's go, Donadze,' Bukia said, standing with an effort and storming to the door.

The car was waiting for them outside the Ministry building.

Bukia sat in the back seat behind the driver, fists clenched on his lap, red-faced and breathing hard. 'Back to the station,' he instructed. 'Donadze, I told you only to speak if invited!'

Donadze turned in the front passenger seat to face Bukia. 'I know what you said, Captain.'

'And you chose to ignore my instructions!'

'I chose to ask the Minister questions relevant to this—'

'Questions like, did he know that prostitution is illegal in Georgia!'

'As you said yesterday, you were doing interviews of this type when I was still at the Academy. So, you understand interrogation techniques. I got his attention. He'll take us more seriously next time.'

'That's not it, Donadze. You don't like him. He was screwing your precious little whore and you're taking it personally!'

'A woman was murdered and it's my job to find her killer. The fact that she was a "whore" is irrelevant and I'm not taking this personally. How could I? I never knew her when she was alive.'

'You're a liability, Donadze! I should take you off this case.'

'That would be your decision, Captain. But not necessarily a good one.'

'Is that a threat?'

'Of course not, how could I threaten you?'

Bukia paused. 'You know that Toreli will kick this up to HQ? We could both be off this investigation.'

Donadze turned to face forward, the driver red-faced

and studiously concentrating on the road. 'I don't think that will happen, you heard what he said about privacy.'

They said nothing more as they were driven back to Mtatsminda Station. Bukia left the car first, loosening his tie and hitching his trousers as he returned to his office. Donadze thanked the driver, apologising for the argument during the trip back. He went to his desk, logged onto the system and updated his case files. With the files up to date he looked at his watch, stood and left the station.

Nino's body had been released by the medical examiner and returned to her mother for burial. Two middle-aged men were standing smoking in the small passageway outside her apartment door, talking quietly, when Donadze arrived. 'You're here for Nino?' one asked and pushed the door open.

She was lying in an open casket on top of the dresser he had seen on his previous visit. The temperature was in the mid-thirties again and he knew that the casket contained a hidden bed of ice. Three chairs had been arranged in the narrow space between the dresser and wall and two were occupied by women he guessed were family members, their role to mark Nino's passing with a visible display of grief.

The funeral directors had skilfully restored Nino's beauty and she lay, arms crossed, in a simple blue dress with white shoes, silver chain and a crucifix around her neck. Her mother stood against a wall, her pride and sorrow evident as she watched Donadze pay his respects by walking around the casket.

'Thank you for coming, Lieutenant.'

'I wanted to come. Your daughter was beautiful, I'm sorry you lost her. Are you taking her to Rustavi Cemetery?'

'Yes, she'll be beside her father, it's a nice location. I couldn't do much for her when she was alive, but I can take good care of her now.'

'You did all you could, Mrs. Adamia. Don't be hard on yourself.'

'Do you still think you'll find the man who did this?'

'Yes, as I promised.'

She looked closely at Donadze. 'How about you, Lieutenant, are you alright?'

'I'm okay, Mrs. Adamia.' He pressed an envelope into her hand. 'To help with the funeral costs...' he said, leaving to shake hands with the men at the door.

EIGHT

The skies were heavy after the heat of the day as Donadze drove to his apartment. He left his car in the underground car park and walked the short distance to Pekini Avenue. People were walking slowly through the thick, humid air, diverting without complaint or comment around the cars which had been illegally bumped onto the pavements. He crossed the road to his favourite supermarket and bought food and a bottle of wine for his evening meal.

He walked slowly back to his apartment, a wave of cool air washing over him as he opened the front door. He was unpacking his purchases when a text alert buzzed. It was from Avto. *'Meet me at 8, same place.'* He checked his watch, time to eat before returning to Rike Park.

He finished his meal and added the dishes and cutlery to the collection in the dishwasher, deciding to run it even though it was less than half full. The thought of driving through the congested streets was unappealing and he called a taxi. Avto was sitting on the same park bench, hunched over and clearly nervous. He looked up as Donadze approached. 'I should never have agreed to do this,' he said.

Donadze sat beside him. 'I said I won't let anything happen to you. Do you have something to tell me?'

'Maybe... there were a couple of guys at the casino today—Russians. They were in to see Kaldani...'

'Okay, what about them?'

'Something about them was off. It's hard to describe but I've never seen Kaldani behave that way before.'

'What do you mean?'

'You know him, he's arrogant, doesn't give a shit about anyone. But there was something about them... the way he was with them.'

'Try to be specific,' Donadze said. 'What was he doing that was unusual?'

Avto paused as he appeared to gather his thoughts. 'It just wasn't like him. He seemed very respectful, but more than that. Nervous maybe.'

'How did you know they were Russians?'

'Kaldani was speaking Russian with them. But it was obvious anyway, the way they looked and the clothes they were wearing.'

'Can you describe them?' Donadze asked.

'They looked like guys you wouldn't want to mess with. Thirty, thirty-five, maybe. Tall—one was about one eighty-six, the other about one ninety. Pretty athletic, looked like they were in good shape. My type in different circumstances,' he joked.

Donadze didn't return Avto's brief smile. 'Did you get any names?'

'There weren't any introductions—you could tell they already knew each other.'

'What did they say?'

'I didn't hear much. Gio took them to Kaldani's office. He came out to meet them and took them in. They looked like they were pissed off.'

'Did Gio go in with them?' Donadze asked.

'No, Kaldani shut the door on him.'

'You said you didn't hear much. What exactly did you hear?'

'The usual stuff when they met up. But I did hear something.' Avto paused then added hesitantly, 'You're not going to like this.'

'Tell me.'

'I heard your name. I heard one of the Russians say your name.'

Donadze looked at Avto closely. 'What else did he say?'

'I couldn't make out anything else, just your name. You'd better be careful, Lieutenant.'

Donadze smiled with fake confidence. 'Thanks, Avto. You've done well. Keep your eyes and ears open but be careful as well. Remember, you can call me any time.'

'Nino's killer—when will you find him, Lieutenant?'

Rain had started to fall as Donadze stood to find another taxi. 'Soon, I hope,' he said.

It was after nine when the taxi dropped Donadze outside his apartment block. Rain was falling heavily now and he dashed for the covered entrance and took the elevator to level four.

His apartment was cool and he shivered in his damp clothes as he slid the balcony door open, towelled his hair dry and deeply inhaled the cleansed city air. Avto's account of the Russians' visit to the Dream Casino had added complexity to his investigation in ways he didn't understand. He needed a different perspective.

Gloveli was out of hospital and recuperating under the watchful eyes of his friends in Shindisi. He answered after a few rings, 'Ramaz.'

'How are you feeling?'

'You usually ask smarter questions than that. What do you need?'

Donadze recounted his conversation with Avto. 'The thing is, Major, this case could be more complicated than I'd thought. I reckon Avto's account is reliable. He heard my name being mentioned by these Russians. But how do I connect to them and Kaldani?'

'You've been sniffing around the casino. Do you think there could be Russian money tied up in the Dream?'

'It did occur to me. When I met Licheli, I implied I'd be taking an interest in their licence renewal, maybe that got their attention.'

'Maybe, but you don't think you could actually stop them getting it renewed, do you?'

'I know I couldn't. Too much money and political capital backing them up. But I'd let Licheli rattle me and I was hitting back.'

'Well, don't let him get to you—you need to rise above it.'

'I know. The other thing I don't understand is what these Russians could have on Kaldani that would make him nervous?'

'Yes, it's not like him. What are you planning on doing next?'

'I was hoping you could help. Is your old network still in place?'

'Network? You mean my former colleagues from Soviet times? Not sure I would call it a network as such.'

Donadze knew that the Major was sensitive about his work during the period that Georgia was a Soviet republic. 'That's what I meant, your KGB buddies,' he teased.

'The KGB was wound up in 1991, Donadze... What, specifically, are you looking for?'

'Can you find out who these Russians are, who they're working for. Any other information you can get on them.'

Gloveli paused. 'Okay, I'll see what I can do. I'm not sure if I'll be able to get much—but give me a couple of days.'

'Thanks, Major. Have you taken any precautions in case Kaldani's men come back?'

'As I said, you usually ask smarter questions than that, Donadze.'

He ended the call and returned to the open balcony door. The rain had stopped, and the traffic below was manoeuvring on the flooded roads. Pedestrians were jumping over the puddles and rivulets which were washing across the pavements. The air was stirring through the trees below, it would be another hot day tomorrow. Donadze took a last deep breath before sliding the balcony door shut and getting ready for bed.

There was little food in his apartment and Donadze had breakfast of stale bread and *sulguni* cheese with an apple and a large mug of strong black coffee. He was trying to cut back his sugar consumption but, feeling the need for energy, added three spoons to the mug. He was walking down the stairs to the underground parking when a text came through from Tamuna '*Can we meet for dinner. King David at 7? T xxx*'

Pausing on the stairs, he texted back. '*Great, see you there*'

Donadze arrived at Mtatsminda Station at nine fifteen and was surprised to see Bukia was already in his office, talking to a younger man. He sat at his desk and began typing up his notes, glancing occasionally towards Bukia and the other man. After a few moments, Misha Arziani came over with two mugs of coffee and gave one to Donadze. 'Hey, Ramaz,' he said.

'Thanks, Misha,' Donadze said. 'What's this going to cost me?'

'Not a *tetri*. He nodded in the direction of Bukia's office. 'The Captain said he wants to see you.'

Donadze looked up. Bukia was still in conversation. 'Looks like he's busy at the moment. Who's he talking to?'

'Don't you know? That's Colonel Meskhi.'

'Really? I don't think I've seen him before.'

'Well, it's not like he comes here very often.'

'I wonder why he's here now.'

'It looks like you're about to find out.'

Bukia was gesturing to him through his office window. Donadze stood and walked to his office. 'You wanted to see me, Captain?'

'Yes. You know the Colonel?'

'Of course,' Donadze lied.

Meskhi was in his late thirties or early forties and must have been promoted rapidly to have reached his current position. By Donadze's reckoning that made him either exceptionally good at his job or very well connected or possibly both. Sitting in the same cramped office, his physical appearance was in sharp contrast with Bukia's. The Colonel was very tall and lean, with closely cropped dark hair and an aquiline nose perched over tight thin lips. He was wearing a dark suit with highly polished black leather shoes. He pulled in his legs to make room for Donadze. 'Sit down, Lieutenant,' he said.

'Thank you, sir,' Donadze said.

'Your Captain has been bringing me up to speed with the Adamia case and with your unfortunate conduct when interviewing Minister Toreli. To be frank, Donadze, you wouldn't have been my first choice for an investigation of this sensitivity.'

'Sensitivity, sir? I'm sorry, I don't quite understand.'

'Oh, I think you do. No need to be cute with me. But let me be clear, we have investigated the murders of women like Adamia before. By this stage in the investigation I would have expected you to have either brought charges or to have categorised the case as unsolved. Your performance has disappointed me.'

'I'm sorry to hear that, sir. But, possibly Captain Bukia hasn't been able to give you a full briefing on our progress to date?'

'It's your fault if your commanding officer is lacking information. Your job is to keep everyone up to speed. We work as a team.'

'Whose team are you on, Colonel?' Donadze said, immediately regretting his words.

The Colonel smiled. 'I see what you mean now, Captain,' he said. 'Listen carefully, Lieutenant. You have three days to bring charges in this case. Failure to do so will result in you being re-assigned. Do you understand?'

'Yes, sir.'

'Get back to work, Donadze,' Bukia said, smirking behind the Colonel's back.

NINE

Donadze returned to his desk, glancing up occasionally to observe Bukia and Meskhi talking. On one occasion he had looked up to see both men staring directly at him and he had quickly looked away. He wasn't surprised that his superior officers were discussing him. He wondered if Meskhi had given him the three-day deadline in retaliation for his disrespect and, if so, realised that he had only himself to blame. He considered going back to the office to apologise but decided not to, as he had no way to justify his words and, in any event, he judged that the damage had already been done.

Meskhi left after about ten minutes, walking past Donadze without speaking or looking in his direction. Bukia stayed at his desk, chewing on his morning snack and staring at him through his office window. Donadze's fingers had been resting immobile on his keyboard for several minutes. Now, no longer prepared to be scrutinised like a fish in a bowl, he stood and walked to Arziani's desk. 'Come on, Misha,' he said. 'We're going out.'

Donadze was in his car waiting, the engine running, when Arziani caught up with him. He got in the passenger seat.

'Put your belt on,' Donadze said.

Arziani buckled up. 'Where are we going?'

The car pulled away, sputtering blue smoke and noxious drops of liquid in its wake. 'Out of here.'

Arziani looked at him uneasily. 'Are you okay, Ramaz?'

'Yes, fine.' Donadze followed the road along the right bank of the River Kura and stopped near the dry-stone bridge.

'This is where Adamia was found?'

Donadze nodded. 'Let's take a look.'

They stood by the low wall, the hot sun in their faces, looking down on the bank where Nino's body had been pulled out of the water.

'Do you want to go down? Do you think we've missed something?' Arziani asked.

'You're a graduate aren't you, Misha?'

'Yes, law degree from TSU. Why are you asking?'

'Good degree then. So why the Police? Why not take your degree and make real money working in business or for the government?'

Arziani frowned and looked at Donadze quizzically. 'Why the Police? It's a long story, and to be honest, I'm not sure I want to discuss that with you right now.'

'But do you feel that you're doing good?'

'Of course, don't you?

'Most of the time. Don't worry, Misha, I'm not going mad. Let's go back to the station.'

The King David Restaurant was almost full when Donadze arrived. Tamuna was already seated at a corner table and stood to kiss him. 'Hey, Ramaz,' she said.

'You're here early, quiet day at the Clinic?'

'Not particularly, I just wanted us to spend some time together.'

'Me too, how are things at your apartment? Is my mother behaving?'

'You're mother's lovely. She's taking good care of me actually.'

'Really? That's good to hear. Not that you need much taking care of.'

'Not usually anyway,' she smiled.

The waiter approached their table and left menus. 'Would you like to order drinks?' he said.

'*Tsinandali*?' Donadze asked.

'Just water for me,' Tamuna told the waiter.

'I'll have the same,' Donadze said.

'How have you been?' Tamuna said.

'I'm okay, a bit tired, this case is full on and I'll have to pick up the tempo. It's very political, I've been speaking to some big shots and it's not going down well. My bosses have given three days to bring charges.'

'Well, don't overdo it. Listen Ramaz, do I still need Police protection? Having a car parked outside my apartment is a bit unsettling. Do you—'

'It's not really protection, Tamuna. And it won't be for long. It makes me feel better if nothing else.'

'Well, so long as *you* feel better...' She stopped herself, then added, 'Sorry, I don't want us to row.'

'I don't either.' He took her hands in his. 'I'm sorry as well. Try to ignore the car, I'll take it away as soon as I can.'

'Don't worry, it's not that important. Ramaz, I wanted to see you this evening because—'

'Your water,' the waiter said, opening the bottle. 'Have you chosen your meal?'

'Five minutes, please,' said Donadze. 'Do you know what you want to eat?' he asked Tamuna.

'You choose, I'm not very hungry. Listen, as I was saying, I wanted to see you this evening... Ramaz, are you listening to me?'

Donadze had glanced across the restaurant and noticed Toreli's legal counsel at a table in the opposite corner. It took him a moment to remember his name—Alex Jibuti. He was talking with a middle-aged man who Donadze didn't recognise. The conversation seemed to be intense with Jibuti leaning in towards the other man and pointing with his finger. At that moment, Jibuti looked up to see Donadze staring at him. His face hardened momentarily, and he said a few words before leaning back in his chair.

'Ramaz?' Tamuna said.

'Sorry, what were you saying?'

'It's not important. Let's order.'

The waiter returned and Donadze ordered their favourite dishes to share. He kept an eye on Jibuti's table and after about ten minutes, both men left. He tried to focus on Tamuna during their meal but was conscious that she was carrying most of the conversation as his thoughts continually returned to the investigation. They finished eating, Tamuna declining dessert and coffee. Donadze called for the check and paid.

Tamuna was picking up her handbag. 'Shall I come back to your place tonight?' he said.

'No, it's not a good idea.'

'Well, let me drop you off then.'

'It's okay, I'll get a taxi.'

'If you're sure. It was lovely seeing you.'

Tamuna leaned over and kissed Donadze on the cheek. 'Was it? You weren't even here,' she said, walking towards the door.

Donadze stood, staring at her back before following her out the restaurant. *No. I wasn't,* he thought.

Gloveli called the next morning. 'Ramaz, I've tracked down the two Russians we discussed. They've been in and out of Georgia for at least three months, travelling through Tbilisi Airport as far as I could make out. Edik Nikitin and Dmitr Banasik—they claim to be traders, buying copper ore for export to Ukraine. But that's not who they are and it's also not what they are. Their real names are Pavel Lobodin and Danya Pilkin and they're both SVR agents. You'll have their pictures on your phone within the hour.'

'Russian Foreign Intelligence? Why would they be speaking to Kaldani?'

'I don't know. I had to burn some serious political capital to even get their names. These people are protected at the highest levels and my source was really nervous even talking about them.'

'Why Georgia?' Donadze asked.

'Well, it won't be to foster better relations, that's for sure. We should assume the SVR has been operating here for some time now, certainly before the 2008 war.'

'Wasn't the SVR suspected of the Litvinenko poisoning in England?'

'Yes, the SVR doesn't like defectors. Especially defectors who accuse Putin of running a "mafia state". They're authorised to conduct what is termed, "special measures" abroad.'

'Russian spies killing Georgian citizens in Tbilisi?'

'Don't get ahead of yourself, Donadze. All we know so far is that two SVR agents met with Dato Kaldani. We don't know why they met or what they were discussing. It won't have been innocent, but it might have nothing to do with the Adamia murder.'

'Do you believe that, Major?'

'I don't know what to believe, you shouldn't either.'

'Investigating foreign spies is outside normal Police work—should I inform the GIS?' said Donadze, referring to Georgia's intelligence service.

'I think that decision goes beyond your pay grade. You need to take this higher. But not to Bukia, not if you don't want to tip off Kaldani.'

'Colonel Meskhi then? What do you know about him?'

'Gabi Meskhi? He served as a detective under me for a

while. I don't know him very well, but I do remember that he was very bright. I also didn't have any reason to worry that he was corrupt. But that was some time ago though, things can change. You do need to take this up the tree and Meskhi is probably your best bet. But, listen carefully, Ramaz. Information can flow in more than one direction. You now know that the SVR has agents operating in Georgia. You know their names—but from what you told me a couple of days ago, they know *yours* as well.'

'Understood, do you think they have your name as well, Major?'

'It's possible, but I'm not too concerned for myself. You should be careful though. If the SVR can take "special measures" against a high-level defector in England, they wouldn't worry too much about a Georgian pain-in-the-butt Police lieutenant.'

'Understood, thanks,' Donadze said, ending the call.

It took Donadze over an hour to reach the Ministry of Internal Affairs' HQ on Gulua Street. He drove steadily through the ill-disciplined and bad-tempered traffic, planning how to conduct his conversation with Colonel Meskhi. He had decided he would have a better chance of getting the Colonel's attention if they spoke face-to-face. He hadn't, however, requested a meeting as he didn't want a record of their conversation appearing on Meskhi's digital schedule.

Parking his car, Donadze entered the MIA building, presented his ID at Reception and requested directions to

Meskhi's office. He took an elevator to the fourth level and walked past several private offices and open plan work areas before arriving at a closed door bearing Meskhi's name and rank. He took a deep breath, knocked three times and opened the door.

Meskhi was sitting on a comfortable looking leather swivel chair behind a large desk, facing dual LCD monitors. Both his hands were poised over a keyboard. He stopped typing and looked up as Donadze entered, 'Lieutenant?' he said, sounding surprised.

'*Gamarjoba,* sir. I apologise for the interruption, but I need your advice on a sensitive and confidential matter,' Donadze said.

'So sensitive and confidential that you couldn't request a meeting with me?'

'Yes, sir.'

'I see, and no doubt your commanding officer has approved you coming here unannounced?'

'I haven't discussed this matter with Captain Bukia.'

'And why is that?' Meskhi asked.

'With respect, sir, I would prefer not to say at this stage.'

'Well, this is very unusual but then, I suppose, you are a very unconventional Police officer.' Meskhi glanced at his wall clock. 'Ten minutes,' he said, indicating a small conference table in the corner of the office.

Donadze stood by the table and waited until being invited to sit.

'Ten minutes,' Meskhi repeated.

'Thank you, sir. During my investigation into the Adamia murder I obtained information which indicates that at least two Russian SVR agents are conducting a covert operation here in Georgia and I would appreciate your advice on how to proceed.'

Meskhi leaned back in his chair and stared at Donadze for a long moment. 'Russian spies operating in Georgia? That's hardly surprising I suppose. What do you think they're up to?' he asked.

'I haven't been able to ascertain that yet.'

'I see. And how did you come by this information?'

'Dato Kaldani is a person of interest in my investigation. A source alerted me that the Russians had met with Kaldani at the Dream Casino.'

'And you obviously think they weren't there just to play the tables. Have you therefore deduced that Kaldani is somehow involved in this covert operation?'

'I think that's likely, sir.'

'Tell me, what led you to the conclusion that these Russians are SVR agents?'

'They're in the country under false identifies, posing as copper ore traders.'

'That doesn't tell me how you know they are SVR,' Meskhi persisted.

'An acquaintance was able to ascertain their real names and their membership of the SVR.'

'Your acquaintance being?'

'With respect, sir, I would prefer not to say at this stage. He is however a reliable source.'

'And I have to take your word for that?'

'I apologise but, as indicated, this matter is extremely sensitive.'

Meskhi straightened and nodded thoughtfully. 'So, to recap,' he said. 'This is a tale about two Russians whom an unnamed acquaintance has told you are spies. You have inferred that they are working with Dato Kaldani on a covert operation—purpose unknown. You have gone outside the chain of command by not clearing this with Captain Bukia and you don't trust me enough to give me all the facts. Is that a fair—'

A uniformed policewoman opened Meskhi's door and looked over to the conference table. 'Excuse me, sir. Your team performance review is ready to start.'

'Please apologise on my behalf—I'll be five minutes late,' the Colonel replied. He waited until the door was closed. 'As I was saying, Donadze, is my summary of our conversation accurate?'

'It's not how I would have characterised it, sir,' Donadze said.

'Wouldn't you? So, what exactly did you hope to achieve by coming to see me today?'

'I'm confident these Russians are SVR operatives and that they are connected to Kaldani and possibly to the Adamia murder. I need to know what to do with that information. I would specifically like to know if we should inform Georgian Intelligence. If we do, who has jurisdiction in a case like this?'

'The GIS... I see your dilemma. We certainly want to bring this case to a successful conclusion, especially if it gives us some leverage against Kaldani. Bringing in the GIS would shift the focus, possibly tip Kaldani off.'

'That's my concern.'

Meskhi paused. 'Very well, let's keep this as a Police investigation for now,' he said. 'I want you to report directly to me.' He took a card from a drawer and wrote on the back. 'You can get me on this number at any time. I want regular updates and to be told immediately if there are any significant developments.'

'Thank you, sir. And Captain Bukia?'

'Bukia remains your commanding officer but he does not have to be informed of this arrangement for now. Anything else?'

'My deadline to bring charges, given developments that could—'

'The deadline remains. You're dismissed.'

'Thank you, sir. I appreciate you time.' Donadze stood and walked to the door, feeling Meskhi's eyes on his back.

TEN

S weat was running down Donadze's face as he left the MIA building and walked slowly to his car through scorched air, the concrete baking under his feet. He hadn't been able to find a shaded parking place and the car's internal surfaces burned when touched. He started the engine and gratefully felt cool air drying his skin, leaving it gritty with crystallised salt.

The meeting with the Colonel had gone as well as Donadze could have hoped—but had still left him feeling uneasy. Up to this point, only he and Gloveli had known that the SVR was operating in Georgia. Meskhi now also had that information. If corrupt, he could inform the Russians that their operation had been exposed—allowing them to silence anyone with knowledge of their plot before escaping the country.

Donadze felt out of his depth. There was too much he couldn't control. For a moment he wished he'd never been on call when Nino's body had been found, that the case had been assigned to someone else. He pulled the sun visor down, slid the vanity mirror cover open and scrutinised himself in the small rectangle of glass. *One step at a time, Ramaz, one step at a time*, he told himself.

Donadze thought about his meal with Tamuna the previous evening, remembering how badly it had gone. She probably didn't realise how much he loved her, probably because he had rarely told her so. He had only ever had a few girlfriends and he had been with Tamuna much longer than any other.

Like all police officers, Donadze understood the strain created by his work. Some could manage it, but Donadze knew his obsessive nature was particularly damaging and would stop him being with Tamuna for the long term— unless he could change.

The future scared him. He looked at many of his older colleagues and saw how their work had cost them their marriages, their families, and their friends. Had cost them everything except each other. They would huddle together at their favourite bars and restaurants, re-telling their war stories—all the time being drawn more deeply into the job. With no escape possible, they dreaded the day they would retire to lonely old age and early lifestyle-induced death. Donadze had resolved to avoid that fate but could feel the same forces pulling on him.

But he wasn't there yet, he still had a chance. As the temperature in the car dropped, he felt his resolve grow. Lifting his phone, he punched out a text to Tamuna. *'Sorry I was distracted yesterday. Can I come around to your apartment this evening, say 7?'*

He slid the driving seat closer to the wheel, buckled his seat belt, adjusted the rear-view mirror and manoeuvred onto the road. *Time to stir things up*, he thought as he drove towards Marjanishvili.

Parking was tight as usual and Donadze left his car in a restricted space on Petersburg Street. He re-traced his route to the United Energy office, approached the front desk and, showing his ID, interrupted the receptionist who was helping another visitor. 'I would like to speak to Mr. Morton,' he said.

The receptionist glanced at the other visitor who shrugged. 'Let me see if Mr. Morton is available,' she said coldly, reaching for her phone.

A few minutes later, Morton's personal assistant arrived at Reception.

'Lieutenant! Welcome back to UE. Rob is in the office today, but his diary is full until six. You didn't schedule a meeting?'

'No. Please tell Mr. Morton I need to speak with him urgently. I can wait ten minutes, no longer.'

'He's in a conference call until five.'

'As I said, ten minutes, no longer.'

'I'll check if Rob can see you. Please wait here.' She looked across to the receptionist, 'Please give the Lieutenant a visitor's pass.'

The assistant returned as Donadze was receiving his

pass. 'Please come with me,' she said, taking the stairs to Morton's office.

Morton wasn't smiling and remained seated behind his desk. Donadze sat opposite without being invited. 'Good afternoon, Mr. Morton. Good of you to see me on short notice,' he smiled.

'What would have happened if I hadn't? Would I have been arrested?' Morton said, his gaze on Donadze.

'Hopefully not. I have some follow-up questions for you.' He placed prints of the two SVR operatives on Morton's desk. 'Have you seen these men before?'

Morton kept his gaze on Donadze. 'You have an unfortunate manner, Lieutenant. We talked of this before. My office has already registered UE's concern about how you conduct your business.'

'I'm sorry you don't like my manner, Mr. Morton. But I think it's more than unfortunate that a young woman has been murdered. A woman you were acquainted with, perhaps your office should consider that?'

'Ask me your questions!' Morton snapped.

'Thank you.' Donadze tapped the two prints in turn. 'Have you seen these men before?'

Morton picked up the prints in both hands, held them close to his face and looked between the two. He shook his head and returned them to the desk. 'No, I don't think so. Who are they?'

'Persons of interest in this case. Do you know a Dato Kaldani?'

Morton paused. 'There's a businessman I met called Kaldani, operates a casino in Tbilisi?'

'Yes, that's him. How did you meet?'

'The American Chamber of Commerce has a branch in Tbilisi. Local businessmen attend. I probably met him there.'

'How about Giorgi Licheli?'

Morton paused again. 'No, I don't think so.'

'Given your relationship with Miss Adamia, do you have any thoughts on why she was murdered?'

'There you go again... Maybe we are losing something in translation but, as I said previously, I did not have a relationship with Miss Adamia. I was seeing her. Yes, for sex, as you pointed out. But no, I have no thoughts on why she was murdered. She was a sweet girl and I wish I could help you more.'

'Well, maybe you will,' said Donadze as he stood. 'I'm sure we'll speak again.'

Donadze's mother had prepared a meal as he arrived at Tamuna's apartment. A variety of Georgian dishes covered the small table and a bottle of *Tsinandali,* along with bottles of water and lemonade, stood in the centre, condensation running down the cold glass.

Donadze kissed his mother. '*Gamarjoba, Deda.* The food looks good. Your own *lobio*?' he said, bending to smell the beans, onions and herbs which were still bubbling slowly inside their clay pot.

'Of course. Have a seat and pour yourself some wine. Tamuna's just had a shower and she's getting dressed. She'll be out in a minute.'

'You've only set two places?'

'Yes, you and Tamuna should have some time on your own. Anyway, I have to go to my apartment to pick up some things.'

'Why not wait and I'll drive you there?'

'I'll get a taxi there and back. Don't worry, I'll be fine.'

'Stay and eat with us.'

'No, I'm not hungry. Enjoy your meal. I'll be back in a couple of hours,' she said, picking up her bag to leave.

Donadze looked at his watch, noted the time she had left then walked to the closed bedroom. 'Hey, Tamuna,' he said.

'Come in,' she replied.

She was sitting at the dresser wearing a knee-length cotton shift dress, with bare feet, brushing her long dark hair which was still damp from the shower. 'You look gorgeous,' Donadze said, meaning it. He leaned over and kissed her neck. 'I've missed you.'

'Yes, well, I've missed you too. But it's difficult just now with your mother staying here and the Police car outside. I'm not complaining though. Let's have some food,' she said, putting her brush down and standing.

They sat at the table and Donadze passed her the salad bowl. 'Wine?' he asked.

'Just water for me, thanks.'

Donadze filled her water glass and poured water and wine for himself before transferring cheese to their plates. 'How are you coping with the heat?' he said.

'Not too bad. It's nice and cool at the Clinic. How's your case going?'

'It's a bit tricky but let's not talk about that tonight. I

could do with forgetting about it for a while.'

She put her knife and fork down and took a sip of water. 'Ramaz, there's something we need to talk about.'

'What? You're not breaking up with me, are you?' he asked, anxiously.

'No, nothing like that...Ramaz, you're going to be a father.'

Donadze held her gaze for a moment. He put his hand over hers and swallowed hard, 'You're pregnant...'

'Yes, I've been trying to find the right time to tell you.'

He stood, pulled her to her feet and drew her in tightly, inhaling the fresh, perfumed smell of her hair. 'That's wonderful, wonderful...thank you.'

'Well, thank you too,' she laughed.

Donadze also laughed and hugged her again before drawing back and kissing her on the lips. 'And you're well?'

'Yes, both of us are fine.'

'I can't believe it. When's the baby due?'

'I'm at eight weeks, so late April probably.'

'And I'm guessing my mother knows about this already...'

'What do you think? I've called my mother as well, they're both really excited.'

'Ah, you girls. Speaking of which—'

'Far too soon—but do you want to know?'

'You can decide that one, I really just want what you want.'

'And you're happy?'

'I can't remember when I've been as happy. What about you?'

'Yes, of course I am, but it's going to mean big changes. For both of us.'

'Yes, we'll have to talk about the future, what we want to do about our work, where we'll live.'

'We will. But not right now. Let's finish our meal and see your mother when she gets back. Stay over, but just for tonight. There's a lot to take in. Let's not rush things.'

They sat at the table, passing food to each other and eating and drinking slowly, keeping the conversation light with long comfortable silences. They were in the kitchen cleaning up after their meal when Donadze's mother returned, knocking on the apartment door, even though he knew she had a key. He let her in and turned to see Tamuna give her a slight nod. She threw her arms around her son's neck, drew him down and smothered his face and head with kisses. 'It's wonderful news, *Ramazi*. So exciting. I'm so happy for you both.'

'And maybe a little happy for yourself?' he joked.

'I'm definitely happy and more than a little. Oh, but listen, that heat has tired me out. I have to go to bed.' She kissed Donadze again before walking over to hug and kiss Tamuna as well. '*Dzli nebisa*,' she said.

'*Dzli nebisa, Deda.*'

He made tea as his mother was preparing for bed and took two cups to the living area. They talked a little longer before Tamuna put her empty cup down and stood to take his hand.

Donadze felt like he had come home as they gently made love in the hot room. Later, as Tamuna slept, he lay beside her, the sweat drying on his back, his thoughts turning to the future. He had been completely honest when he had told her how happy he was that they were having a baby. But what now? Should they get married? Where would they live? Would Tamuna want to keep working? She earned more than he did—could they get by on his salary? Could he be less obsessed with his work and what would happen if not? What really did he have to offer? He raised himself on his elbow and looked down on Tamuna as she slept, her face slightly flushed, breathing softly through her open mouth, his baby growing inside her. *So much to think about*, Donadze thought. *But nothing that can't wait until tomorrow.* He watched her a moment longer then lay back and, with his head on the pillows, closed his eyes and slept.

ELEVEN

Tamuna had showered and dressed and was preparing breakfast with his mother when Donadze went through to the living area. Both women smiled at him. 'Sleep well?' his mother said.

'Very well, thanks.'

'Good, have a coffee and something to eat. I'm going out. I want to do some shopping before it gets too hot,' she said, looking at Donadze defiantly.

'You've not eaten,' Tamuna said.

'I'll get something when I get back. I'll see you soon,' she said, kissing her son.

Tamuna watched the apartment door close. 'Is she safe going out on her own?'

'Yes, she'll be okay at this time of day. She won't go far anyway.'

'You know she's only going out to give us some space?'

'Yes, I realised that. I didn't know she could be so discreet.'

'You know she worries about you, don't you?'

'I know she does.'

'So, how are you feeling this morning, *mamik'o*?' she smiled.

'About becoming a father? I can't believe it. I'm so excited. I can hardly wait till April.'

'Well, you'll have to. You know Ramaz, last night...'

'I know, it was a one-off until my mother's back home. I'll go to my own apartment tonight.'

'Good, and let's have that talk about the future. Not today, but soon. And please, let's keep our news to ourselves, at least for now.'

'Yes, definitely.'

'I'd better get into work. Enjoy your breakfast. I'm not having anything—I've started to feel a bit nauseous in the mornings.'

'Okay, well, keep your strength up. Call you this evening?'

'Please,' she said, kissing him and walking towards the door.

Donadze ate quickly then shaved and showered. He shut his eyes and kept his mouth tightly closed as the warm water washed over his head and shoulders. He couldn't remember a time when he felt so positive. He was delighted at the prospect of becoming a father and felt that the baby had already brought him and Tamuna closer. *Just don't mess it up this time*, he thought.

It was eight forty-five when Donadze arrived at Mtatsminda Station. He logged onto the Police system and considered how he should update his case files. The Colonel's instructions had been to keep information about the Russian operatives confidential and he updated the files accordingly.

Bukia arrived at nine thirty, squeezing past desks on his way to his office. He stopped beside Donadze. 'I thought you were getting tired of this station, Lieutenant.'

'Sir?'

'Come to my office in ten minutes.'

Donadze waited twenty minutes. Bukia was wedged behind his desk, leaning back in his chair to see the keyboard which was partially obscured by his overhanging belly. He looked at his watch and frowned. 'Sit down.'

'Thank you,' Donadze said, sitting opposite.

'Go ahead, Lieutenant.'

'Sorry, Captain?'

'I assume you wish to tell me why you visited Colonel Meskhi at his HQ yesterday'

'Did the Colonel tell you I had visited?'

'Any conversations I have with the Colonel do not concern you, Donadze. Why did you go to see him?'

Donadze had anticipated Bukia getting to hear of the and had planned his explanation. 'I had hoped that the Colonel would re-consider the three-day deadline he had given me to bring charges.'

'And you asked him to do that?'

'Yes.'

'What did he tell you?'

'He said that the deadline remains.'

Bukia snorted derisively. 'As I would have expected. What else did you discuss?'

'I gave him a general update on the investigation to date.'

Bukia's face reddened. 'Did you consider giving your commanding officer an update first? Or to ask permission before going above my head. Tell me, Donadze, do you have *any* respect for the chain of command?'

'Certainly. And the Colonel himself reminded me it must always be respected.'

'Of course, he did,' Bukia said. 'It says a lot about your character that you needed that reminder. I have to say that this is very unprofessional conduct. You've let everyone at this station down.'

'I'm sorry if that's the case.'

'It's certainly the case. Tell me, your three-day deadline expires tomorrow doesn't it?'

'Yes.'

'And is it likely that you will have brought charges by then?'

'It's possible, a lot can happen in two days. But it'll be difficult.'

'So, should I be thinking about who to give your case to? Who would you recommend?'

'I couldn't say, Captain.'

'Well, I'll give it some thought. Anyway, I've wasted enough time with you. Let me be clear on this matter. You are not to have any further communication with the Colonel unless authorised by me first. Is that understood?'

'Yes.'

'I'm recording this conversation in your personnel file. Failure to follow my instructions in this matter will result in disciplinary action. Now get back to work.'

Donadze returned to his desk, passing Misha Arziani, who winked at him conspiratorially. He smiled back, grateful for the implied support. Bukia seemed to have accepted Donadze's account of his meeting with the Colonel, which suggested that the substance of their conversation had been kept confidential. Meskhi had however instructed him to provide updates and Donadze intended doing just that, despite Bukia's threats.

Donadze wanted to speak with Minister Toreli again to ask him about any connections he had to the Russian agents. He doubted if Bukia would help set up a second meeting and, in any event, he could not spare the time to go through formal channels.

He had called Toreli's office and was told that the Minister wouldn't be able to speak to him as he was flying to Germany on government business. He had then checked flight schedules and had guessed that Toreli would be flying Georgian Airlines from Tbilisi to Berlin Schoenefeld Airport. He was waiting outside the Ministry building on Sanapiro Street when Toreli and his counsel, Jibuti emerged, walking briskly towards the government SUV which was waiting for them with its engine running and blue lights flashing in the grille.

Donadze walked in a direction to intercept Toreli, one hand held high and open, the other holding his ID for the benefit of the security officer who was scanning the short route from building to car. 'Minister Toreli, I need to speak with you.'

Toreli stopped and spoke to the security officer. 'It's Okay, Tomas, I know this man. It's Lieutenant...'

'Donadze, sir. I need just a few minutes of your time.'

'That won't be possible, Lieutenant,' Jibuti said, 'The Minister has a flight to catch.'

'I wouldn't have bothered you if it wasn't important,' Donadze said, ignoring the attorney.

'I see you're on your own today. Did your Captain have more pressing duties? Or does he not know you're here?' Toreli said.

'As Captain Bukia mentioned, I'm lead investigator on this case, which I would remind you involves the murder of a young woman you were acquainted with,' Donadze said.

Toreli shook his head. 'Let's give him the benefit of the doubt, Alex,' he said to his counsel. 'We can talk in the car.'

'Thank you, sir, very much appreciated,' Donadze said.

Toreli and Jibuti sat in the back two seats, leaving Donadze to join the driver in the front. As the car accelerated away, he turned to face the Minister who had opened his briefcase on his lap.

'You remember our discussion about respecting the Minister's privacy, Lieutenant?' Jibuti said, nodding at the driver's back.

'Did you enjoy your meal at the King David Restaurant, Mr. Jibuti?'

'I beg your pardon?'

'We were both there two nights ago.'

'Really? You should have said hello.'

'I doubt your dining experiences have any relevance here. Can we get on with this?' Toreli said.

Donadze took the pictures of the SVR operatives out of a folder and passed them back to Toreli. 'Do you know these men?'

'They do look familiar. Alex?' Toreli passed the pictures to Jibuti.

'Yes, traders, I think. Looking to export ore to Ukraine. I can't quite recall their names.'

'Where did we come across them?' Toreli asked.

'Your office, about six weeks ago, I think. It was a courtesy visit.'

Toreli handed the pictures back to Donadze. 'Yes, I remember now. Is that all, Lieutenant?'

'What did you discuss?'

'The Minister's discussions with foreign investors are—'

'That's okay, Alex,' Toreli interrupted. 'We're familiar with the Lieutenant's methods by now.' He smiled at Donadze. 'As Mr. Jibuti said, it was a courtesy visit. I don't recall the details, but we probably spent about ten minutes together. They told me that they were looking to set up some trades involving export of copper ore. I'm sure I wished them luck with their venture and offered them the support of my office if required. Standard stuff.'

'Do you know if Nino Adamia had any connection to these men?' Donadze said.

Toreli glanced at the driver's back. 'I think we'll wind it up at that, Lieutenant,' he said. He tapped the driver on the shoulder, 'Lieutenant Donadze is extremely busy, pull over and let him get back to work.'

The SUV stopped on the inner lane of the George W Bush Highway, the fast road connecting the city to the airport. Donadze got out the car and stood on the grass bank, buffeted by traffic which was passing at speed—wondering how he would get back to the city.

Arziani picked Donadze up and took him to the Ministry building to collect his car. 'Can we keep this between the two of us?' Donadze had asked.

He drove back to his apartment on Kandelaki Street. He had two calls to make, the first to Tamuna as he had promised. He had seen her that morning and, as they didn't have a lot more to say, the call only lasted five minutes.

He then called Colonel Meskhi who answered after two rings, 'What do you have for me, Lieutenant?'

Donadze provided an update on his interviews of Morton and Toreli. He was surprised not to be censured for approaching a high-profile businessman and senior politician without permission.

'I heard that you had spoken with Morton. You might have advised me that you wished to speak with Toreli, but I think you were justified in doing so,' Meskhi said.

'Thank you, sir. Captain Bukia was aware that we had spoken yesterday...'

'Yes, I told him. I'm sure he would have found out anyway. Was he angry?'

'Yes, he said that I was not to have any further direct contact with you.'

'And yet, here you are talking to me now. Have you any more information on these Russians?'

'Morton claimed he doesn't know them. Toreli said he met them briefly when they were posing as traders.'

'Did you believe them?'

'Difficult to be sure. They were certainly both worried about their liaisons with Nino Adamia becoming known. Morton didn't seem concerned when I asked about the Russians, but I thought Toreli and his attorney tried a bit too hard to stress that their relationship was purely professional.'

'Interesting. But, as far as Adamia is concerned, we are policemen, not priests. I don't see any reason why their liaisons, as you put it, *should* become known, do you?'

'Only if it becomes pertinent to the case.'

'Clearly. What's your next move?'

'I think we need to get more information on the Russians. I can't ask Captain Bukia for help. Would you be prepared to set up surveillance on them?'

'Don't you think I would have done that already?'

'Using good people, I hope? They'll disappear back to Russia if they think their cover has been blown.'

'Yes, Donadze, that had occurred to me.'

'Sorry, sir.'

'Anything else?'

'The three-day target you gave me to bring charges...'

'Not a target, a deadline. I take it you won't be bringing charges tomorrow?'

'Highly unlikely, sir.'

'Well, that's unfortunate,' Meskhi said, hanging up.

TWELVE

'   vto?' Donadze said as he put down his coffee cup
and answered his phone.
        There was a long pause. '*Gamarjoba,*
Lieutenant.'

'Kaldani!'

'Yes.'

'What do you want?'

'I'm calling on behalf of your friend.'

'Avto? What have you done to him?'

'Me? Nothing—but I'm afraid he's been beaten.'

'Beaten! Who would have done that if not you?'

'How would I know? He was found in the Dream's car
park by my barman.'

'Tell me what happened.'

'Who knows? Maybe a homophobic attack. You know
how some people are.'

'And now you have his phone.'

'He told my barman that he didn't want an ambulance, that he should call you. Of course, nothing happens at the Dream that I don't get to hear about. So, I said I would call you myself. Lucky for Avto he has you as a friend, don't you think? How did you come to know him?'

'Where is he now?'

'I've had him taken to the casino's first aid room. He's being looked after.'

'I'm coming over now. Keep him safe, Kaldani.'

'I'm not sure I like your tone, Lieutenant. But it's understandable, you're probably very upset.'

Donadze hung up and headed for his apartment door, arriving at the Dream Casino within thirty minutes. Licheli was waiting at the entrance, a smirk playing on his lips.

'Where is he?' Donadze said.

Licheli turned without speaking and sauntered through the casino lobby, Donadze following closely behind. They reached a door with a red cross on the outside, the smell of disinfectant sharp on Donadze's nostrils. He barged past Licheli and threw the door open. Avto was lying on the treatment couch, stripped to his underpants and looking very young and vulnerable. His pale thin body was a mass of bruises, his chest wrapped in compression bandages, his face swollen, and his eyes closed to slits. A middle-aged woman was standing at the foot of the couch. 'You're Lieutenant Donadze?' she said.

Donadze put his hand on Avto's arm. 'What happened?' he said. Getting no response, he turned to Licheli who was leaning against the wall on the other side of the couch. 'Who did this?'

'No idea. Could have been a boyfriend I suppose. Maybe he's been playing around, you know how jealous these queers can get.' He straightened, stepped to the treatment couch and shouted into Avto's ear, 'Hey, Avto, tell the Lieutenant who did this to you.'

'Get away from him!' Donadze said. He turned to the woman. 'Please call an ambulance, he's going to the hospital.' He put his hand back on Avto's arm. 'Don't worry. You're safe now.'

'How sweet,' Licheli said.

Donadze raced around the couch, pushed Licheli back hard against the wall and jammed his forearm under his chin, forcing him onto his toes. 'Say that again!' he said.

Licheli didn't resist and Donadze pressed harder. 'Say that again!'

'Lieutenant, please!' the woman said.

Donadze released Licheli, who slumped forward, rubbing his throat. 'Assault in front of a witness,' he said hoarsely, 'Probably not your smartest move.'

'I'll see you in court then. Where's your CCTV records.'

'Take that up with the boss. But anyway, the system doesn't cover the car park.'

Donadze turned again to the woman and gave her his card. 'Let me know where he gets taken. Please look after him until the ambulance arrives.'

'Don't you think I would have done that anyway,' she said coldly.

He leant down and spoke softly to the injured young man, 'You'll be safe at the hospital. They'll take good care of you and I'll see you soon.'

Avto turned to look at Licheli and started to speak but Donadze placed his hand on his shoulder. 'Just rest for now, I'll see you later.' He glared at Licheli who was still rubbing his throat. 'Where's Kaldani?'

'In his office. Up the stairs, turn left.'

Donadze nodded to the woman then left the first aid room. His adrenalin had spiked, and he wished he hadn't attacked Licheli. He wasn't worried about charges being brought but he knew that anger clouded good judgment. He tried to compose himself as he crossed the lobby and climbed the stairs. He arrived at Kaldani's office, opened the door without knocking and went in. This office was much smaller than the one at Rustaveli Avenue—probably not required to impress criminal associates and corrupt politicians, Donadze thought. Kaldani was sitting behind a small functional desk and nodded to him to sit opposite.

'Why?' Donadze said.

'Are you recording this?'

Donadze took his phone out of his pocket and placed it on the desk, face up.

'Why?' he repeated.

'Why was your friend beaten? Let's assume for now it had nothing to do with his, what shall we call it—lifestyle. That being the case, you could probably ask yourself that question.'

'What do you mean?'

Kaldani smiled. 'You know, Lieutenant, Georgia is a very conservative country—not everyone is as tolerant as you and me. But your young friend was doing well at the Dream.

I gave him a job, treated him properly, didn't interfere in his life or make judgments about how he lived. All I asked in return was loyalty. But then, someone turned him against me.'

'So, you had him beaten because he was disloyal to you.'

Kaldani raised his hands. 'Your words, not mine. You asked me why he was attacked. Maybe someone took advantage of him and put him in harm's way. That person should be asking himself these questions.'

'That person being me?'

'Only you would know that.'

'What now?'

'Well, I'm sure your colleagues will want to investigate this assault. For my part, I'm assuming that he either had a fall-out with a boyfriend or it was a homophobic assault. As I said, I have nothing against these people, but I must protect my business interests. He won't be returning to the Dream.'

Donadze stood. 'Just so we're clear, I'll take it very personally if Avto is hurt again. Tell that to your thug, Licheli,' he said.

'No need for threats, Lieutenant.' Kaldani smiled. 'On a more positive note, I hear that congratulations are in order. Please pass on my best wishes to Tamuna.'

Donadze felt blood rising to his face as he snatched up his phone, turned and strode out the door.

The casino was starting to fill with early morning gamblers as Donadze returned to his car. An ambulance had pulled up at the front entrance and he watched as paramedics went in with a stretcher. He felt that he should go with them to make sure Avto was being treated well, to keep him safe, to let him know he had someone on his side, to say sorry. Instead, he started the engine and accelerated hard for the exit, smoke blowing through the old car's exhaust system, a blue haze billowing in its wake.

He drove to Tamuna's apartment and pulled up beside the patrol car which was parked outside her block. He didn't recognise the two officers inside but one wound down his window. 'Lieutenant.'

'Anything to report?'

'Nothing, all quiet. Doctor Losava has left for work and your mother's inside.'

'Thanks. Stay alert.'

Donadze walked quickly up the stairs to the third level, arriving outside Tamuna's door short of breath and with sweat prickling his brow. He knocked and his mother opened the door without using the security chain.

'Come in *shvilo*. Tamuna's at work.'

'You should have used the chain, *Deda*. But it's you I wanted to see.'

'Is something wrong? Let me get you a drink.'

'No, thanks. I can't stay. *Deda,* this case I'm working on. You know that it involves some dangerous people?'

'Yes, of course. That's why I'm here, isn't it, why your Police car is parked outside?'

'Yes, I wanted to make sure that you and Tamuna are okay.'

'So, what's happened?'

'Well, I'm a bit more worried now. Someone got hurt.'

'And you're worried the same thing could happen to Tamuna or me? Is this to do with her being pregnant, because, you know—'

'No, nothing like that. And I don't want you to worry, you're both still safe. I just want to take an additional precaution.'

'You want to move back in.'

'Well, yes. I'd feel better—'

'And you want me to persuade Tamuna to allow you.'

'No, not to persuade her, just to speak to her, help her to—'

'No! This doesn't sound like you, *Ramazi*. Do you want to lose her respect? If you have something to say, you say it to her yourself.'

'This isn't about me.'

'Well, I think it might be. And more to the point, Tamuna might think that as well.'

'Why should she? She knows I just want her and the baby to be safe.'

'Of course you want them to be safe, but that's not all you want, is it?'

'I don't know what you mean.'

'Yes, you do. You're using this person getting hurt as an excuse to get closer to her. It's not the right way to do it.'

Donadze's head dropped. 'You've no idea what I'm up against, *Deda*. I can't do my job properly if I'm worrying about Tamuna and you.'

'Come on, Ramaz,' she said sternly. 'We've been through worse than this, haven't we? You're strong, you'll be fine. And so will Tamuna and I.'

Donadze stared at his mother and shook his head. 'I can't remember the last time you spoke to me like that.'

'Well, it won't be the last time, I can promise you that,' she laughed.

'I'd better behave then. And Tamuna?'

'We didn't have this conversation.'

He stood and kissed his mother. 'Take care, *Ramazi*,' she said.

'I will. And please use that door chain.'

Donadze left Tamuna's apartment and took out his phone as he stood outside and listened to his mother locking and bolting the door. The woman from the casino's first aid room had texted to say that Avto had been taken to Tbilisi International Hospital on Chachava Street. He walked quickly down the stairs and out to his car, knocking on the patrol car's roof as he passed.

Traffic was heavy and it took fifty minutes to arrive at the hospital. He walked to Reception, showed his ID and was told that Avto was being assessed in the Emergency Department. A doctor was standing outside the acute assessment ward, writing notes in a case file, as Donadze approached and showed his ID again. 'I would like to see Avto Sabauri,' he said.

'Yes, he said you would be here.'

'How is he?'

'Comfortable. We've given him a high dose of codeine

so his pain's being managed for now. We'll keep him on that dose for the next few days. He's suffered trauma to his left kidney, and we'll have to keep an eye on that. He also has a broken rib which makes breathing painful. His face is quite swollen, and he's lost two teeth, but it looks like there's nothing which will give him problems long term. He'll be here for a couple of days at least but he's going to be stiff and sore for the next two or three weeks.'

'Can I go in?'

'Yes, but don't stay long.'

Avto had been given a hospital gown which hid the bruises Donadze had seen at the casino, but his face was a mass of blue and purple, his head bandaged, and his eyes shut. Donadze pulled a plastic chair close to the bed, sat down and put his hand lightly on his shoulder.

'I'm very sorry,' he said.

Avto's lips moved and Donadze bent closer to hear. 'I didn't want to do this,' he whispered, struggling to speak.

'But we were doing it for Nino, weren't we?'

'How has this helped her?' he said faintly.

'Avto, please stay awake. Can you tell me what happened?'

'Was walking through the car park, got grabbed from behind. They didn't say anything. One held me... other hit... Was thrown onto the ground, kicked. Passed out... Next thing, Zura was helping me up.'

'Zura from the bar? Did you see their faces?'

'Wearing hoods... but I know them, Kaldani's men.'

'Why did they do it?'

'It's obvious... because I was helping you.'

'But why now? Did you find something?'

'No.'

'Are you sure, someone you saw, something you heard?'

'I said no.'

'Why did you ask for me after you were attacked?'

'I didn't... you were the last person I wanted to be seen with.'

'But Kaldani said you asked for me...'

'And you believed him...'

'I'm sorry. Is there anything I can get you? Anything I can do?'

'Yes. Speak to my mum and dad... Tell them what happened. I want to go home.'

'Okay, I'll speak to them. I'll be back to see how you're getting on. I'm sorry this has happened but you're safe now. Try to rest.' Donadze straightened, looked down on Avto's battered face then stood and left the ward.

THIRTEEN

There was little chance that Donadze would be able
to bring charges against Nino's killers that day and
he decided to go to Mtatsminda Station and face
Captain Bukia. The Captain was in his office speaking to
Detective Soso Chichua. Chichua was a similar size to Bukia
and the two men had difficulty squeezing into the restricted
space.

Donadze logged onto the system to check how the
assault on Avto was being treated. There had been no
connection made to Nino's murder and the investigating
officers surmised that it had probably been a homophobic
assault and had given it a low priority. He searched for an
address for Avto's father and copied it to his notebook,
intending to visit him that evening.

Chichua left the office and walked to Donadze's desk.
'Hey, Soso,' Donadze said.

'He wants to see you,' Chichua said. 'Sorry, Lieutenant.'

'That's okay.'

Donadze stood and walked to Bukia's office. 'You asked to see me.'

Bukia had rolled up his shirt sleeves and his fleshy forearms rested on the desk.

'Sit down.' He made a show of completing and sending an email before turning his attention to Donadze. 'It's four thirty and I take it you are not ready to bring charges in the Adamia case?'

'At this point, no.'

'At what point will you be ready?'

'Difficult to say. It's complex and I haven't been given enough time.'

'That's not what the Colonel thinks.'

'So, you're re-assigning my case to Chichua.'

'You've left me no choice.'

'Don't you mean Kaldani's left you no choice?'

'What's that supposed to—'

'How did you find out about Avto Sabauri?'

'Sabauri? What are you talking about?'

'You're not much of a liar, Bukia. What did you think would happen to Avto after you talked to Kaldani? Or didn't you care? How much was that information worth to him?'

'This is gross insubordination! I should suspend you!'

'Yes, you should. But you won't. Suspend me and this goes to HQ. Maybe even outside the department. Who's going to pay your pension then—Kaldani?'

'If only I'd had a witness to this conversation...'

'Bring Chichua in and I'll repeat it.' Getting no response, Donadze continued. 'I thought not. This is the way it'll be. The Colonel wants me off the Adamia case—fine. You and I both know that you're in Kaldani's pocket. Stay out of my way and that goes no further. But, if anyone else gets hurt because of you selling him information, I'll burn you—badly. Is that clear?'

Bukia sat immobile, his face red and his eyes bulging, a small vein on the side of his head throbbing rapidly. 'I've never—'

'Thanks for your support, Captain,' Donadze said loudly as he stood. He walked to Chichua's desk. 'Looks like you've been handed the poisoned chalice, Soso,' he said.

'Yeah, Bukia told me. Can you bring me up to speed?'

'No problem, but let's leave it till tomorrow.'

The sun was low in the sky and the day cooling when Donadze arrived in Rustavi. He parked his car outside Avto's parents' apartment block and took the stairs to the second level. His mother opened the apartment door. 'Is Avto okay?' she asked anxiously after Donadze introduced himself.

'Can we talk inside?'

'Please tell me what's happened to my son.'

'He's going to be okay. Let's go inside.'

She held the door open and Donadze went through into the small living area. A battered leather reclining chair was placed in front of a disproportionately large television showing a popular Georgian medical soap, the volume turned up very high. The chair was occupied by a man who Donadze thought was about forty. He was short, very thin and dressed in grubby white track suit bottoms and a worn Georgia rugby top, his feet bare and dirty. A thick tumbler sat beside the chair, half full of cloudy home-made wine.

'Mr. Sabauri?' Donadze said.

'Yes,' he said, operating a lever on the chair to sit upright.

'Excuse me,' Donadze said, picking up the remote control and turning the television off. He motioned to the woman. 'Please sit down.' He took the last free chair and glanced around. The room was clean and tidy, the walls decorated with Orthodox icons and framed prints of Georgian mountain scenes.

'Will you please tell me what's happened to Avto?' Mrs. Sabauri asked again.

'He'll be okay,' Donadze paused before continuing, 'but he's recovering in hospital.'

'Recovering from what?' Sabauri said.

'He's been beaten, I'm afraid. And he asked me to speak to you.'

'Beaten! Who would do that? And why him?' Mrs. Sabauri cried.

'It's under investigation, but we might never be able to prove who did it or why.'

'Where is he now?' she said.

'The International Hospital in Tbilisi. I visited him this morning, he's in good hands.'

'And he's asked for us? We need to see him,' she said, looking at her husband.

'Why? We've not seen him for, what, two years?' Sabauri said, reaching for his glass.

'I saw him two weeks ago. We've been meeting regularly in Tbilisi,' she said.

Sabauri jumped up and strode a few short steps to stand over his wife, his fists bunched at his side. 'You stupid bitch! I told you we were to have nothing more to do with him!'

Donadze also jumped up. 'Sit down!' he ordered. Sabauri glared at Donadze and snorted derisively before returning to his chair and reaching for his glass again. Donadze softened his tone. 'Avto said that you had told him to leave,' he said. 'But he needs you now. He needs you to take him back.'

'Yes,' Mrs. Sabauri said, 'of course we will, he's our son.'

'No, he's made his choice, he can stay in Tbilisi with his queer friends. He's no son of mine.'

'Of course he's your son,' Mrs. Sabauri said in a pleading voice. Getting no response, she continued scathingly, 'You look down on him but he's a better man than you. How do you think I've been paying for the food you eat? It's not as if you've been bringing any money home.'

'You think you can speak to me like that because of him,' Sabauri said, jabbing a finger at Donadze.

'No, it's not about us. Our son needs us, and we have to help him.'

'You don't have to decide now,' Donadze said. 'Let me take you to the hospital. I'll drive you there and back. Speak to him.'

'Why are you involved in this?' Sabauri said. 'Since when does the Tbilisi Police come out to Rustavi?'

'I'm trying to help. He might have come to harm because of an investigation I'm running.'

'Well, that makes him your responsibility, not mine.'

'Thank you, Lieutenant. I'll come with you,' said Mrs. Sabauri.

'Suit yourself,' Sabauri said, reaching for the television controller, 'but don't bring him back here.'

Mrs. Sabauri gathered up a small bag of fruit to take to the hospital and walked with Donadze to his car. They drove without speaking. He took her to the ward where Avto was being cared for and stayed in the waiting room while she visited her son. The waiting room was empty, and he took the opportunity to call Tamuna.

'Ramaz,' she said. 'I'll have to speak quietly, your mother's having a nap.'

'You should join her. How are you feeling?'

'Great thanks. How about you?'

'I'm fine. Listen Tamuna, can we meet up tomorrow for dinner? We need to talk.'

'Yes, we should, but let's go somewhere quiet. How about your apartment, say at eight?'

'Okay, but don't expect me to cook. I'll order something in.'

'That's a relief,' she said lightly. 'I've got my first antenatal appointment booked as well. I'll tell you about it tomorrow when we meet.'

Donadze's phoned buzzed—Colonel Meskhi was calling.

'Ramaz?' Tamuna said.

'That's great, Tamuna... I'm sorry, but there's a call I need to take. Can I get back to you after that?'

She hesitated, 'No need, I'll see you tomorrow.'

'See you tomorrow, take care,' he said, accepting the Colonel's call.

'When had you intended giving me your update, Lieutenant?'

'Update, sir? I'm off the case. Your decision, I thought.'

'Come to HQ tomorrow, my office, 8:00 a.m.—clear?'

'Yes, sir, can I—'

'8:00 a.m.' Meskhi repeated, hanging up.

Mrs. Sabauri had stayed with Avto until being asked to leave by the nursing staff. She had been upset to see her son so severely injured but relieved when the doctor said he would make a full recovery.

Donadze had driven her back to Rustavi and she had talked incessantly, telling him some of their family history. Her husband had never been close to Avto but had rejected him completely when told by an interfering neighbour that she had seen him with another boy. She was certain that her husband wouldn't let him return home, but that she would continue seeing him regardless.

Donadze asked if she would be safe at home after the row with her husband. She gave an evasive answer, which told Donadze that she probably wouldn't be. *Got to choose my battles*, he thought.

It was after midnight before he returned to his own apartment. He went straight to bed but couldn't sleep, his mind racing, trying to think why the Colonel had summoned him. He eventually gave up, made a coffee and sat on his balcony, enjoying the relatively cool air and the silence which was broken only occasionally by drivers uncaringly blasting their horns or by policemen in cars, blipping their sirens in resentful protest at having to work the night shift.

By seven fifteen he was sitting in his car outside the MIA HQ wondering how to put in the time until his appointment with the Colonel at eight. *Life's too short,* he thought as he got out his car and made his way to Meskhi's office. He knocked on the door and entered. The Colonel was sitting at the small conference table reading a document, a highlighter pen in his right hand. He put the highlighter down, leaned back in his chair and looked at his wall clock. 'You're early.'

'Yes, sir.'

'Sit,' he said, indicating a chair opposite. 'Tell me the latest on Adamia case.'

Donadze quickly provided an update including the call he had received from Kaldani on Avto's phone and the extent of the beating.

'And Kaldani admitted to doing that?'

'Nothing we could take to court, but effectively, yes. He found out that Avto had been passing information to me.'

'So, let me see where we are. We have a murdered woman—a prostitute who was working for Dato Kaldani. Your source inside the Dream Casino told you that she had been scared because Kaldani had involved her in a blackmail scheme. He also told you that Kaldani had met with two Russians who you have now identified as SVR agents. They are posing as traders and we don't know if they are connected to this case or not. Yesterday, your source was beaten up on Kaldani's orders, because Kaldani had identified that he was passing information to you. Is that an accurate assessment?'

Donadze was impressed with the Colonel's grasp of the case highlights and his ability to express himself so clearly. 'Yes, sir, perfectly accurate,' he said.

'How do you think Kaldani realised you had a source at his casino?'

'I'd rather not say, sir.'

'I didn't ask you to state your preferences. You obviously have a theory, tell me what that is.'

Donadze paused. 'Only a few people knew that I was receiving information from inside Kaldani's organisation. I believe one of these people told him.'

'These few people being the source himself, Captain Bukia, you and me,' the Colonel stated.

'Yes, sir.'

'Well, I think we can rule out you and your source. Do you think I was the leak?'

'No.'

'Thank you, Lieutenant. I understand your discretion. You were told yesterday that you have been taken off this investigation because you didn't bring charges by the deadline I set.'

'Yes, but with respect, the time allowed wasn't realistic for—'

'I agree. But you're still off the case—officially at least.'

'I don't understand.'

The Colonel pushed the document he had been marking to one side and leaned towards Donadze, his arms folded on his desk. 'I have instructed Captain Bukia to re-prioritise the Adamia investigation. My assessment is that her occupation was inherently dangerous and that, in all probability, led to her death. You have been given a reasonable amount of time to investigate and have not been able to bring charges. The case is therefore to be re-assigned to another detective and worked part time on a low priority basis. All case files will be updated to reflect this reality.'

'But, sir—'

'As for you, I have told Captain Bukia that I am disappointed with your performance and concerned about your insubordination and general attitude.'

Donadze didn't respond and the Colonel continued, 'I have just described my official position. Kaldani will get to hear about it and think he's off the hook. As will the SVR agents if they're involved. *Unofficially*, this case remains a top priority and I want you to keep working it. We have an opportunity to take down a major crime organisation. And I'm also not having Russians coming to this country to make trouble.'

'But how will I be able to investigate if I'm off the case?'

'I didn't say it would be easy. You might take some personal damage in the short-term. You're going to carry on despite your orders. If necessary, we'll say you've become obsessed with this investigation and gone rogue. You have something of a reputation already so that will be believable at least. You might be transferred or disciplined, but ultimately I will protect you.'

'And all this will be verbal, nothing on-record. I'll be completely exposed.'

'Yes. I know what I'm asking. And that's why I'm giving you the opportunity to refuse.'

'I'll do it,' Donadze said.

'Good. You have my contact details. You will report only to me. Call me anytime. Don't return to this office unless I instruct you to do so.'

'Thank you, sir.'

'Good luck, Lieutenant,' the Colonel said. 'You're dismissed.'

FOURTEEN

Donadze drove to Mtatsminda Station and found Chichua at his desk. 'Hey, Soso. Let's get a coffee and I'll bring you up to speed with the Adamia investigation.'

'Thanks, Lieutenant,' Chichua said. 'Sorry you were taken off it.'

'Not your fault.'

They sat at Chichua's desk and Donadze briefed him on the case, omitting to identify Avto as an informant and the Russians' true identities as SVR agents.

'Good luck,' Donadze said. 'Let me know if there's anything I can help you with.'

'Thanks. Bukia's told me not to spend much time on it, probably going to be archived soon.'

'Yeah, pity.'

Donadze was facing the door and saw Bukia enter the detectives' bureau. He was carrying several paper bags of food. He stopped at Chichua's desk and looked down on Donadze, the smell of warm pastry and cheese mingling with the stale sweat of yesterday's clothes. 'You've handed over the Adamia case?'

'Yes.'

'Then come to my office in twenty minutes.'

Chichua made a face as Bukia waddled towards his office. 'I don't think he likes you,' he said.

Donadze waited five minutes. Bukia had made coffee and had just taken a large bite of his *lobiani* as he spoke, 'You wanted to see me.'

Bukia took a swig of coffee to help him swallow. 'I told you twenty minutes,' he spluttered, particles of bread and beans landing on his shirt.

'Let's do this now,' Donadze said, shutting the office door and sitting down.

'Listen, *Lieutenant*, I don't want you to get into any more trouble. You know the Colonel's already looking at you. One word from me and you're out.'

'Possibly. But remember our conversation yesterday about you and Kaldani. If I'm out, then you're coming with me. I might not have a job, but you'll be locked up. How long would you survive in Ksani Prison?'

'You've got nothing on me, Donadze.'

'Haven't I? Try me and see.' He paused, trying to read Bukia's face. 'What did you want to talk to me about?'

'Your new assignment. And to tell you that I'm taking the patrol car away from your girlfriend's apartment.'

'I've been putting in a lot of unpaid overtime with the Adamia case and I'm taking some time off. We can talk about new assignments after that. As for the patrol car, it stays for now.'

Bukia stared at Donadze, his face an unhealthy shade of purple. 'When the Colonel gets—'

'Save you breath,' he interrupted. He stood and opened the office door. 'Thank you, Captain. I'll get on that immediately,' he said loudly.

Donadze felt unsettled after his row with Bukia and wanted to clear his head. He had threatened to disclose that the Captain had a corrupt association with Kaldani but had no real evidence to support that allegation. Bukia however seemed to accept the threat as real and Donadze hoped that had given him enough space to continue investigating Nino's murder and to keep Tamuna and his mother safe whilst doing so.

He left the station and walked slowly to his car. He started the engine and ran the air conditioning against the late morning heat and humidity. He was about to drive away when his mobile phone rang, and he fumbled in his pocket to retrieve it, accidentally cutting off the caller. He was checking the call history when the phone rang again, the number withheld. He answered, 'Donadze.'

'*Gamarjoba*, Lieutenant. My name is Tatyana Rokva. Could we speak with you about a case you're working on?'

'We?'

'My colleague and I.'

'Who are you?'

'Let's discuss that face-to-face. Can you come to East

Point? Go to the McDonald's restaurant. Buy yourself a burger and sit at an empty table near the back. Thirty minutes?'

'How will I find you?'

'Don't worry, we'll find you.'

Donadze took the Kakheti Highway and arrived at East Point in only fifteen minutes. The mall was based on an American model and was one of several which had recently been constructed in Georgia. He parked in a shaded area, consulted a wall-map and walked the short distance to the McDonald's restaurant. It was located beside a large fountain which incorporated perimeter seating and he sat outside, trying to spot Rokva and her colleague as customers entered and left.

'Aren't you hungry, Ramaz?' Donadze peered into the sun to see an attractive woman smiling down at him. She looked about thirty, slim with shoulder length dark hair and wearing dark trousers and a white shirt which hung loosely below her waist.

'Rokva?'

'If you're not hungry, let's go to your car,' she said, turning to walk in the direction of the car park.

Donadze stood and followed as she led the way to Donadze's BMW. A man was leaning against the car and held out his hand as they approached. He looked about the same age as Rokva and was casually dressed in khaki shorts, light blue T-shirt and canvas loafers. His black hair was stylishly cut and gelled, with designer sunglasses nesting on top. 'Gia Pataraia,' he said. 'Let's talk in your car.'

'Who are you?'

Pataraia flashed his ID. 'Georgian Intelligence Service,' he said.

'What do we have to talk about?'

'Let's do it in the car,' Rokva said.

Donadze opened the car and sat behind the wheel. Rokva joined him in the front, Pataraia sitting in the back. 'Can we have some music, fairly loud please,' he said.

'You think someone's listening?' Donadze said, turning his radio on.

'Unlikely, but we're creatures of habit. Besides, Tanya and I like music while we work. Cool air would be good as well.'

Donadze started his engine. 'What can I do for you?'

'Let's discuss what we can do for each other,' Pataraia said. 'We have what appears to be an interface issue.'

'You'll have to explain that to me.'

'I will, but I suspect you know what I'm talking about. You're investigating the murder of Nino Adamia.'

'I was, but I'm not on that case now. It's being wound down, probably won't be solved.'

'As I said, you are investigating her murder.'

Donadze didn't reply and Rokva picked up the conversation, 'We were a bit surprised you didn't come to us when you found out about Lobodin and Pilkin.'

'Who?'

'Come on, Ramaz,' Pataraia said impatiently. 'We're on the same side here. We've been watching these two since they arrived in Georgia over three months ago. The thing is, we haven't been able to figure out what they're up to. Maybe we can help each other.'

'Go on.'

Rokva leaned towards Donadze. 'This is the way we see it,' she said. 'You had what looked like a straightforward murder investigation. But it's become a bit more complicated and you're effectively on your own, with no backup from your own people. You've been focussed on possible criminal connections, thinking that Dato Kaldani could have ordered the murder. You've also identified that the SVR has been talking with Kaldani, but you don't know if that's connected to your case or not. You need some answers, but you'll find that dealing with the SVR is difficult. We can help.'

'Help do what?'

Rokva smiled. 'Keep tabs on them, see where they go, who they talk to, intercept their calls, listen in on their conversations. Standard stuff for us, but not so easy for you.'

'Didn't it occur to you that we've already got surveillance on them?'

'We know you do, Ramaz. And what have you found? Not much I bet. That's not your fault. It's difficult for the Police—we don't have the same constraints,' she said.

'And you'd pass all your information on to me. Why so generous?' Donadze asked.

Rokva put her hand on Donadze's arm. 'We can help each other, Ramaz. You'll continue investigating all other aspects of the case. We'll share information and put our heads together and try to figure out the big picture. If something is going on—and it is—we'll have a better chance of stopping it if we work together. And you'll have a better chance of finding who killed Nino Adamia.'

'Why do you need me? Why not just run the whole thing yourself?'

'Well, for one thing, we don't have jurisdiction,' Pataraia said. 'But more importantly, we can't spook Lobodin and Pilkin and have them running back to Russia until we know what they've been up to. If we start poking about in your investigation, it'll get back to them through Kaldani and we'll lose them. Similarly, your methods won't work on the SVR. Look on us as a resource if it helps.'

'I'll have to think about it. How do I reach you?'

Pataraia took out his phone and dialled. When Donadze's phone rang he ended the call. 'You'll get us on that number. Explain all this to Colonel Meskhi, he'll understand. Good talking with you. We're going for these burgers now,' he said, opening his door to leave.

'He loves his food,' Rokva smiled, following behind.

Donadze watched Pataraia and Rokva saunter back into the mall. They looked like a couple on a day out, which was probably their intention he thought. He took out his phone to call Colonel Meskhi then, realising that his car might be bugged, walked to an open area of the car park before dialling. The Colonel answered after two rings and he updated him on his encounter with the pair.

'So, you're speaking with the GIS after I told you to report only to me,' the Colonel said.

'Yes, sir, but they approached me, and I didn't tell them anything they didn't already know. They were very well informed.'

'Evidently, including the fact that you are now working directly for me on this case. What worries me is how they are getting their information and who else could have it.'

'It's possible that they've planted bugs at the Dream Casino. They found out that the Russians were speaking to Kaldani and they wanted to know what it's about.'

'It's what they do I suppose. But if they did get bugs into the Dream, it sounds like they didn't get the answers they were looking for, otherwise there would be no need to work with you.'

'Yes, but they *do* want to work with me and maybe we can turn that to our advantage.'

'I wanted to keep this as a Police investigation. My focus is to bring Kaldani down and the GIS will have different priorities, despite what they told you.'

'Yes, sir. I agree, but I think we have a better chance of success with their help.'

'So, we should collaborate?'

'On balance, I think it would be beneficial.'

The Colonel paused. 'Okay, get back to them. Tell them that I've agreed that you can share information. It must be on an equal footing—they can't hold out on us. Any games and the deal is off,' he said, ending the call.

Donadze went into his call history and dialled the number Pataraia had given.

It was Rokva who answered, 'So Meskhi's agreed?'

'Yes, with conditions. Our priority is to catch a killer and to go after Kaldani. If I think working together compromises that, then we go our own way.'

'Okay, let's keep in touch. Anything else?'

'Yes, has my car been bugged?'

'Not by us. To be honest, we had thought about it but decided it's not a good way to build trust.'

'No, it's not,' said Donadze, hanging up.

It was cooler inside his apartment than Tamuna liked and Donadze adjusted the thermostat to raise the temperature. He was tidy by nature but had been too busy to keep on top of housework and the surfaces had accumulated a fine layer of dust, which he quickly wiped down. He went to his bedroom and cleared away some dirty clothes then changed the towels in the ensuite shower room. Donadze was hoping that Tamuna would stay the night but he thought that was unlikely. He adjusted the lighting then connected his phone to a wireless speaker and started music playing. His front doorbell rang, and he saw Tamuna through the spyhole, smiling. He opened the door and gave her a hug and a kiss. 'Did you forget your key?' he said.

'No, I have it,' she said, entering the apartment.

'You're looking well.'

'I'm feeling well, a bit sick in the mornings, but nothing serious.'

'Are you hungry? If I order now, the food will arrive in about thirty minutes.'

'Okay, what will we have, pasta?'

Donadze ordered some dishes for delivery from a local Italian restaurant. He placed cutlery and glasses on the breakfast bar and put plates in hot water to warm. 'What would you like to drink?' he said.

'Water please.'

He poured two glasses of water and joined her on the sofa. They clinked their glasses together. 'Here's to you and the baby,' he said.

'Here's to *us* and *our* baby,' she corrected.

He smiled. 'You were telling me you have a doctor's appointment. Is that routine?'

'It'll be my first pre-natal appointment, tomorrow at four and, yes, it's routine. I'm being looked after at the Clinic, so it's very convenient. Can you come?'

'Of course. Shall I meet you at, say three forty-five? We can go in together.'

'Good idea... You said you wanted to talk.'

Donadze lifted his glass, took a drink and turned on the sofa to face her. 'Yes,' he said, placing his hand over hers. 'You know that I love you and always want to be with you. And I'm so happy that we're having a baby together. Somehow, it just makes what we have perfect. But we must think what is best for the baby as well as ourselves. Children need stability, a mother and a father who are committed to each other. I want us to make that commitment. Tamuna, will—'

'Wait Ramaz, don't say any more... Having a baby with you is wonderful but it won't solve any of the problems we have—it might even make them worse.'

Donadze took both her hands in his. 'I know we have things to sort out. But if we start with a commitment then we should be able to figure out the rest,' he said.

'Well, we haven't so far,' Tamuna replied, squeezing his

hands. 'And I'm not saying it's all your fault. But it's not just the two of us now. I need to know that our child will have a father who will be around for her.'

'For *her*?' Donadze said.

'I don't know, just a feeling. Your mother thinks the same. But anyway, girl or boy, we both need to be there.'

'I know, and we will be, nothing is more important to me than you and the baby.'

'I know you mean that when you say it but sometimes the reality is—'

'Tamuna, you're right,' Donadze interrupted. 'I want us to get married. But I'm not going to ask you tonight. Give me a couple of weeks to close this case. It's one of the toughest I've had but I can work on it and still be there for you both. If I let you down, you won't have to tell me, I'll know already. But I won't do that, I promise.'

Tamuna put her hand behind Donadze's head and drew him forward, kissing him on the lips. 'Please don't think I'm judging you, Ramaz. You're a good man and you care about people. I know you care about us. I want this to work as much as you do. Let's just make sure it does.' She looked at her watch and smiled. 'When's that food coming, don't you know I'm eating for two?'

FIFTEEN

Donadze's was in a deep sleep when his phone rang. He groped for the bedside light, sat up on the bed and answered. 'What's happened, Major?' he said, shaking his head to wake up fully.

'I've called this in,' Levan Gloveli said. 'But I'm letting you know before our colleagues from the city arrive. I had a couple of visitors tonight—one of them is now dead.'

'Visitors? What do you mean?'

'Same two thugs as before. They had masks last time but I'm pretty sure it was them, and I was ready. I had some help from friends in the village but I'm keeping them out of this.'

'Tell me what happened.'

'I got word that a strange car was in the village. Pretty stupid of these people to think that they could drive into Shindisi at that time in the morning without being noticed. Anyway, a couple of us were sitting here, waiting. They came in the front door about ten minutes ago, the one in front had his pistol drawn. He got it in the gut from my Remington. The other ran. He made it to his car, and we let him go.'

'Are you okay, no injuries?'

'Nothing new anyway.'

'Sounds like a clear case of self-defence to me. The dead guy definitely had his pistol drawn when he came in?'

'He's lying on my floor with a gun in his hand.'

'Not quite what I asked... Did you give a warning before you fired your Remington?'

'I put a shot into the ground and told him to drop his weapon.'

'Before or after shooting him in—'

'Don't ask.'

'Understood. And presumably you were out of bed, probably getting a drink when you heard noises outside the house?'

'Something like that.'

'What about your friend?'

'I've got lots of friends, who are you talking about?'

'Good. What about the one who ran off?'

'He'll have to explain this mess to Kaldani. It won't be an easy conversation.'

Donadze paused to think. 'And these were Kaldani's men? They must have been coming to finish the job, to kill you. Why would Kaldani need to do that?'

'It has to be something to do with the information I gave you on these Russians. Someone found out I had made the connection to the SVR. Kaldani will be pissed with me but it's got to be more than just revenge.'

'When you say someone...'

'Who else knows about the SVR connection?'

'I told Colonel Meskhi as we agreed. I also showed Morten and Toreli the pictures you sent me but didn't say anything about them being SVR. I also had a visit from the GIS yesterday. They told me they've been keeping a watch on these guys for a couple of months now.'

'GIS? When were you going to tell me about them?'

'They only approached me yesterday. They want to pool information, help us keep tabs on these Russians. I think it's a good idea and Meskhi agrees.'

'And you trust them?'

'We're on the same side, even if we have different priorities.'

'How about Meskhi, do you trust him?'

'I think so, he's got some good qualities, he's pretty sharp, seems to work hard. Why, do you think he could have tipped off Kaldani?'

'No, I'm not saying that. Just be careful who you pass information to.'

'Understood. How can I help you now?'

'Get me a lawyer, someone good. I'll be taken to a station in Tbilisi, find out which one and send him there. I'm not spending any more time in a cell than I have to.'

'Good luck, Major,' Donadze said. He hung up and called Misha Arziani.

'Ramaz, I was about to call you,' Arziani said breathlessly.

'Why, what's going on?'

'It's Captain Bukia—he's dead!'

'Bukia! How?'

'He was found in his apartment. Neighbours reported suspicious noise and some uniforms checked it out. His throat's been cut… Soso Chichua should be there by now.'

'Chichua told you about this?'

'Yes, but why did you call me?'

Donadze gave a brief account of events at Shindisi.

'So, the murder and attempted murder of a serving and a retired Police officer,' Arziani said. 'Both on the same night. They must be connected.'

'Of course they're connected. Has anyone called around, made sure everyone else is safe?'

'It's what I've been doing, that's why I was going to call you. Ramaz, how do you fit into this?'

'What do you mean?'

'Bukia and Gloveli and you—does this tie back to the Adamia case?'

Donadze paused before speaking. 'It might. It feels like someone is trying to clean house, to tie up loose ends.'

'Then you need protection, you could be next.'

'I'm okay, Misha. I'm taking precautions, don't worry about me.'

'If you're sure,' Arziani said. 'I'm here if you need me, call any time.'

'Thanks, I appreciate that. Has Colonel Meskhi been informed?'

'Yes, of course, he's on his way here now.'

'I'm coming in as well. I'm going to drop by Bukia's apartment first.'

'I thought you were on leave?'

'I was. Could you do me a favour?'

'Sure.'

'Find out which station Gloveli is being taken to. Speak to their Shift Commander, tell them to take it easy. He's one of us.'

'Will do, but why not do that yourself?'

'I need to keep some distance from this for now. Let me know where he's being taken and I'll get a lawyer lined up,' Donadze said, hanging up. He put the phone on his bedside table and started to dress, his mind racing. *What's going on, Kaldani?* he thought. *What's got you so rattled that you'd pull a stunt like this?*

A swarm of Police cars guarded the entrance to Bukia's apartment. Donadze parked his car away from the entrance and walked to the control barrier, produced his ID and took a single flight of stairs to the apartment door. The uniformed officer who was guarding the door recognised him and he was nodded through.

The entrance led directly to the kitchen and living area and he took two paces, paused and looked around. Bukia's body lay on its side in a corner of the kitchen, his face turned towards greasy cabinets. A large pool of blood had coagulated around his head and upper body. He'd only been wearing white shorts and a vest which had ridden up his back and sat bunched and bloody beneath his arm pits. Donadze thought the sight pitiful and he felt a sharp pang of sympathy for the murdered man and guilt over the arguments they had had.

He looked away from the body and studied the living area. The only sofa in the room, a two-seater, had been turned over, a small wooden table lay in pieces on the floor alongside a smashed lamp, and a framed print of an ancient church was hanging precariously on its hook.

The mood inside the apartment was sombre. Metreveli was the medical examiner and he glanced up from the corpse to see Donadze, nodded to him then continued directing the technician who was collecting the data which would eventually confirm the cause and time of death.

Chichua was standing by the window in the living area speaking into his mobile phone. Donadze walked over to him, keeping to the room's perimeter to avoid contaminating evidence. 'Soso,' he said.

Chichua end his call. 'Lieutenant,' he formally replied.

'What happened?'

'Are you taking over this investigation?'

'Of course not, why?'

'Just wondered why you're here.'

'Why? It's obvious isn't it? Bukia was our commanding officer.'

'Was he? You never showed him that respect when he was alive.'

Donadze looked closely at Chichua. 'Are you angry with me, Soso? You think this is my fault somehow?'

Chichua turned to look at Bukia's corpse then back at Donadze. 'We're not stupid, *Lieutenant*. We know you couldn't take orders, couldn't make progress in the Adamia case, resented me taking it over. We've all seen your bust-ups with the Captain. And now he's dead.'

Donadze was aware that their altercation was attracting attention and he lowered his voice. 'All right, Detective, give me your report.'

Chichua made a show of consulting his notebook. 'The Captain lived alone, never married. A neighbour reported a disturbance at about 1:00 a.m. and the uniforms got here about forty-five minutes later. They didn't know a detective lived here. The door wasn't locked, and they went in. They found Bukia and called it in. The footprints indicate two assailants. There was a struggle, but the Captain must have been overpowered. His throat was cut, and he bled out. Nothing's been taken as far as we know.'

Donadze looked at the apartment door. Like most front doors in Tbilisi, it was manufactured from steel and fitted with substantial locks. 'The door wasn't locked? That probably means Bukia unlocked it. Why would he do that? Do you think he knew his killers?'

'Maybe, but you can't read anything into that.'

'Did you find his pistol?'

'In its holster by his bed.'

'Can you think of a reason why an experienced Police officer would open his apartment door to two strangers at that time in the morning—unarmed?'

Chichua didn't reply.

'Anything else?' Donadze said.

Chichua hesitated. 'Yes, there was a package taped underneath a drawer in his bedroom. Fifteen thousand dollars.'

'Okay, Soso. Thanks,' he said, offering his hand.

Chichua put his own hands in his trouser pockets and

didn't reply. Donadze turned to leave, feeling Chichua's eyes burning his back.

Despite it being early morning, there were only a few parking spaces left when Donadze arrived at Mtatsminda Station. He entered the building nervously, uncertain if the other detectives shared Chichua's belief that he had somehow been responsible for Bukia's murder. It was nonsense of course, the stash of dollars taped under a drawer confirmed, in Donadze's mind at least, that Bukia had been on the take and that, somehow, had led to his death.

He was certain that Bukia's murder and the attempted murder of Gloveli were linked and that Kaldani was behind both. If things had gone to plan, Gloveli would also be dead and both assassins would have escaped, undetected. But Gloveli wasn't an easy target and identification of the two, one of whom he had killed, should be straight forward. Identifying Bukia's killers wouldn't be easy however, unless fingerprints or traceable DNA was found. Donadze thought that was unlikely as the hit appeared to be professional.

The detectives' bureau was full, although no one seemed to be doing any work. Colonel Meskhi was in the Captain's office, talking into his mobile phone. Donadze looked for Misha Arziani and saw him at his desk, drinking coffee. He walked over, sensing a chill from the other detectives who were huddled in small groups, telling each other that Bukia had been one of the good ones and promising to find and take revenge on his killers.

'God, what a night,' Arziani said.

'Yes, terrible... Did you find out where Gloveli was taken?'

'Dzveli Tbilisi. No problem, the cops there think he's a hero. He's being well looked after.'

'Thanks for doing that, he'll need a lawyer all the same.'

'What's going on, Ramaz? Who's behind this?'

'I've got a good idea who's behind it. Proving it or finding a motive is another matter.'

'Kaldani?'

'Yes.'

'Why him though?'

'As I said, I don't have a motive yet.'

'And you think Kaldani has a connection to the Adamia case?'

'I really don't know. But in any event, you know that Soso is looking after that investigation now, Meskhi took me off it,' Donadze said nodding towards the Colonel.

Arziani sighed. 'Okay, if you say so. You've probably got your reasons for not telling me more.'

The Colonel had finished his call and was staring at Donadze and Arziani.

'I think he wants to talk to me,' Donadze said.

Despite the early hour, Meskhi was cleanly shaved and smartly dressed in a suit with white shirt and blue tie. He had plugged in his own laptop, the lid open, a steady stream of emails pinging their arrival to his inbox. He had tidied up Bukia's office, a large black plastic bag was sitting outside the door awaiting disposal. The office certainly looked more business-like but Donadze thought that a clear-out so soon after Bukia's death was insensitive. 'Close the door, Donadze,' he said, pointing to the chair opposite his own. 'What did you find at Bukia's apartment?'

Donadze provided a summary of his observations including his view that Bukia must have known his killers, that it was a professional hit and that a large amount of US dollars had been found hidden under a drawer.

'And you have assumed that was a pay-off of some kind? Did you consider Bukia's killers might have planted it to discredit him?'

Donadze hesitated. 'Speaking frankly, I believe that Captain Bukia had been passing information to Kaldani. We can't rule out that the money was planted but I think that's unlikely. But, anyway, I'm not sure that matters now.'

'You're suggesting we cover up apparent corruption?'

'No, it's just that the Captains is dead, and I can't see any value in damaging his reputation.'

'Let me be clear, if we find evidence that Bukia or any other officer was corrupt, that information *will* be disclosed. Understood?'

'Yes, sir.'

Meskhi paused. 'And you think Kaldani ordered the hit?'

'I'm sure of it. It was Kaldani's men who tried to kill Major Gloveli. It's too much of a coincidence to think that the Captain's murder wasn't connected.'

'I agree, but killing two Police officers, even if one's retired? That's a very risky move and Kaldani's not stupid. The stakes must be incredibly high for him.'

'Major Gloveli believes the connection could be that he

and Bukia both knew about the SVR operating in Tbilisi.'

'How would Bukia have found out about that?'

'From Kaldani probably. Nothing else seems to make any sense at this point.'

'I know Gloveli well and respect his opinion. We'll bear it in mind.'

'Where do we go from here, sir?'

There was a pause before the Colonel spoke. 'I'm assembling a team to investigate Bukia's murder and the assault on Gloveli. I want you to lead it.'

'Of course, sir. But I thought you wanted me to continue investigating Adamia's murder.'

'I do. I am going instruct Detective Chichua that our priority is to catch Bukia's killers and that the Adamia case is to be shelved. But I want you to keep working it in the background. I have authorised you to share information with your contacts in the GIS, subject to the conditions I stipulated. But, remember, there were only a few of us who knew about SVR involvement. One's dead and the other only narrowly escaped being killed. I'm not losing any more. Understood?'

'Yes, sir.'

'Carry on, Lieutenant,' the Colonel said, turning to his email.

SIXTEEN

'All right, quiet please.' Donadze looked around the Major Incident Room and the team of detectives and administrators he had assembled.

Each desk contained a telephone, note pad and pens. The walls were covered in cork boards and whiteboards. Flip charts with new paper pads and coloured pens stood ready in each corner. Case material including crime locations had been posted onto the cork boards and other boards contained headings for items still to be identified, including timelines, suspects identified and alibis to be checked and verified.

A projector displayed an organisation chart onto a wall mounted screen, its focussed light making the airborne dust sparkle. As Senior Investigating Officer, Donadze's name was at the head of the chart with a reporting line to Colonel Meskhi. The atmosphere in the room was gloomy, charged with frustration and anger, and scented with the odour of stale smoke and sweat.

'Before you begin, Lieutenant, I'd like to speak to your team,' the Colonel said in an even voice. He was standing at the head of the incident room, his height accentuated by the low false ceiling, its halogen lights shining onto his head and throwing his narrow face into sombre shadow. The remaining conversation stopped as the investigation team leaned forward to listen. 'I didn't know Captain Bukia well. He was only under my command for a few months. But he was one of us. We *will* find the people responsible for his death and we *will* bring them to justice. Is that understood?'

Meskhi paused as the detectives stirred. Soso Chichua hammered his desk and shouted, 'Yes, sir!'

The Colonel continued. 'We also nearly lost Major Gloveli. He was my commanding officer early in my career and is one of the finest Police officers I have ever known. There is no doubt that whoever was responsible for Bukia also tried to have Gloveli killed and we will bring these people to justice. He paused at looked around the room. 'But when I say justice, I mean just that. We are *not* vigilantes. When we find these men, they are to be treated like any other suspect. I want no planted weapons, no punishment beatings, no suicides in cells, no one *accidentally* falling downstairs. I hope *that* is understood?'

The Colonel paused and slowly scanned the room again, the detectives avoiding his gaze. 'Now, I would normally have asked the Station Commander to lead an investigation of this significance but that is obviously not possible. I do however have complete confidence in Lieutenant Donadze, and I want you to give him your full cooperation. I will remain at this station until we have these killers in custody and will continue to support you all as necessary. Let me stress, this case has our highest priority. Do you have any questions?'

The Colonel scanned the room once more as the detectives shook their heads or looked away. 'Carry on, Lieutenant,' he said and walked out.

Donadze quickly described how the investigation would be conducted. He stressed the need to comply with recognised incident management principles. He had appointed Misha Arziani as Deputy Senior Investigating Officer and he asked him to detail the immediate actions to be taken to preserve evidence and the forensics acquired at both crime scene.

Arziani ran through their near-term objectives: witnesses were to be identified and interviewed while events were fresh in their memories, suspects and their motives were to be identified. Arziani stated that he was confident the assailant who had escaped from Gloveli's house would be identified, but that he was probably in hiding by now. He reminded the detectives that prompt and effective action would lead to the early resolution of the case and successful prosecutions.

Donadze resumed the briefing. He stressed that they were dealing with a ruthless criminal gang who would intimidate or kill if they felt threatened. He told the detectives that their own safety was paramount. As he spoke, he sensed the mood in the room lift. Satisfied that his team was properly briefed and motivated, he set them about their task.

Donadze left the incident room and went to the detectives' bureau. The Colonel had vacated Bukia's office and he entered and closed the door. He dialled the number Pataraia had given him. Rokva answered after two rings, 'Hey, Ramaz, long time!'

'Not that long, can we meet?'

'How could I refuse? Same place, thirty minutes?'

'Fine.'

'But Ramaz, don't disappoint me.'

'What do you mean?'

'I really want a burger this time, see you soon,' she said, hanging up.

Donadze drove to East Point Mall, parked and made his way to the McDonald's restaurant. Rokva was already sitting in a quiet area at the back of the restaurant, trying to keep the contents of her burger within its bun as she raised it to her mouth. He sat on the chair opposite as she nodded a greeting, swallowed the food in her mouth and took a sip from her cold drink.

'I got you the same,' she said, gesturing towards a plastic tray. 'They're really good.'

'Thanks,' he said, unwrapping his burger and taking a bite. 'Where's Pataraia?'

She froze, looked around theatrically and fixed Donadze with a stare. 'State secret, need to know basis only.' She paused a moment then laughed, 'Got you! No, he's having a day off, some family business to take care off.'

'Very funny. Did you hear what happened?'

'Yes, I'm sorry. Is that what you wanted to discuss?'

'Partly, what do you know about it?'

'Why don't you tell me what you're thinking?'

'Kaldani ordered Bukia's murder. He also attempted to have Gloveli killed,' Donadze stated.

Rokva didn't respond but nodded and took a sip of her drink.

'I don't have proof and I'm not clear on motive. But I think it's tied to the SVR somehow,' Donadze added.

'Seems likely.'

'Have you had the Russians under surveillance?'

'As you would expect.'

'And they weren't personally responsible for Bukia?'

'Both were out of town when it happened.'

Donadze returned his burger to its tray as he gathered his thoughts. 'Kaldani must have known how we would react to this. Is he taking instructions from the SVR? And what's so important that he would risk war with the Police?'

Rokva looked up from her food. 'Come on Ramaz. Kaldani's a big-time gangster but he's no match for the Russians and the resources they have. If they wanted something done badly enough, Kaldani would do it.'

They both ate silently for a moment. 'How are you progressing with the Adamia investigation?' she said.

'It's not gone any further, still trying to make connections. It won't get any easier now that it's officially on the back burner.'

Rokva looked longingly at her remaining piece of uneaten burger before wrapping it in its paper and dropping it back on the tray. 'These things really are *too* good,' she said, standing. 'Nice talking to you, Ramaz. Keep in touch.'

'Thanks for lunch,' Donadze said as she stood to leave.

Donadze arrived at the Medifirst Clinic on time and went straight to the Orthopaedic Department. Tamuna was in her office wearing scrubs and writing up notes. 'Hey, darling,' he said. 'You don't look ready for our appointment.'

'Oops, got a bit distracted. Just as well you're here to remind me,' she smiled. 'Give me a minute.'

He took out his phone and read his texts and emails until Tamuna returned wearing her own clothes. 'Ready,' she said. He quickly finished sending an email as she held the door open for him. They walked a short distance to the Obstetrics Department and sat together in the waiting area.

'So, tell me what's going to happen today,' he said.

'Well, you'll get to meet Lela, the obstetrician who'll be looking after me. She's a friend—you'll like her too. She'll do the usual stuff: height, weight, blood pressure. She'll also take a urine sample and test for signs of pre-eclampsia and diabetes as well as doing an initial blood screen. There's a hormone in blood that will give an accurate estimate of my due date, so you'll have a better idea when you are going to be a father...' She looked at Donadze. 'Do you really want to know all this?'

'Well, you are making me a bit nervous,' he said. 'But it's all routine?'

'Completely. Lela might want to talk about general health care, like diet and exercise but she may give me a pass on that.'

'Because you're a doctor? No, take everything offered.'

'Don't worry, I'll look after our girl.'

'Girl? You're convinced we're having a girl.'

'It must come from being around your mother, she's certainly convinced.'

'Female intuition maybe? Well, look after our *girl* but look after yourself as well.'

'Tamuna! Congratulations, such wonderful news!' A woman of about thirty strode quickly towards them and held out her arms. Tamuna stood and the two women hugged.

'Ramaz, this is my good friend, Lela.'

Donadze also stood. Lela was very attractive and he felt intimidated by her looks and her energy. He held out his hand, but she stepped forward and hugged him as well. 'So exciting,' she said. 'Come on through.'

She held open the door to her surgery and indicated two chairs on the other side of her desk. 'Well, Tamuna,' she said, bringing up a file on her screen, 'you'll know a lot of this stuff already but, bear with me. I've got to go through the motions.' She continued by telling Tamuna the purpose of the appointment and the tests she would be doing.

Donadze had put his phone on silent but felt it buzzing in his trouser pocket. He took it out and held it discreetly in his lap. Colonel Meskhi was calling. He declined the call but kept the phone in his hand. Tamuna glanced at him, frowning. Lela smiled inquisitively then continued discussing Tamuna's medical history. His phone buzzed again. 'Do you need to take that?' Lela asked.

'No,' he said, declining the call and turning the phone off. 'I don't.'

SEVENTEEN

D onadze had both been pleased and excited to attend the ante-natal clinic. He felt it somehow made the pregnancy more real. Tamuna had returned to her office to complete some paperwork and they had agreed to meet later that evening for dinner at her apartment. He returned to his car and called Colonel Meskhi.

'Why didn't you answer my call, Donadze?'

'Sorry, sir. I had some personal business to attend to.'

There was a long silence when Donadze failed to elaborate. Meskhi eventually spoke, 'I want to turn up the heat on Kaldani.'

'Yes, sir, I think that's an excellent idea.'

'I'm glad you concur,' Meskhi said dryly. 'We're going to interview Kaldani. But we'll have to be careful. He has a lot of political influence in this city, so anything we do must stand scrutiny. I know how to hurt him though.

Politicians—they share one thing in common—what they hate, above all else, is to be associated with tarnished goods. I'm sure the media will hear that Mr. Kaldani is helping us to progress our investigation. His friends in Parliament won't be so keen to answer his calls after that. It should take some heat off you and your team.'

'That could be useful, sir. But we'll have to justify the interview.'

'Yes, and what do you see as justification?'

'Well, Gloveli's assailants are known to us. One's dead and the other hasn't been found yet. Both worked at the Dream. We could ask Mr. Kaldani for his help in trying to understand why they attacked the Major and to help us find the missing suspect.'

'That seems very reasonable to me. Kaldani's a public-spirited individual, I'm sure he'll want to help. You and I will conduct the interview. Set it up for tomorrow.'

'Yes, sir. Should I ask him to come to the station?'

'His choice. We shouldn't inconvenience an important businessman like Mr. Kaldani unnecessarily. Set it up and let me know tomorrow.'

Donadze got into his car and drove to the International Hospital. He enquired at Reception and was told that Avto had been moved from the acute assessment ward to a private room for recuperation. He followed directions and was about to knock on the door and enter when he heard two male voices inside.

He thought that Avto's father had decided to visit and he put his ear close to the door to listen. There seemed to be a heated conversation between Avto and the other man. The sound was distorted, and he didn't recognise who Avto was talking to.

'You say you love me,' he heard Avto say, 'and this is what you do?'

'It wasn't what I wanted—you've got to know that. Kaldani was going to have you killed for speaking to that cop. I stopped that happening.'

'And then *you* had me beaten up instead.'

'Yes, but I had to do it. You've got no idea what he's capable of. Better a few bruises than dead—he would have had us both killed.'

'You'd be dead if he knew you were here with me now, wouldn't you? Doesn't he know you like boys?'

'Don't say that! I don't. You're the only one—I don't know why that is.'

'You're fooling yourself, Gio. All that business with Nino. Who was that for? Yourself? Kaldani?'

Donadze suddenly realised that Avto was arguing with Giorgi Licheli.

'It didn't mean a thing,' Licheli continued. 'Listen, when you get out of hospital, I'll find you a nice apartment, visit when I can.'

'No.'

'What do you mean, no?'

'I mean no. I'm not scared of you anymore. You're a monster and I hate you and all you stand for. Stay away from—'

'Not scared of me you little queer! You should be!'

Donadze burst through the door. Licheli was leaning over the bed, his weight bearing down on a pillow pressed to Avto's face. Avto was writhing frantically, his arms and legs kicking up the sheets and blanket, his panicked cries muffled by the pillow.

Donadze rushed to the bed, bent and put his left arm around Licheli's neck, locked it with his right to apply a choke, then straightened, lifting Licheli off the bed. Licheli tried to break the choke by elbowing him in his ribs. Donadze took a short step back, released the choke and jabbed him twice to the right kidney. He let Licheli fall forward onto his knees then punched him on the back of his head, knocking him unconscious.

'What's going on here?' A nurse shouted from the open door.

'Police,' Donadze said, reaching for his ID. 'This man is under arrest. Check your patient.'

Avto had thrown the pillow off his face and was wheezing painfully, trying to catch his breath. 'I'm okay,' he gasped.

The nurse looked uncertain. 'I'll call the doctor,' she said.

'Thank you. I'll wait here.' Donadze said.

'How about him?' the nurse asked, nodding at Licheli.

'Don't worry, I'll keep an eye on him.'

The nurse left and Donadze patted Licheli down, finding a short-barrelled revolver and flick knife. He dragged Licheli to a sitting position at the base of the bed, picked up a water jug and threw the contents in his face.

'What are you doing?' Avto said. 'Get him out of here, he nearly killed me.'

'Wake up, Gio,' Donadze said, slapping Licheli's face. 'We need to talk.'

Donadze placed a chair in front of Licheli and sat down. He showed him the revolver and knife as he came to. 'Stay where you are,' he said.

'You won't be able to prove a thing,' Licheli whispered through his damaged throat. 'It's your word and the queer's. And he's not going to say anything, are you, Avto?'

'I'd be a bit more careful about who you're calling queer if I were you. But don't worry, I'm not going to have you charged.'

Licheli remained silent, a lopsided smile on his face.

'Avto asked if Kaldani knows you like boys. I'm pretty sure he doesn't know, but what if I told him? I might also tell him why you didn't want Avto killed. What do you think he'd do to you then?'

Licheli's mouth turned down in a sneer. 'I've been loyal. He'd stand by me.'

'Well, we can put that to the test. But not tonight. Go home and think about it. I'll be in touch tomorrow. Now get out!' He stood over Licheli as he dragged himself to his feet and hobbled to the door, wincing with the pain from his bruised kidney. He watched the door close and turned to Avto. 'He's mine now,' Donadze said.

The nurse returned with a woman wearing hospital scrubs. 'There was a fight when I came in, Doctor.' She pointed at Donadze. 'He nearly killed the man who was visiting Mr. Sabauri,' she said.

'It was a misunderstanding,' Donadze said. 'How's Avto doing, Doctor?'

'Surprisingly well, considering.' She turned to Avto, 'We could release you tomorrow if you feel up to it. Do you have someone who can keep an eye on you for a week or so?'

'Tomorrow? I thought—'

'That'll be fine, Doctor' Donadze said.

'No more fighting, please, even if it is a misunderstanding,' the doctor said, leaving the room.

The nurse straightened the bed and made sure her patient was comfortable before following the doctor out.

Avto waited until the door had closed then turned to Donadze. 'Why did you tell her that? I've got nowhere to go. I don't have a job. I can't afford to stay in Tbilisi and my dad's not taking me back. I've got nowhere to go...'

'Yes, you do, you're staying with me for a while.' Donadze said. 'I'll pick you up tomorrow evening.'

It was late in the evening when Donadze arrived at Tamuna's apartment.

His mother answered the door, 'Are you hungry, *Ramazi?*' she said, kissing him.

'Always,' he replied.

'We waited for you,' Tamuna said, standing to kiss him.

'Go and wash your hands then come to the table,' his mother said.

'Do you mind if I watch this first?' Donadze had heard a familiar voice on the television which was playing in a corner of the room. Channel 1 TV was reporting on a trade conference which had been held in Tbilisi earlier that day. The centre of the stage was occupied by Minister Toreli. His legal counsel, Jibuti, was sitting slightly behind the Minister, speaking into his ear. The rest of the stage was occupied by business leaders, including Robert Morton of United Energy, who was answering a question from a reporter through his perfectly white smile.

'Yes, of course UE has a huge presence in Georgia,' he said. 'You may not know it but about thirty percent of the gas used in your kitchens comes from our pipeline,' Morton continued, smiling as his answer was translated.

'You need to come up with some new straplines, Rob,' Donadze told the television.

'Can you confirm that your new pipeline will be routed through Georgia?' a reporter asked.

Morton looked thoughtful. 'Not at this stage, I'm afraid—the routing decision hasn't been made yet.'

'Minister Toreli, how important is this pipeline to Georgia?' another reporter asked.

Toreli paused, 'It's incredibly important and my officials and I are in constant contact with Mr. Morton and his management team. This government is focussed on attracting new inward investment as well as growing existing businesses. My ministry has successfully developed a favourable business environment and we are starting to see real results. We are determined to do all we can to develop the national economy and create jobs for our people. United Energy is an important partner and this government is working hard to encourage more high calibre companies to invest in our country.'

'Our future Prime Minister...' Donadze said to himself.

'Do you want to keep that on while we eat?' his mother asked.

'No, sorry,' he said turning the television off. 'The food looks great.'

Donadze joined his mother and Tamuna at the small table and was helped to more food than he could eat. He had a small glass of *Tsinandali* at his mother's insistence but declined Turkish coffee. They talked about Tamuna's antenatal appointment, both women still referring to the baby as *she*. Donadze knew his mother was concerned that he and Tamuna weren't married but she, wisely, didn't broach the subject. It was after ten when they finished eating, his mother insisting on tidying up while Donadze and Tamuna continued talking.

'Do you want to stay tonight?' she asked.

'I'd love to, but I've got an early start tomorrow. I don't want to disturb you. Anyway, what would my mother think?' he asked, smiling.

'Well, I *am* pregnant, I don't think she would be too shocked. Don't worry about disturbing me, I'll be up early anyway.'

'Well, if you're sure,' he said, putting his hand over hers.

'How did you bruise your hand?' she asked.

'It's nothing, let's get some sleep,' he said.

EIGHTEEN

Donadze was up at six, beating Tamuna to the shower but lagging behind his mother who had prepared breakfast for them all. He ate some bread and cheese and drank a hasty cup of coffee before kissing the women goodbye and walking to his car.

He arrived at Mtatsminda Station and went immediately to the incident room. He noted that the cork boards, white boards and walls had been populated with flow diagrams, names, places and dates. Misha Arziani was briskly typing a report on his laptop and another detective was sleeping with his head on his desk. 'Hey Misha, feel like a coffee?' Donadze said.

Arziani rubbed his stubbled face and rolled his shoulders. 'Absolutely.'

Donadze made them both a drink, placed them on Azania's desk then pulled up a chair. 'Can you give me an update?'

'Yeah, it's going reasonably well so far. I've been to see Gloveli. He's being released today, no charge, acted in self-defence of course. We got the dead guy's ID from his wallet and Gloveli was able to identify the one that ran off—Nikoloz Shengelia and Luca Mamedov respectively. Both listed as security officers at the Dream Casino. Mamedov's an Azerbaijani national and he's done a runner, most likely to Shida Kartli. We've not done so well on Bukia. We've been out trying to find witnesses, looking at CCTV, the usual stuff. Nothing firm so far.'

'Great work, Misha. Positively connecting these two to the Dream is useful. Gives us a good excuse to interview Kaldani.'

Arziani looked up. 'We're interviewing Kaldani? When's that happening?'

'Today if I can set it up.'

'Do you want me with you?'

Donadze paused, knowing that Arziani was ambitious and, as Deputy SIO, might legitimately expect to be present when high profile interviews were being conducted. 'Sorry, Misha, the Colonel has already told me he only wants the two of us there.'

'Glory seeker?'

Donadze chose to interpret the question as a reference to the Colonel. 'I don't think it's that. He's got a good feel for these things. I think we need to trust him.'

'Not like you to respect authority, Lieutenant.'

Donadze was surprised at Arziani's observation. 'Really, is that what you think?'

'It's not just me who thinks it. Anyway, don't worry.

Let me know how it goes.'

'Will do. Did you get any sleep?' Donadze asked.

'Not really, I'm going to my apartment now. I'll be back in the early afternoon. The guys know the plan and I'll catch up with them later today.'

'That's great, I'm around if anyone needs help.'

Arziani looked at Donadze. 'And the Adamia case?' he said.

Donadze shrugged. 'Speak to Soso, but as far as I know, it's shelved for now.'

'If you're at the Dream later today you might want to try your luck at the poker tables. You've got the face for it.'

'Sorry?'

'Catch you later,' Arziani said, turning to complete his report.

Donadze walked to the detectives' bureau. It was empty and he went into the Commander's office, closed the door, took out his phone and called Licheli.

There was no answer and he texted, '*Call me back now*'

He put his phone on the desk, leaned back in the chair, closed his eyes and waited. His phone rang six minutes later. 'Hey, Gio. How are you feeling today?'

'What do you want?'

'I'll be speaking to your boss later today. But I want to talk to you first. I think you'd prefer it to be private.'

There was no reply and Donadze continued. 'Tell you what, Gio. I'll be at Mushthaid Park at eleven, I think you should be there as well. Take a seat on a bench between the trees, I'll find you.'

'Fuck you, Donadze.'

'Mushthaid Park at eleven. See you there.'

The park was quiet when Donadze arrived. He smiled to himself when he saw that Licheli had taken a seat on a bench near the park entrance, not between the trees as he had instructed. *Small victory for you, Gio*, he thought. He sat at the end of the bench and faced Licheli. 'Hey, Gio,' he said, his tone seemingly friendly. 'It's a little bit cooler today, don't you think?'

Licheli didn't reply but turned to face Donadze. He was dressed in black trousers and a white shirt which were tailored to tightly fit his lean frame. His hair had defied his styling gel and had fallen forward over his pock-marked forehead. A twitch had developed under his left eye.

'I hope you're feeling better after our little disagreement yesterday?' Donadze said with mock concern.

'Don't flatter yourself, Donadze. I've put down much better men than you.'

'Well, if you feel that way, let's just get down to it. Tell me about Shengelia and Mamedov.'

'I don't have to tell you a fucking thing.'

Donadze smiled. 'You know you do, or you wouldn't be here. You've screwed up, Gio. You know I'll talk to Kaldani. You could try running but he's got a long reach. How would you rate your chances?'

Donadze made himself smile again as he observed Licheli's lips tighten and his hand slide down his leg. 'I'd leave that knife where it is if I were you,' he said.

He continued watching carefully as Licheli's adrenaline spiked and his defeated brain surrendered. His shoulder slumped and he turned to face the park and away from Donadze. 'What are you offering?' he said.

'Give me the information I need, and I keep your sexual preferences to myself.'

Licheli's lips moved but he said nothing.

Donadze waited until a young couple had passed their bench. 'Tell me about Shengelia and Mamedov.'

'I want immunity.'

'No, no immunity. When the time's right I'll speak to the Prosecutor's Office, but only if I get your full co-operation now.'

'Kaldani will kill me if he finds out.'

'He won't hear anything from me.'

Licheli said nothing for a long moment then continued in a flat voice. 'Shengelia and Mamedov. Worked at the Dream—security. Shengelia's dead, that old cop was waiting for him, shot him without warning.'

'Not the way I heard it. Where's Mamedov?'

'I don't know, didn't report in, and hasn't answered my calls. We're looking for him. Kaldani doesn't like loose ends.'

'He could be a witness against Kaldani?'

Licheli nodded. 'Screwed the job up as well, fucking amateur.'

'I don't want him harmed.'

Licheli shrugged. 'Not much I can do about that.'

'And they both worked for you.'

Licheli nodded again. 'Part of my team at the Casino.'

'You know what I meant—what did I say about co-operating? You sent them to Shindisi.'

'Nice try. You could charge me for attempted murder if I admitted that.'

Donadze nodded. 'Okay, I'll accept that for now. Who killed Bukia?'

'No one that I know. Kaldani took care of that one himself. I think he brought some talent from out of town, Chechens I heard.'

'Why do that, he has plenty of resources in Georgia?'

'You're supposed to be the detective, aren't you? Shouldn't be too difficult to figure it out. Killing a cop—wouldn't you want the best? Wouldn't you also want them to disappear afterwards?'

'Was Bukia on the take?'

Licheli shrugged. 'Nose in the trough for years.'

'So why have him killed?'

'Couldn't figure that out. He was already in Kaldani's pocket. Maybe he become unreliable, maybe going to tell tales, who knows? It must have been something pretty serious though—this is going to be *really* bad for business.'

'Tell me about Nikitin and Banasik,' Donadze said.

'Never heard of them.'

'I won't give you too many more chances, Gio.'

Licheli sighed. 'A couple of Russian traders. Or so they said. I had them checked out. Turns out they're SVR. Kaldani had some business with them. They were at the Dream a couple of times to meet him.'

'What kind of business?'

'I don't know, he doesn't tell me everything.'

'You had them checked out, knew that they weren't traders. Didn't you want to know what they were really up to?'

'No, that kind of curiosity can get you killed.'

'You're not giving me much here, Gio. Maybe this isn't such a good idea.'

'I can't tell you what I don't fucking know! All I do know is that they had a deal going with Kaldani. Whatever it was went wrong and they wanted it cleaned up.'

'Did that include killing Nino Adamia?'

'What? No, why would it?'

'So why was she killed?'

'I've got no idea, and I don't think you can pin that one on Kaldani either.'

'Why don't I believe you, Gio?'

'Believe what the fuck you want, Donadze!'

More people were beginning to come into the park. 'Look at me, Gio,' Donadze said. Licheli put his hands in his pockets but didn't turn. 'I said, look at me!'

Licheli turned and fixed Donadze with a stare, his eyes narrowed, lips tight, left eye fluttering sporadically.

'You're working for me now. Get back to the Dream, keep your head down and your eyes open. I'll be in touch. Now go.'

Licheli continued to stare at Donadze for a long moment before springing to his feet and striding to the park's exit.

Donadze watched him leave. 'Nice talking to you,' he said quietly.

It had become uncomfortably hot in Mushthaid Park and Donadze walked to a shaded bench to call Kaldani at his office in Rustaveli Avenue. His personal assistant answered, and he asked to be put through. He was on hold for about five minutes before being connected. Petre Melua, Kaldani's attorney answered, 'How may I help you Lieutenant?'

'I asked to speak to Kaldani.'

'I'm with Mr. Kaldani but I have advised him that he should conduct all conversations with the Police through me.'

'Why?'

'Why? Last time you were here, Mr. Kaldani agreed to help and he answered all your questions openly. You were quite abusive in turn and made several unwarranted accusations. I won't allow that to happen again. Please address your questions to Mr. Kaldani through me.'

Donadze imagined Kaldani's office—the two men sitting side by side at the large conference table, the lawyer leaning into the desk phone to speak, Kaldani frustrated, all his instincts telling him to take control, to dominate.

'Well I'm sorry I offended you, Dato. But we do have to speak,' he said, ignoring the lawyer.

'Could you please get to the point of your call, Lieutenant,' Melua said.

'It's a shame you have to hide behind your lawyer, Dato,' Donadze said, again ignoring the lawyer. 'We need to speak, and it has to be today. You can choose the time and place. Unless you want Melua to choose for you?'

'Lieutenant, as I told you, Mr.—'

'The Dream, 2:00 p.m.' Kaldani snapped, hanging up.

Donadze took the phone from his ear and smiled, picturing Kaldani beating his chest like a silver-back gorilla, a classic alpha-male. He called Colonel Meskhi to pass on the meeting place and time. Meskhi instructed him to return to Mtatsminda Station to allow them to travel to the Dream Casino together.

Arziani was parking his car at the station as Donadze pulled into an adjacent bay. They walked into the building together and Donadze told him about the planned meeting with Kaldani, but not about his conversation with Licheli at Mushthaid Park. They split inside, Arziani heading for the incident room and Donadze going to the detective's bureau to speak to Meskhi.

The Colonel was in the Commander's office, copying information from his laptop to a notebook. 'We'll leave at one forty,' he said. 'I have cars organised.'

'Cars? We need more than one?'

'Yes, remember the point of this interview. It's unlikely we'll get any useful information from Kaldani, but we can, at least, embarrass him. We want our visit to be noticed. How are your media skills?'

'Media skills?'

'Yes. I think it's likely that the media will hear that we're speaking to Kaldani. They'll probably want to ask you some questions.'

'Ask *me* questions?'

'This is getting tedious, Donadze. Be ready to leave at one forty.'

'Don't you want to discuss tactics?'

'No, let's play it by ear. One forty.'

Donadze was waiting at the station exit as the Colonel came out. Three marked cars were waiting in a row, blue lights flashing. 'Ready, Lieutenant?' he said. 'We'll take the second car.' They got in the middle vehicle. 'Let's go,' the Colonel said to the driver. 'Lights and siren.'

The Colonel sat back in his seat and closed his eyes as the cars sped off. It took about twenty minutes to force their way through the crowded streets. 'Park at the entrance, screen anyone going in or leaving, leave your lights on,' he instructed.

Licheli stepped out of the shade to meet them. 'What's going on here?' he said, pointing to the Police cars. He stared at the Colonel and said, 'Who's this?'

'Take us to Kaldani,' Donadze said.

Licheli made a point of sauntering through the casino but Donadze overtook him, remembering the route. 'This way,' he said to the Colonel, crossing the lobby.

Kaldani was standing at the door to his office. He turned and went in, taking a seat at his small round conference table. Licheli stood outside, looking uncertain. 'You can go, shut the door.' Kaldani said.

Petre Melua was waiting inside and pointed to the remaining two chairs. 'I don't believe we've met,' he said, extending his hand to the Colonel, who ignored it.

'This is Colonel Gabrieli Meskhi, an old friend. How are you Gabi?' Kaldani said.

'I'm fine, thanks,' the Colonel said evenly. 'Lieutenant Donadze has some questions for you, Dato.'

Donadze was stunned to hear the friendly exchange between the two men but tried to remain impassive as Kaldani smiled at him.

'Before you begin, Lieutenant, please be aware that this conversation is being recorded. I also want to state, for the record, that Mr. Kaldani is co-operating with your investigation in good faith and on a purely voluntary basis,' Melua said.

Donadze was struggling to collect his thoughts. 'You won't mind if I record the conversation as well then,' he said, starting the memo app on his phone and placing it on the table. 'You know why we're here. Let's start with the attempted murder of Major Levan Gloveli by Shengelia and Mamedov. Both employees at the Dream Casino.' He paused and looked at Kaldani.

'Do you have a question?' Melua said.

'Why did two of your employees try to kill Gloveli?'

'Former employees, I think, would be the more accurate term,' Kaldani said. 'I employ about five hundred people across my different businesses. I don't know them all and I can't guarantee their behaviour. I was shocked to hear that these two had attacked Gloveli. I remember him as a fair and conscientious officer.'

'Behaviour? That's an unusual way to describe attempted murder.'

'Do you have a question, Lieutenant?' Melua repeated.

Donadze glanced at the Colonel who was leaning back in his chair, hands in his lap, staring straight ahead and remaining silent. 'Tell me how you came to employ these two men,' he said to Kaldani.

'I didn't, not directly anyway,' Kaldani replied. 'My security manager would have hired them.'

'Do you know where Mamedov is now?'

'No, he didn't come back to the Dream, didn't even clear his locker.'

'Did you order the hit on Major Gloveli?'

'Don't answer that Dato!' Melua said. 'Lieutenant, that is an outrageous—'

'Save your mock indignation for someone more gullible,' Donadze snapped. 'Answer the question, Kaldani.'

'Dato, I don't like Lieutenant Donadze's tone. I think we should end this interview now,' Melua protested.

'It's all right, Petre. The Lieutenant is clearly upset. To answer your question, no, of course not. I'm a businessman. I don't order hits on anyone.'

'There are four of us in this room and we all know that's not true.'

'Lieutenant—' Melua began.

'Let's talk about Bukia. He was killed on the same night that Gloveli was attacked. Do you agree that's an unlikely coincidence?'

'Well, I couldn't say for sure but, yes, I agree it's unlikely,' Kaldani conceded.

'Good. So, we've established your connection to the Gloveli incident through your two employees. You agree that Bukia's murder wasn't coincidental so that tells me you have a connection there as well.'

Kaldani held up a hand as Melua spluttered his objection. 'Very clever, but no, you haven't established connections to either incident—because there aren't any.'

Donadze was unsettled by the Colonel not engaging in the interview and made a show of consulting his notebook while he gathered his thoughts. 'How well did you know Captain Bukia?'

'I know you better, why do you ask?'

'I'm trying to understand why you would want him dead.'

Melua slammed his hands on the table, 'Dato, I really insist—'

'Give me the names of the men who killed him.' Donadze interrupted.

'I think that will suffice for now,' Meskhi said. 'Dato, Mr. Melua, thank you for your time and co-operation. We'll see ourselves out.'

Melua was red with indignation 'This behaviour has been outrageous! I'll be advising Mr. Kaldani to make a formal complaint,' he said.

'No, no need, Petre, the Lieutenant was only doing his job,' Kaldani said, offering his hand to the Colonel who took it.

Donadze ignored Kaldani's offered hand and walked to the door, allowing the Colonel to lead the way out of the casino.

Two TV news crews and several reporters were waiting at the entrance. 'Is Dato Kaldani a person of interest in the

Bukia murder?' a reporter shouted.

'Lieutenant Donadze is lead investigator on this case. He'll be happy to answer your questions,' the Colonel said, walking towards the cars.

NINETEEN

T he Colonel and two of the cars had left before
Donadze had finished answering the reporters'
questions. He was glad that he had been given a
heads-up that they would be waiting. He had faced the
media before and was generally satisfied with his
performance on this occasion. He knew that Kaldani would
be furious that he was being openly associated with Bukia's
murder, even though he had been careful not to make that
connection explicit.

He got in the remaining car, instructed the driver to
return to Mtatsminda Station and walked straight to the
detectives' bureau. The Colonel was in the Commander's
office, working on his laptop, his long fingers hitting the
keys at an enviable speed. He didn't stop typing or
acknowledge Donadze's presence at his door. Donadze
coughed awkwardly to attract his attention.

'Are you coming down with a virus, Lieutenant?' the
Colonel said.

'I hope not, sir. Bad timing if I am. I was hoping we could debrief.'

Meskhi stopped typing and indicated the chair opposite. 'Tell me how you think it went,' he said.

Donadze felt awkward sitting closely beside the Colonel in the small office. He quickly pulled his feet back when they touched his. He cleared his throat again. 'I think it went very well, generally. We didn't get any new information, but it was good to have the face-to-face. Kaldani seemed to keep his cool but I think he'll be secretly rattled. And he wouldn't have liked these reporters setting up outside his premises— his friends in Rustaveli Avenue won't be keen to pick up the phone when he calls now,' he said, referring to the politicians whose favour Kaldani purchased.

'And have you drawn any conclusions?' Meskhi asked.

'I'm totally convinced that Kaldani is behind Bukia's murder and the attempt on Gloveli's life.'

'So am I, proving it will be a different matter. How about the Adamia case? Anything new on the SVR?'

'No further forward but things are looking more positive.' Donadze briefed the Colonel on Licheli's obsession with Avto and how he was using that to turn him against Kaldani.

'Your GIS friends are teaching you some novel investigation techniques,' the Colonel observed dryly.

'You don't approve?'

'I didn't say that. Be careful though, I know Licheli's type. He's like some breeds of dog. You think they're tame and friendly right up to the time they wrap their jaws around your throat. He's also been with Kaldani a long time, betraying him will come very hard. And don't discount the possibility that they're both playing you.'

Donadze blinked in surprise, embarrassed that he had missed an obvious possibility. 'Thank you, sir. Good advice.'

'Are you too close to this, Donadze?'

'Sorry, sir. I don't understand.'

'You were extremely aggressive with Kaldani and Melua.'

'Yes, deliberately, I knew what I was doing. I know Kaldani. You need to get under his skin, get him rattled and make him react. We go back a long way.'

'Well, I think it was effective on this occasion. Keep him on his toes but don't let your judgement become clouded.'

'No, sir.'

Donadze remained sitting while the Colonel returned to his laptop. 'Something else you wanted to ask me, Lieutenant?' he said.

'If I may...' He cleared his throat again. 'Kaldani described you as an old friend. You were calling each other by your given names. I was a little surprised—'

'Tell me, Lieutenant, why do you think Kaldani is so successful?'

'He's clever, completely ruthless, rules by fear, knows how to play people...'

'Knows how to play people... He just played you, don't you think?' The Colonel paused and fixed Donadze with a stare. 'Make sure it doesn't happen again.'

Donadze stood to leave, tripping on the leg of his chair, colour coming to his cheeks. *It won't*, he thought.

Misha Arziani was briefing the investigation team when Donadze entered the incident room. Arziani looked at him expectantly and he nodded and walked to the front. 'Sorry, I've been out most of the day,' he said, looking around the tired faces.

'We saw you on TV1,' Arziani said. 'Good job, Lieutenant.'

'Thanks Misha. It was the Colonel's idea to interview Kaldani and to make it high profile. We didn't expect a confession of course but we're both convinced he's behind Captain Bukia's murder and the attack on Gloveli.'

Donadze gave the detectives a summary of their visit to the casino. He didn't want to disturb Arziani's briefing any further and thanked the team for their hard work then left.

He was walking towards the car park when Soso Chichua caught up with him, his large frame heaving from the exertion. 'Soso?' he said warily.

'Lieutenant, the other night at the Captain's apartment...'

'Yes?'

'I want to apologise. I couldn't believe that Bukia had been killed that way. And when we found the hidden money and couldn't explain why he had let these guys into his apartment? There was only one real explanation but I didn't want to believe he was dirty. You were only doing your job. I'm sorry.'

'Thanks, Soso. Don't worry, we're going to get Kaldani,' Donadze said, offering his hand to Chichua who took it briefly before turning to the incident room.

He continued walking to his car then called Licheli, who answered after a long delay. 'What?'

'No more games. I want to see you tomorrow morning at seven. Mushthaid Park— find a bench between the trees,' he said, not waiting for an answer before ending the call. He then took a deep breath and called Tamuna.

'Hey, darling,' she said.

'Hey, how are you?'

'Tired, you?'

'I'm fine. Are you busy this evening?'

'No, just sitting in with your mother.'

'Can I come over? There'll be two of us.'

'Of course. You're bringing a friend?'

'Something like that. See you about eight.'

Donadze drove to Tbilisi International Hospital and went straight to Avto's room. A nurse was sitting on the bed writing up the forms required for his discharge. He was dressed in tight designer ripped-and-repaired denim trousers, an equally tight white tee-shirt and black leather boots, his quiff carefully gelled into place.

'You're feeling better then,' Donadze stated.

The nurse looked up. 'This is your friend?' she asked Avto curtly.

Avto smiled and looked at Donadze, who answered, 'Not really a—'

'Yes,' said Avto.

The nurse shook her head slightly and put her pen in

her breast pocket. 'He'll need to rest for a week or so, no heavy exertion and pain killers as directed. You're free to go, Mr. Sabauri,' she said primly, gathering the forms and leaving the room.

Avto watched her go. 'I get that a lot,' he said.

'It's not because you're gay, it's because you're irritating. Anyway, let's get out of here.'

'That's my bag, Zura picked it up for me,' Avto said pointing to a large, very full bag in the corner of the room.

'Zura, the barman from the Dream? Found you in the car park?'

'Yes, he's really nice.'

'Are you and he...'

'Involved? No chance, not that I wouldn't be interested. He's firmly a ladies' man, unfortunately.'

Donadze hefted the bag by its handle. 'Didn't you have something with wheels?' He watched uneasily as Avto got gingerly to his feet, the pain from his injuries and the exertion evident on his strained face. 'I'd better take your handbag as well,' he said, putting the strap of a brown leather bag over his shoulder.

Avto took a tentative step forward. 'Thanks, but it's called a man-bag,' he said.

Donadze led the way along the corridor to the elevator, out of the hospital and to his car. Avto shuffled behind, leaning forward, his left hand protecting his broken rib, his face pale and strained. He eased himself into the passenger seat as Donadze held the door open. It had taken more than twenty minutes to get to the car. 'I'm not sure this is a good idea. I'll go back in and speak to the doctor, get you re-admitted,' he said.

'Don't, I'm due my pills soon. I'll be fine, it'll just take time. Please, let's go.'

'If you're sure.'

They drove in silence for a few minutes before Avto spoke. 'Why are you doing this?'

'You haven't told me everything.'

'What do you mean?'

'You didn't tell me about Licheli. Tell me what else you know.'

'So *that's* why you're doing this. Still trying to use me to get at Kaldani. I should have known.'

'What aren't you telling me?'

'Nothing. I shouldn't have agreed to help you. Take me to Zura's. I'll stay with him tonight and go to Rustavi tomorrow. My dad will have to take me back.'

'No forget it. He won't have you.' He glanced over. A solitary tear had run down Avto's pale face and pooled on his chin, ready to fall. 'I'm sorry. Let's leave it for now.'

They travelled the rest of the way to Tamuna's apartment in silence and Donadze parked illegally outside the building entrance.

'I thought you lived on Kandelaki Street,' Avto said.

'How did you know that?'

'You must have told me.'

'No, I didn't.' He paused. 'We're visiting—be on your best behaviour.' He helped Avto out of the car and led him into the apartment building, walking slowly up the stairs to the third level. Avto followed behind, gasping with each step taken. They reached Tamuna's door and Donadze rang the bell.

The door was opened immediately by his mother who was about to hug Donadze when she saw Avto leaning against the wall, eyes closed, sweat dripping off his hair and falling onto his face. 'Tamuna!' she shouted, then gently to Avto, 'Come on, child, let's get you inside.'

Avto was being led through the hall when Tamuna appeared, professionally appraising his condition and giving Donadze a cold look. 'What's your name?' she said.

'His name's Avto, he'll be staying—'

'Nice to meet you, Avto. Sit there,' Tamuna said, pointing to the sofa.

'Could I please have a drink, I have some pills to take,' Avto said, carefully sitting down.

Donadze's mother hustled to the kitchen and came back with a glass of water.

'Codeine,' Tamuna said, watching Avto take the pills with a long swallow of water. 'Don't take more than you need.'

'Tamuna's a doctor,' Donadze said.

'What were you thinking of, Ramaz? He's exhausted, why did you bring him up these stairs?'

'Well, I hadn't realised. The hospital said he was okay, and I wanted to see you. He'll be staying with me for a while until he finds a place of his own.'

'He's not going anywhere tonight. Avto, you can sleep on that sofa, Ramaz will pick you up tomorrow. He'll be staying in his own apartment tonight.'

Avto looked at Donadze and smirked. 'Is that okay with you, Ramaz?'

'You're enjoying this, aren't you? It's Lieutenant Donadze to you and, yes, I suppose it has to be.'

'You must both be hungry. Ramaz, help Avto to the table. I've made you *lobio*,' his mother said, returning to the kitchen.

TWENTY

Mushthaid Park was still in shadows when Donadze arrived. There was no sign of Licheli and he picked a bench under the trees, ran his hands over the wooden slats to displace some of the dew and sat down. He waited impatiently for a few moments longer then angrily reached for his phone, found Licheli in his contacts folder and called his number.

The call connected and a loud, harsh ring tone sounded close behind. Donadze flinched then jumped to his feet, spinning around rapidly and reaching for his pistol.

Licheli was standing on the grass two metres behind the bench, phone in hand and smiling. He swiped the screen to answer the call and lifted the phone to his face. 'Sorry I was late,' he spoke into the phone.

Donadze felt his heart race and his knees soften as adrenaline coursed through his blood. He took a moment before speaking, trying to keep his voice even.

'Congratulations, you managed to sneak up on me. It's a useful skill if you don't have the balls to go head to head, I suppose.'

'No sense of humour, Lieutenant? But, now I'm here, tell me what you want.'

'Sit down.'

'No, I'll stand.'

'It's not a request.'

Both men continued standing and staring at each other across the park bench for a long moment before Donadze turned and started to leave.

'Wait,' Licheli said. Donadze turned and watched as Licheli walked around the bench, wiped it with his hand and sat down.

Donadze returned to the bench and sat beside him. 'Good,' he said. 'It doesn't have to be like this, Gio. You know you're done with Kaldani. Even if I don't tell him about you, he'll find out somehow, you know that, don't you?'

Licheli didn't answer and Donadze continued speaking. 'You can salvage something from this. I said I'd help with the Prosecutor's Office, speak on your behalf when you go to trial. You'll do jail time but that's nothing for you. I'm sure you've got money stashed away—you'll be able to start again.'

Licheli remained impassive. 'Say something,' Donadze said.

He watched the conflict play out in Licheli's face before he spoke. 'How do I know you'll keep your word?'

'You'll have to trust me. But I think you know I'm good for it.'

'What do you want from me?'

'I told you to go back to the Dream and keep your eyes open, but I want more than that now. We're on the same side and we'll bring Kaldani down together. I want to know what he is doing every day, who he sees, anything you hear, any documents you come across. Bring me everything you can. It doesn't have to be connected to Bukia, Gloveli or Adamia.'

'Adamia? I told you he had nothing to do with Nino being killed.'

'Maybe—then you won't have anything on him for that. But bring me information and any evidence that can be used in court and I'll help you as much as I can.'

Licheli paused a moment then nodded.

'I need to hear you say it, Gio,' Donadze said.

Licheli nodded again. 'Okay, yes, yes... I'll do it,' he said.

Most of the investigation team were out when Donadze returned to the station and he asked Arziani to bring him up to speed. Limited progress had been made. CCTV video had been found which showed two suspects entering Bukia's apartment building shortly before his murder—but it hadn't been possible to identify them yet. Arziani thought that they were aware of the cameras as their heads were covered and they had never looked up. Gloveli's assailant, Luca Mamedov also hadn't been found and Arziani thought that he had either left Georgia or that Kaldani had found him first and he was now dead.

'I may be able to help you,' Donadze said. 'Bukia's killers, the two guys you have on video, were probably Chechens, brought in by Kaldani and possibly back in Chechnya now. Professionals—they won't have left you anything to work with and it would be nearly impossible to get them back to Georgia, even if we could identify them. You think Mamedov might have left Georgia? I'll try to get that confirmed but I'm not sure where we would go with that either. We won't be able to extradite him if he's in Shida Kartli but I might be able to find out if he's still alive.'

Arziani looked puzzled. 'How did you get all that information, Ramaz?'

'Sorry, Misha, I can't tell you.'

Arziani shook his head. 'Tell me if I'm wrong then. You've got someone inside Kaldani's organisation.'

'Why do you think that?'

'I know you've been meeting someone, working on your own, not involving the team.'

'As I said, there are things I can't tell you, at least not for now.'

'Now's exactly when we need it.'

'I said no, you'll have to trust me.'

Arziani shook his head again. 'I need to get back to work,' he said in a flat voice.

Donadze watched as Arziani walked away. *I know, Misha,* he thought. *'Trust should go both ways.'*

The Commander's office was empty and Donadze went in, closed the door and called the number given to him by Pataraia. 'Ramaz, I was just about to call you,' he answered

'That was lucky then. What's Rokva doing today?'

He paused. 'State secret, need to know basis—'

'I've heard that one already.'

'Just kidding, Ramaz. She's actually in the car with me.'

'Hey, Ramaz, want to meet at the usual place?' Rokva said.

'No—no burgers. Let's meet at Dedaena Park, by the monument. I'll be there in one hour.'

Donadze parked by the Flea Market and walked to the Mother Language Monument. He thought he had chosen the meeting place at random but it occurred to him that there might be a subliminal connection, given that the monument was erected to celebrate resistance to Russian dominance, in this case Georgian being preserved as the country's primary language.

He saw Pataraia and Rokva approaching the monument and the three simulated a chance meeting of friends who had then decided to take a stroll around the park.

'You're looking tired, Ramaz,' Rokva said.

'I'm fine. What were you going to call me about?'

'Exchange of information. You?'

'Yes, same thing, trying to make progress in this case.'

'You go first then.'

'You've got the Dream Casino bugged,' Donadze stated.

'Let's say that's possible.'

'You heard Meskhi and me interviewing Kaldani.'

196

There was a pause as Pataraia glanced over at Rokva, obtaining her unspoken agreement to continue. 'Yes, it was quite entertaining,' he said.

'What did Kaldani do after we left?'

'Well, we've only got audio, but poor Dato seemed to be quite upset. Shouted at his lawyer, maybe even slapped him around a bit. He got even more upset watching you on TV. Great move by the way, Kaldani's brand is toxic now.'

'What else?'

'Let's hear what you've got first,' Pataraia said.

'I've a source in Kaldani's organisation.'

'Yes, we know—Giorgi Licheli.'

Donadze was startled. 'How did you know that?'

'It's what we do. Don't worry, it won't go any further.'

'It'd better not. Licheli would be dead in a heartbeat if Kaldani found out.'

'And you'd lose your source. We understand that. What has he told you?'

'Well, he's confirmed that Kaldani was behind Bukia's murder. Kaldani organised that one himself, professional hit by a couple of Chechens he brought in. He's also certain that Kaldani wasn't behind Nino Adamia's murder.'

'Okay.'

'It's the gaps in his knowledge that are frustrating. He does not know why the hits were ordered. He does know that Kaldani is speaking to the SVR but he does not know, and does not want to know, what business he has with them.'

'Interesting, and you're putting pressure on him to fill these gaps?' Pataraia said.

'Of course—your turn.'

'Well, we can help you a little. After you left, Kaldani got on his phone and called his SVR friends. It was a short call, but with more than a few expletives. The message was clear, pretty much along the lines, *"I've done what you wanted. We're through."*'

'Did he elaborate, say what it was that he had done?'

'Why would he? They obviously already knew what that was.'

'But you think the Russians wanted Gloveli and Bukia dead and that they got Kaldani to do their dirty work.'

'Looks likely.'

'But why?'

'You're the detective, let us know when you've figured it out—speak soon,' Pataraia said, keeping up the pretence of a friendly meeting by giving Donadze a hug goodbye.

'Great talking with you, Ramaz. Let's get burgers next time,' Rokva said, reaching up to kiss him on the cheek.

Donadze drove around the area close to Tamuna's apartment, trying without success to find a parking place before joining the other cars illegally abandoned on the pavement. He stopped the engine, pulled down his visor and looked at himself in the mirror. Rokva was right, he really did look tired—tired *and* dishevelled. He promised himself he would get his hair cut soon. He rubbed his hands briskly over his stubbled face, trying to restore some colour to his cheeks. He stepped out of the car. August was coming to an end and he looked forward to the cooler and drier months of autumn. He climbed the stairs and rang Tamuna's doorbell.

Avto opened the door. 'Lieutenant,' he said. 'Come in.'

'Thanks,' Donadze said dryly. 'Are you ready to go?'

Donadze's mother kissed him on the cheek. 'Let's have something to eat first,' she said.

Tamuna was sitting on the sofa and Donadze leaned over to kiss her. 'Are you okay?' he asked.

'Never better. Avto's been keeping us entertained. Avto, tell Ramaz that story about your first boyfriend.'

'I think I've heard it. Very funny.'

'Funny? It was so sad,' his mother said.

'Well, Avto, it looks like your overnight stay hasn't been too much of an imposition, but I think we'd better go now.'

'Of course, Lieutenant. It's just that your mum has made us a lovely meal and I didn't want to be rude.'

'Ramaz, it's you who is being rude. Sit down and have something to eat. You can go after that if you're in a hurry,' his mother said sternly.

Donadze looked across at Tamuna who smiled and said, 'Do as your mother asks, Lieutenant.'

The food was as good as usual, and the two women were clearly fascinated by Avto who was charming and entertaining in equal measure. They finished eating and Donadze declined coffee for Avto and himself. He started to help tidy in the kitchen but was dismissed by his mother who told him he should go home and rest. She and Tamuna followed Donadze and Avto to the door and hugged and kissed them both, telling Avto he was welcome any time. The walk down the stairs was laborious and Donadze had

Avto wait at the building entrance while he retrieved his car then helped him in.

'We're going to your apartment now?' Avto asked.

'Yes, you can stay there until you're feeling better. I've got a spare room. You'll be okay in a week or so.'

'You know I've got no money.'

'I guessed that—it's not a problem.'

'Tamuna told me she's having a baby.'

'Yes.'

'She's lovely, your mum as well.'

'I'm a lucky man.'

'Why are you helping me, Ramaz?'

'It's Lieutenant Donadze to you. And I really don't know why. Maybe you deserve a break. Anyway, it's been a long day, let's get to the apartment and we can both get some rest.

TWENTY-ONE

Avto was still sleeping in the spare room while Donadze ate breakfast. He made a mental note to buy extra food for his guest—who was already starting to be irritating. Donadze kicked his boots under the table and moved his bag into a corner of the room. He could hear snoring through the bedroom door as he finished breakfast and rinsed his plate and cup. *It's going to be a long week,* he thought, then texted Tamuna, '*Dinner this evening, King David at 8?*'

She replied immediately, '*Okay, bringing Avto?*'

Donadze responded, '*Definitely not,*' adding a smiley-face emoji. He picked up his ID, pistol, keys and wallet, scribbled a note telling Avto not to leave the apartment and took the elevator to the underground car park.

Misha Arziani was alone at the station and he looked up as Donadze entered, 'Hey, Ramaz,' he said.

'Long night?'

'Yes, can't say it's been productive though. No new leads or witnesses. Our guys are feeling down. Doesn't help that the Captain's funeral's tomorrow.'

'Tomorrow? You're going?'

'Of course, we all are. Aren't you?'

'I'll do my best.'

Donadze's phone rang, the caller ID indicating that Pataraia was calling. He was about to step out of the room but, after a moment's thought, swiped to answer instead. He put the phone on speaker, holding his hand up to indicate to Arziani that he shouldn't speak.

'Donadze,' he said.

'Ramaz, it's Rokva. Are you on speaker?'

'Yes, I'm with a colleague. You can trust him.'

Rokva hesitated. 'Okay,' she said. 'I've got something for you, but you'll have to be quick. Mamedov—he's back in Tbilisi. He did run to Shida Kartli after Gloveli scared him off. But he's back at his girlfriend's apartment this morning, probably picking her up and collecting his escape money. He won't be there long.'

Donadze motioned to Arziani to write down the apartment's address, thanked Rokva then ended the call. 'Bring him in, Misha,' he said.

'Who was that?'

'I can't tell you and I want you to keep that conversation to yourself. I'm trusting you.'

'Will do. Are you running the arrest?'

'No, this one's yours. Just make sure you bring him back in one piece. Get going, you might not have much time.'

Arziani grinned. 'Thanks, Ramaz, I'll call you with updates.'

'Do that but be careful. Mamedov will be armed and he's got nothing to lose.'

'Understood,' Arziani said, striding for the door.

Donadze called the Colonel who answered immediately. He appraised him on the tip off from Rokva and said that an arrest was imminent.

'Well, that's exceptionally good news. You'll be leading the arrest I take it.'

'No, sir. I have instructed Detective Arziani to take the lead.'

'Really, let's hope it goes well then.'

'I'm sure it will.'

'And the tip off came from your GIS contacts. Why didn't we know about Mamedov's girlfriend?'

Donadze lips tightened. 'We should have known, of course. We should have been watching her apartment.'

'Yes, you should have been. Let me know when you've made the arrest,' the Colonel said, hanging up.

Donadze took his phone from his ear and glared at it. *How did we miss that?* he thought. Pushing self-criticism to one side, he called Major Gloveli and told him that the arrest was underway.

'He won't be able to tell you anything you don't already know,' Gloveli said.

'Maybe not, but he'll be able to confirm his orders came from Licheli and Licheli is the link to Kaldani.'

'I suppose so. Anyway, it's good that you've found him. Makes for good press and keeps the pressure on Kaldani.'

'Are you going to Bukia's funeral?'

'Yes, of course.'

'I'll pick you up, save you getting the bus.'

'Do that, you can try some of my wine.'

'As long as I don't have to try your *chacha*.'

'You should be so lucky. You'd better get back to work.'

Arziani called Donadze on his way back to the station. Mamedov's arrest had gone well. He had been in bed with his girlfriend when the Police had rammed their apartment door open. Neither had been in any position to resist and Mamedov's pistol was well out of reach, should he have been foolish enough to try to use it. A news crew had been waiting outside Mtatsminda Station as Mamedov had been brought in, another tip-off by Colonel Meskhi, Donadze thought. He had smiled as he watched footage of Arziani, striking a heroic pose, leading his prisoner past the reporters to be charged with attempted murder.

Donadze and Arziani interviewed Mamedov at the station. He had realised that Gloveli, a retired Police major, would make a very credible witness and was keen to co-operate in return for leniency from the court. He confirmed that the order to kill Gloveli had come from Licheli but was not able to make a further connection to Kaldani.

Donadze sensed the pressure Kaldani would be feeling. He pictured him in his office at the Dream, furious but calculating, anxious but at some level enjoying the game, convinced that he would be the ultimate winner—as he always was. *Arrogance might be your undoing, Dato*, he thought. *Better not let it be mine.*

Tamuna was seated at their favourite table when Donadze arrived at the restaurant. He thought she looked tired as she stood to kiss him. 'Did you come straight from the Clinic?' he said.

'Yes, it wasn't worthwhile going home so I caught up on some admin. How's Avto?'

'Getting on my nerves. Do you want him back?'

'You're not as hard as you pretend,' she laughed. 'What will he do after he moves out of your place?'

'Not sure. He should be able to find a job in Tbilisi then get somewhere to live. Or maybe his father will take him back.'

Donadze was feeling good after Mamedov's arrest and the positive publicity that had followed. When the waiter arrived, he checked with Tamuna that she didn't mind him ordering a glass of *Mukuzani* as she was restricting herself to water. They ordered a selection of their favourite dishes and chatted while waiting for the food to arrive.

Donadze was finishing his wine and wondering if he could order another when he heard a customer speaking to a waiter in loud nasally English. He turned in his seat and saw Robert Morton with a woman about Morton's own age. They'd been shown to a table on the other side of the restaurant. Morton was taking his seat when he glanced up and noticed Donadze looking at him. He nodded slightly in acknowledgment then shook his head slightly—silently imploring Donadze not to approach.

'Who's that?' Tamuna asked.

'Robert Morton, General Manager of United Energy.'

'We saw him on television, didn't we? How do you know him?'

'He had some information about the case I'm working.' He paused. 'Back in a couple of minutes, sorry.'

Donadze thought Morton looked like a deer caught in headlights as he approached his table. 'Good evening, Mr. Morton,' he said in English. 'It appears that we have similar taste in restaurants.'

He offered his hand to Morton who flashed a very white smile, took it briefly and said with synthetic warmth, 'Good to see you, Lieutenant.'

Donadze turned to Morton's companion. She was slim, with carefully styled shoulder length blond hair, and wore a black sleeveless dress with a gold chain. He held out his hand. 'Ramaz Donadze,' he said.

'*Gamarjoba.* Erin Morton.'

'Your Georgian accent is excellent, Mrs. Morton.'

'Thank you, please call me Erin.'

'We've been taking lessons,' Morton said with forced jocularity.

'Lieutenant? Is that military or police?' she asked.

'Police, I'm a detective.'

'How do you two know each other?'

'The Lieutenant needed some background information on a case he was working. I couldn't help much.'

'That's very modest of you, Mr. Morton. You were more helpful than you realise.'

'Would you care to join us, Lieutenant?' Erin Morton said.

'Thank you, but I'd better get back. Enjoy your meal.'

'Good talking to you, Lieutenant' Morton said.

'*Nakhvamdis*,' his wife said.

Donadze returned to his own table and sat down. 'You know so many people,' Tamuna teased.

'It's an occupational hazard.'

'But the General Manager of United Energy? A television celebrity as well. You should have introduced me,' she continued.

'I wouldn't have been doing you a favour, believe me,' Donadze said.

Donadze was eating breakfast prepared by Avto when Rokva called. He stepped onto his balcony and closed the sliding door before swiping to answer.

'Hey, Ramaz,' she said. 'We need to talk.'

'Let me guess, burgers?'

'It's a bit early, even for me. How about same place as before? One hour?'

'One hour,' Donadze confirmed, opening the balcony door to see Avto staring at him from the cooking area.

'You're going out?'

'Yes.'

'At least finish your breakfast first. I thought you liked poached eggs?'

'You're not my wife or my mother, Avto.'

'Five minutes, it can't be that important.'

'You need to get your own place soon,' Donadze said,

seeing hurt register on Avto's face. He thought about apologising but left the apartment instead.

He arrived at Dedaena Park early and called Misha Arziani who was still on a high after arresting Mamedov the previous day. Arziani said that Mamedov was co-operating with the investigation and that he hoped to obtain more information from him later that day.

Donadze left his car and walked into the park. Rokva was slightly behind, walking towards the monument and she caught up with him and took his arm, simulating lovers enjoying an early morning stroll. 'Pataraia?' he asked.

'Busy,' she replied with no attempt at humour.

'So, what's going on?'

Rokva kept walking for several steps before speaking. 'We've been watching our Russian friends.'

'Lobodin and Pilkin, what about them?'

'You've spoken with Minister Toreli,' she stated.

'Yes, him and his Rottweiler, Jibuti.'

Rokva paused as a runner overtook them and passed out of earshot. 'Toreli has been speaking with the Russians.'

'Okay, but is that a problem? He told me he had met them previously when they were posing as ore exporters. Told me it was part of his job to support foreign investments. He doesn't know that they're SVR.'

Rokva nodded and walked a few more steps before speaking. 'Maybe not...'

Donadze stopped walking and turned to face Rokva. 'Get to the point, Tanya.'

'Keep walking,' she said, taking his arm again. 'It would be understandable for Toreli to meet Russian businessmen if that's what he thought they were. But why would that meeting have to be in secret?'

'Secret? What do you mean?'

'They met in an apartment in Kazbegi Avenue. It's being rented by Pilkin under a different alias. The only people there were Lobodin, Pilkin, Toreli and Jibuti. It was extremely low key, no government SUV for Toreli, no security. It just wasn't right.'

'You had the apartment bugged?' Donadze asked.

'We didn't have time, unfortunately.'

'Do you think Toreli's on the take?'

'He might be, but that's not what this is about. He wouldn't need a clandestine meeting just to receive cash,' Rokva said.

'So, what's your best guess?'

'We think the SVR wants something from Toreli and they're exerting pressure to get it.'

'Bribery?' Donadze asked.

'Or blackmail...'

'They know Toreli was having sex with Nino Adamia and they're using that...'

'Possibly.'

'But for what purpose?'

'That's what we need to determine.'

They walked on in silence until Donadze said, 'Why are you telling me this?'

Rokva paused, 'It could be relevant to your investigation.'

'Yes, but what do you want from me?'

She stopped walking and turned to face Donadze.

'Investigating a government minister is difficult for us, for the GIS. Our bosses worry about political fall-out. Pataraia and I were hoping that you could run with this. If you can, put some pressure on Toreli and Jibuti, see what you come up with.'

'So, it's okay for me to risk my career?'

'We don't see it that way, this fits in with your investigation, doesn't it? No one could criticise you just for following the evidence where it takes you.'

'They could and they probably will,' Donadze said, turning to leave.

TWENTY-TWO

Bukia's funeral was to be held with full Police honours. Donadze had driven to Shindisi to pick up Major Gloveli and had railed about the hypocrisy on the return trip to Tbilisi. Bukia had been incompetent and corrupt, had betrayed his office and was probably killed because of his association with a leading crime boss. He didn't deserve the respect being shown, Donadze had declared.

He had expected Gloveli to agree with his assessment. 'So, you think we're doing Bukia a favour he doesn't deserve?' the Major asked.

'Of course, don't you?'

'He's lying in a box—do you really think he cares?'

'Not literally, obviously.'

'You know, Ramaz, you're a good detective but you'd do better if you could learn to be a bit more open-minded. You, more than most, know the importance of family. The

Police service *is* a family. This funeral isn't for Bukia, it's for us. It gives us a chance to come together and show that we stand strong and united. We serve the public, but we look after our own. We need this—despite what we might have privately thought of the Captain.'

Donadze's instinct was to spit out a retort, but Gloveli's comment about being more open-minded had stung, and they drove in silence for a few more kilometres.

'How's your investigation going,' Gloveli said.

Donadze paused to gather his thoughts. 'I think we're making progress—the pressure is definitely on Kaldani. We know he ordered the hit on you, but we want to get him for Bukia's murder as well. Licheli is clear that Kaldani had nothing to do with Nino's death and I believe him. So, we're no further forward there.' He recounted his earlier conversation with Rokva about Toreli and Jibuti meeting the SVR agents.

'I never get tired of that view,' Gloveli said, gazing out his side window as the landscape opened to show Tbilisi lying in haze at the foot of the hills they were driving over. He turned to face forward again. 'The SVR would need something pretty strong on Toreli. Seeing a call-girl wouldn't be enough to blackmail him—this is Georgia after all. And blackmailing a government minister? It can't be for money— they must want something that's connected to his office. Did you consider they may be investing for the future, spotted him as our next Prime Minister possibly and getting him lined up to do Putin's bidding. What a coup that would be.'

'Yes, it certainly would be. But even if they are lining him up for the future, they must have something on him now. And if they can get him to behave improperly now, then that would strengthen their hold going forward.'

'You say his lawyer was at the meeting? So, he must know what they have on his boss as well.'

'Yes, he'd have to know.'

'So, you're looking more closely at Toreli and Jibuti now?'

'My GIS contacts asked me to do that.'

'Because they don't want to target a government minister themselves?'

'Yes.'

'And do you have a problem with that?'

'No.'

'Didn't think so. But give yourself some cover. Speak to Meskhi, make sure he is up to speed and knows what you're doing. Don't allow him deniability. I don't think he'd sell you out, but don't give him that opportunity.'

The weather turned suitably oppressive for the funeral. The skies over the surrounding hills were black and brooding. In the toxic cauldron below, the air hung dank and heavy, reluctant to stir and give up its oxygen, suffocating the city.

It seemed to Donadze that just about every police officer in Georgia had turned out to honour Bukia. They lined the procession route, sombre and still as his casket passed en route to the cemetery, blocking the already congested streets and daring any driver to protest.

He and Gloveli stood to attention in dress-uniform as the casket was lowered and the firing party saluted their fallen comrade with a rifle volley. The Police family was standing strong and united.

All the seats in the incident room were taken by tired detectives and administrators, most drinking strong coffee and anticipating their next cigarette, as Misha Arziani summarised the status of their investigation and their tactics going forward.

Donadze had given the team the previous night off to allow them all to attend the post-funeral *supra* which was held to honour Bukia. The feast was low-key in keeping with tradition. The toasts followed the expected formula and were well-delivered and appreciatively received. Colonel Meskhi had attended and stayed to talk with Bukia's extended family members and his own officers. Major Gloveli had changed out of uniform and spent time drinking and smoking with old colleagues, a much-loved commander Donadze thought, with a tinge of jealousy.

Arziani was a good motivational speaker and Donadze felt energy coming into the room as he lifted the team out of their early-morning lethargy.

'So why not arrest Kaldani now, charge him with ordering the hit on Gloveli, and sweat the rest out of him?' Soso Chichua asked.

'He's sweating now, Soso, believe me,' Donadze interjected. 'But he won't break easily. We need solid evidence, preferably from more than one source. We've got one chance to get this right or he's free and clear on all charges.'

'Okay, so we've got enough to prove means and opportunity, but what's his motive? What was it that made Kaldani think he had to take out Gloveli and Bukia?' Chichua persisted.

Arziani glanced at Donadze who did not respond. 'It's a good question Soso, and something we need to work on going forward,' he said flatly.

'That sounds pretty vague to me. Is there something we're not being told here, Lieutenant?' Chichua said, looking at Donadze. 'We were all so busy congratulating ourselves on nailing Mamedov that we forgot to ask where the tip-off about him being back in Tbilisi came from.'

'I'm sure Lieutenant Donadze is telling you everything he can.' Colonel Meskhi had entered the room unnoticed and joined Donadze and Arziani to face the investigation team.

Chichua straightened in his chair. 'Yes, sir. It just difficult to get the job done properly if we don't have all the information available,' he said

'Yes, I understand that, Detective. But let me say that everyone on this team has my full confidence and support. It's not a question of trust and you'll just have to take my word on that. Your work to date has been impressive. Let's get this investigation over the line and Kaldani in front of a judge. Lieutenant, get your people back to work.'

'We need to make better progress on this investigation, Lieutenant,' Colonel Meskhi said.

Meskhi had instructed Donadze to join him in the Commander's office and they sat across the small tidy desk, the Colonel's laptop open but pushed to one side to allow room for his notebook.

'Yes, sir.'

Meskhi exhaled loudly through his nose, straightened his long legs to push his chair back as far as it would go, leaned back and closed his eyes.

'Colonel?' said Donadze.

'I'm thinking.'

Donadze sat nervously for a long moment, watching Meskhi until he opened his eyes, sat up and pulled his chair back under the desk. 'It seems to me, Lieutenant,' he said, 'that we need to identify the common factor which connects a crime boss and a government minister to the Russian secret services.'

'Well, of course, that's exactly what—'

'If you would allow me to finish... As we haven't been able to identify that common factor yet, let's look at things in a different way. As Detective Chichua pointed out, we should consider motive.' Meskhi leaned forward and fixed Donadze with a stare. 'The SVR has been calling the shots here. What would motivate Kaldani to do their bidding?' he said.

Donadze resisted leaning back and away from Meskhi's scrutiny as he answered. 'Money, power, licence to expand his empire into Russia and the break-away regions protected by Russia—Shida Kartli and Abkhazia. Fear of reprisals if he didn't do everything they wanted.'

'Yes, all of these things. Why would the SVR need

Kaldani though? They're well resourced, plenty of back-up from Russia?'

'Kaldani knows the terrain better, has access to local talent. He gives the SVR distance and deniability if things go wrong.'

Meskhi changed direction. 'How about Minister Toreli? What would motivate such an ambitious man? A man who has already achieved so much but wants even more?'

'To have that ambition thwarted, to *not* become Prime Minister, to lose what he already has as a government minister—status and power.'

'Not money?'

Donadze shook his head. 'No, money doesn't drive Toreli.'

'Could the SVR make Toreli Prime Minister?' Meskhi asked.

'Not directly.'

'Could they prevent it somehow, say by releasing salacious information about him?'

'Yes, if it was powerful enough?'

'So, he's not being bribed, he's being blackmailed.' Meskhi concluded. 'How about the SVR? It's a Russian state agency, working directly or indirectly for Putin. What would motivate the SVR to run an operation in Georgia?'

'Putin wants to resurrect the USSR or something similar, with him front and centre. He resents us cosying up to the West, doesn't want us in the EU or NATO, wants people to be nostalgic for the old days. He wants us back in the fold.'

'And how might that be achieved?' Meskhi prompted.

'If our people became dissatisfied with the direction our government is taking us. If they don't see any improvement in their daily lives, if they don't have jobs.'

'Something the Minister of Economy could influence—in either direction?'

'Toreli is being blackmailed by the SVR to damage our economy!'

'It's a credible theory.'

'That's treason! Donadze declared.

'If that's what's happening, yes.'

'How do we prove it?'

'Slow down, Lieutenant. It looks like we *may* have identified a conspiracy against our country in which a government minister *may* be complicit. What are we not seeing?'

'Sir?'

'Who else is involved?'

'There's been no one identified, as yet.'

'Not yet. Something for you to work on... Let's move on. We seem to have a reasonable understanding of what's been motivating the key players up to this point. But what's changed?'

Donadze looked down at the desk as he considered the question.

'Have things worked out for Kaldani?' the Colonel coached.

'No, we have Mamedov and can use him to tie Kaldani to the attempted murder. We're on his back, he's had bad press and his business is hurting.'

'How do the Russians feel about that?'

'If we can tie Kaldani to the attempted hit on Gloveli then we can tie them in as well.'

'And?'

'And Kaldani becomes a loose end, a potential embarrassment to the SVR and their political bosses back in Russia!'

'And therefore...'

'He's at risk—the SVR might have him killed!'

'Unless...'

'Unless he gets to them first.'

'Yes, but how feasible would that be?' Meskhi asked.

'Difficult, he'd have to worry about the whole organisation, not just a couple of agents.'

'So, what would be the smart move from Kaldani's perspective?'

'He should try to keep the SVR on-side, help them complete their mission, whatever that is. He can't take on a whole secret service, but he might have found a way to buy some insurance for himself.'

'How would he do that?'

'Classic approach. Provide evidence on what he and the SVR have been up to. To be disclosed in the event of his death or disappearance.'

'Yes, and who would he leave that with?'

'Someone he trusts and knows the system. Someone he wouldn't mind putting at risk. No close family member. A loyal lieutenant or maybe his lawyer.'

'Licheli?'

'No, he's not close enough.'

'So?'

'His lawyer, Petre Melua.'

Meskhi nodded, closed his laptop and put it and his notebook into his briefcase. 'Has this been a useful conversation?'

'Very useful, sir.'

'Did it provide you with anything you didn't already know?'

'Well...'

'I'm not fishing for compliments, Donadze.'

'No, sir. I think you helped me focus.'

'Thank you, Lieutenant. Keep me informed,' the Colonel said, stooping under the door frame as he left the office.

Donadze watched as Meskhi strode through the detectives' bureau, acknowledging the two officers who were at their desks with a nod. He shook his head and, feeling exhausted, slumped back into his chair. He looked at his watch—it was only just after ten. *I need coffee*, he thought, pulling himself to his feet.

TWENTY-THREE

T he change in Licheli was stark. He was dressed in his customary black trousers and white shirt, but the shirt was crushed and sweat stained, the trousers unbelted and slipping off his narrow hips. He had shaved badly—black hair had escaped his razor and was tufted on his chin, neck and under his nose. Donadze struggled not to recoil from the stench of stale alcohol and sweat which cloaked him like a black mood as he sat down on the bench.

'What's happened to you?' Donadze said.

There were only a few people walking or running in Rike Park and no one else in the children's play area, but Licheli looked around anxiously. 'Nothing,' he said.

'Kaldani will know he's got a problem if he sees you like this.'

'He won't see me. I've taken a couple of days off. Anyway, he knows I have a drink sometimes. What do you want?'

Donadze observed Licheli closely as his right foot beat rapidly on the children's soft play surface, his oily hair falling lank over his eyes as he bent forward, hugging himself and shivering in the early autumn evening's warmth. 'Maybe this isn't a good idea,' he said.

'I told you I'm okay! What do you want?'

'All right. Tell me what's been happening at the casino?'

'Business as usual, really. Things got heated after that stunt you and that big cop pulled. Dato was a bit rattled, everyone was in the firing line, me included. But apart from that?' he shrugged. 'I've not seen many VIPs in lately, but there are plenty of others willing to lose a hundred *lari* or so at the slots or pay forty *lari* for fake Scotch—cannon fodder Dato calls them.'

'The two Russians Kaldani met at the Dream—have they been back?'

'Haven't seen them.'

'Remember our deal Gio. You have to convince me to help you. I'm not getting much from you yet.'

'Yeah, I remember. They've not been back but Dato's been to see them. Some place in Kazbegi Street. Got that from his driver.'

'What was it about?'

'No idea.'

'What's Kaldani saying about Mamedov?'

'No one likes a rat. I wouldn't put money on him seeing his next birthday.'

'Is Kaldani planning—'

'Wait a minute,' Licheli's shoulders shook. 'I've just described myself. That's hilarious!'

Donadze struck Licheli hard on his upper arm. 'Listen carefully, Gio. Pull yourself together or we're done. Understood?'

Licheli's laughter turned to dry sobs as he straightened to face Donadze. 'How's Avto?' he said.

'Avto? He's somewhere you can't find him.'

'I know he's at your apartment. He called me. I want to see him.'

'You tried to kill him.'

'That wouldn't have happened.'

'Well, he doesn't want to see you.'

'Don't be so sure, he called me, didn't he?'

'Listen to me, Gio. You're mine until we have Kaldani in a cell. After that, if Avto wants to see you, I won't get in the way.'

Donadze waited until Licheli nodded his agreement before continuing. 'Is Kaldani planning on killing Mamedov?'

'Of course he is.'

'How?'

'I don't know, but it'll happen eventually.'

'Tell me about Petre Melua,' Donadze said.

'Dato's lawyer? What about him?'

'How close is he to Kaldani's business? Does Kaldani trust him?'

'As much as he trusts anyone. They've got connections going back to Shida Kartli. I think he worked for Dato's old man.'

'When are you due back at the Dream?'

'Tomorrow, why?'

'Get yourself cleaned up. If I see you in this state again, Kaldani can have you. Think of that if you ever want to see Avto again.'

Donadze walked to the security door and buzzed Melua's apartment. Construction of the block had only been completed the previous year. Built in the grounds of a former hospital, it was unusual for Tbilisi in having extensive gardens where residents could walk, or their kids could play away from the busy city streets. He thought that the developers would already be eying the gardens greedily, wondering how to get around purchase agreements and build an adjacent block.

'Yes?' Donadze heard indistinctly.

'It's Lieutenant Donadze, could you please let me in.'

'What's this about?'

'I just need a few minutes of your time. It's not official, but you should hear what I have to say.'

There was a pause before Donadze heard a buzz and the door unlocked. 'Level fifteen,' Melua said, providing Donadze with the elevator security code.

Melua was waiting outside his apartment. He turned and walked back inside, leaving the door open. Donadze walked to the apartment and followed him in. 'Through here,' Melua said from the lounge doorway.

The room was sparse, with polished wood flooring unsoftened by any kind of rug or carpet. Spotlights shone brightly from the ceiling, their beams uncompromising and only partially diffused by shimmering atmospheric dust. A modest television sat on an opaque glass table in the middle of a long wall. It was set to a news channel, the volume turned low. Two framed prints were propped on the floor, ready to be hung. 'You've not been here long?' Donadze asked.

'What's this about, Lieutenant?'

'Can we sit?' Donadze said, nodding towards a small dining table which had four chairs placed around it, the arms and legs still wrapped in protective card.

'Go ahead,' Melua said, remaining on his feet as Donadze sat down. 'I want to know what this is about.'

'I think you're a worried man.'

Melua looked at his watch. 'You asked for a few minutes.'

'You're right to be worried. You've been with Dato for a long time, his old man before that. He's hardly put a foot wrong, has he? Built the organisation into what it is today. He's a player right across Georgia and beyond. Made a lot of money. Made you a lot of money too. But more recently? Killing cops—who does that? And all that bad press? His political cover is running for the hills, they've got no choice.'

'Mr. Kaldani is my client, Lieutenant and I cannot and will not discuss his affairs with you. Let me show you to the door.'

'Kaldani's going down, Petre. You know it. He's arrogant, thinks he's bullet-proof. Would his old man have got into bed with these Russians? You know what they are, don't you? People might turn a blind eye to gambling and girls. Where's the harm, right? But betraying your country?

And to the Russians? He's going to jail for a very long time and the question is: who does he take with him? It doesn't have to be you.'

'I'm outraged, Lieutenant! You have come to my home uninvited and made ridiculous and totally unsubstantiated assertions about my client, insinuating that I should compromise our professional relationship.' Melua held up his mobile phone. 'I have a meeting with Mr. Kaldani tomorrow and he'll hear everything you've said.'

'Nice speech, but that's okay, I knew you'd be recording. But what will Kaldani's reaction be when you play that to him? I'm sure he'll appreciate your loyalty. But he might wonder how long that loyalty will last. You know too much, what would be the smart thing for him to do?'

Donadze stood and closed the distance to Melua, crowding his personal space, trying to read the emotions on his face. He prodded him in the chest with his forefinger. 'Why not start thinking like *him*? What's the smart thing for *you* to do?'

Melua held Donadze's stare for a long moment before breaking eye contact.

'Thanks for seeing me, call me when you're ready to talk,' Donadze said, brushing past the lawyer as he walked to the door.

'What were you thinking of when you called Licheli?' Donadze spoke hands-free into his phone as he drove.

'He's not that bad.' Avto replied.

'Yes, he is. He's very bad. He tried to kill you—don't you remember? He had a pillow on your head.'

'He gets mad sometimes, I know that. But he wouldn't hurt me, really.'

'You're going to see him?'

'Probably, yes. But not right away.'

'You're making a big mistake.'

'I know you worry about me, Ramaz. But you really shouldn't—I know what I'm doing.'

'It's Lieutenant Donadze to you and I don't think you do know what you're doing. Listen, I won't be back this evening. I'm going to Tamuna's.'

'That's nice, I'll see you there,' Avto replied.

'You're going as well?'

'I'm here already, your mum invited me. I'm sure she'll keep you some food.'

'How did you get over there?' Donadze asked.

'Taxi, is that a problem?'

'No, but if you're well enough to be socialising then you're well enough to find your own place.'

'I agree and I have. Got a job as well. I've just been telling your mum and Tamuna. It's really exciting. A friend from—'

'Tell me when I get there, I want to hear all the details,' Donadze said, hanging up.

His mother opened the apartment door. She smelled of childhood food and love as she stood on her tiptoes, put her arms around her son's neck and kissed him. '*Ramazi,* come in. You look tired, let me get you something to eat,' she said.

Avto was sitting on the couch with Tamuna's

obstetrician friend, Lela. An Australian soap was playing on the television, the actors' voices dubbed into Georgian. Lela stood to hug Donadze.

'She's in her room,' Avto said, smiling at him from the couch.

Donadze knocked on the bedroom door. 'Come in, Ramaz,' Tamuna said.

She was standing in front of a mirror pulling on trousers.

Donadze stood behind her, put his hands on her hips and kissed her neck, looking at them both in the mirror. 'You look wonderful.'

'I feel fat,' she said, stepping away from Donadze and the mirror.

'You're not fat, you're pregnant.'

'And you're such a smooth talker.'

'I tell it as I see it. But I'd better get back through. I think my mother wants to give *me* a baby-bump before you get yours.'

'Fine, but let's talk first.'

Tamuna sat on the end of the bed and indicated for him to sit beside her. 'Sounds ominous,' he said.

She took Donadze's hand. 'Listen, Ramaz. We may have a problem...'

'A problem? With the pregnancy?'

'Yes, possibly. I've had some bleeding. Spotting it's called. It's not unusual and may be nothing to worry about. But I've spoken to Lela and she's going to give me an ultrasound scan tomorrow and—'

'I should have known,' Donadze said, his head dropping.

Tamuna let go his hand. 'What are you talking about?'

'I should have known. It was too good to be true, nothing that good can—'

Tamuna jabbed Donadze hard on his shoulder. 'Now you listen to me,' she said with quiet anger. 'I told you there *might* be a problem. But equally—there might not be. In any event, I can't do this on my own. I need you to be there with me, and that means you can't panic like that. Whatever happens, we face this together. Do you understand?'

Donadze blinked rapidly then raised his head to meet Tamuna's fierce gaze. He took her hand again. 'I'm sorry,' he said. 'You're right, I did panic. But it's not going to happen again, I promise.'

Tamuna moved closer to Donadze and pulled him to her, 'It's okay, I understand what you've been through, why you reacted that way. But things are different now. Everything's going to be all right.'

Donadze straightened and put his arms around her. 'I know. You and the baby are going to be fine, I'm sure of it. Can I stay tonight and take you for the scan tomorrow?'

'Yes, of course. You're a good man Ramaz, that's why I love you.'

'Good? I'm not so sure about that.'

'I tell it as I see it. Now go and get your *lobio*.'

TWENTY-FOUR

'It all looks good, Tamuna. Baby's size is about right, she's got a strong heartbeat, the kidneys and liver are perfect. Your amniotic fluid volumes are as I would expect. Lela put her hand on Tamuna's shoulder. 'It all looks good,' she repeated.

'Thanks, Lela. That's a relief,' Tamuna said.

'That's really good news, Lela, thanks,' Donadze said. 'And you described the baby as she…'

'Always the detective, eh Ramaz? Yes, I did, but it's really too early to say. I was taking my lead from your mother, I guess.'

'It's always dangerous to argue with her. But everything really is okay?'

'Well, yes, but it's important that you understand this. The scan shows that baby is progressing as well as we would hope. And Tamuna is doing really well. However, although spotting is quite common in the first trimester, it can *sometimes* be a symptom of miscarriage. Now, having said that, Tamuna told me she isn't suffering from other typical symptoms, such as discharge of—'

'That's okay, Lela, thanks. We'd better not overload the poor man,' Tamuna said. 'Ramaz, be grateful. The scan was positive, the baby's healthy. We've got a lot to be thankful for.'

'I know and I am. What about you though? What can I do to help?'

'Tamuna knows she needs to take things a bit easier and rest when she can,' Lela said. 'I'll be keeping an eye on her and I won't be letting her work late. Having your mother stay helps a lot. There are some other practical things which we'll discuss.'

'When I'm not here?'

'Yes, when you're not here,' Tamuna smiled. 'Why don't you go and catch some criminals?'

Donadze left the Clinic and was walking to his car when he sensed movement from behind. He spun quickly, his hands instinctively going up to defend himself from attack. Pataraia stopped abruptly, his hands held low and open. 'Steady, Ramaz,' he said.

Rokva stepped forward and hugged Donadze as an old friend would, speaking quietly into his ear, 'We need to speak with you, it's urgent.'

'We were just going for a coffee—do you have time to join us? It'd be good to catch up,' Pataraia said in a conversational tone.

Donadze made a theatrical show of consulting his watch and said loudly, 'Why not, I could use a coffee.'

Rokva took his arm and said softly, 'Don't overdo it.'

They walked to a nearby coffee shop and sat at an outside table where the rowdy Tbilisi traffic muffled their conversation.

'Tamuna's okay?' Rokva said.

'Yes, but that's not why you—'

'No, it's not,' Pataraia interrupted. 'You tried to turn Petre Melua.'

'Yes. We think he might be holding Kaldani's insurance policy. Something to keep him safe should the SVR start to see him as an embarrassment.'

'Make sense. But it hasn't worked,' Rokva said.

'Why, what happened?'

'It looks like Melua couldn't bring himself to go against his boss. He took the story to Kaldani, played him the recording he made when you turned up at his apartment.'

A waiter approached and took their coffee order. Donadze paused until he was out of earshot. 'You've still got a bug in Kaldani's office?'

'Yes, surprising that he's not had the office swept, but we still have it for now.'

'How did the conversation go?'

'You know, Ramaz, we'd really hoped that we could have worked a bit more closely than this,' Pataraia said. 'It would have been useful if we'd known you were making a play on Melua.'

'I doubt you and Rokva tell me everything you get up to. Anyway, you asked to speak to me. How did the conversation at the casino go?'

Rokva put her hand on Donadze's arm. 'We're on the same side, Ramaz. Let's just try sharing a bit more, please.'

Donadze looked down at her hand resting on his arm. 'Okay, understood...' he said, nodding.

'All right, this is what happened,' Pataraia said, briskly. 'And remember, we only have voice, no visuals. Melua went to Kaldani's office, crashed a call he was on and said he had to speak with him urgently. He told him how you had turned up unannounced then played him the recording. Kaldani was surprisingly calm. He got him to play it again and asked for a copy. It all got a bit emotional from that point onwards. Kaldani asked Melua if he believed what you had told him, that he would ever doubt his loyalty. It sounded like they were both in tears and Melua said something like, no, of course not, and that you, Ramaz, were a fool if you thought that he would ever betray the family. Kaldani then made a speech about how his father had taught him the meaning of loyalty, that Melua was more than his lawyer—that he was his brother. They probably had a manly hug then got into a conversation about you. Melua wanted to make a formal complaint, call in some political support. Kaldani said no, that would stir up more bad press and that getting politicians behind them would be difficult anyway. He told Melua to carry on as usual and not to speak to you again unless it was a formal interview.'

'That's a pity, I thought if—'

'Wait, there's more,' Rokva said. 'Melua left the office and, a short while after that, Kaldani made a call from a burner phone. We don't know who he spoke to and we only picked up his half of the conversation. But it looks like loyalty only goes one way with Dato—despite the tears and Melua supposedly being his brother.'

'He ordered a hit on Melua!'

'Not using words which would stand up in court, but yes—Petre Melua is a dead man walking.'

'Can I hear what was said?'

Pataraia put a USB flash drive on the table. Donadze put it in his pocket, took out his phone and walked to the edge of the pavement.

Arziani answered on the second ring. 'Misha, pick up Petre Melua, arrest him if necessary. Don't let him speak to anyone. Bring him to the station. Do it quietly. Put a guard on him, someone you trust. I'm coming in and I'll explain everything when I see you.'

Donadze pocketed his phone and returned to the table. The waiter had served their coffee and he sat back down. 'You're welcome,' Pataraia said.

'Sorry. Thank you. This will be useful.'

'Well, it was lovely catching up, Ramaz,' Rokva said brightly. 'Give our love to Tamuna, and all the best with the pregnancy.'

Donadze downed his espresso, feeling it burn his throat. He stood, shook hands with Pataraia and bent to kiss Rokva. 'Yes, great seeing you both. I'll be in touch soon,' he said and left to return to his car.

'You two are finished,' Melua said as Donadze entered the

234

interview room and closed the door. The room was just large enough to contain a table and four chairs, all of which were bolted to the floor. Recording equipment was installed in a recess above the table and two CCTV cameras were mounted high on the sound-proofed walls. A large one-way glass panel allowed observation and scrutiny of witnesses and suspects, their body language often giving lie to their words. LED lights shone harshly behind protective metal cages and a ventilation grill noiselessly cooled and freshened the air. Arziani and Melua sat at opposite sides of the table, plastic cups of water in front of both men.

'Thanks, Misha. I'll take it from here,' Donadze said, ignoring Arziani's irritated glance as he stood to leave. He put his laptop on the table and waited until the door was closed before clicking an icon to start an audio file playing.

Kaldani's voice was small and metallic through the computer's speaker. He spoke Russian with an Ossetian accent, only his half of the conversation having been picked up by the GIS bug. '*I have another job for you... I know, but I can't trust these fucking amateurs to get it right... It's my lawyer, Petre Melua... There can't be any connection to me... It needs to look like suicide... I want you to implicate the cops. They've been harassing him. Get him to leave a note and blame a detective called Donadze...Tomorrow at the latest... Okay, but make sure it's clean.*'

Donadze watched the man opposite him as he sat slumped in his chair, trying to come to terms with complete betrayal. 'Your brother, Dato Kaldani,' he said.

Melua straightened and pointed at Donadze. 'No, that wasn't Dato.'

'In which case, you're free to leave.'

Melua remained sitting, his face a mess of conflicting emotions.

'I'll give you a few minutes.'

Arziani was in the adjacent observation room, facing the one-way glass panel.

'Did you hear all of that?' Donadze said.

'Yes, I almost feel sorry for him.'

'Don't, he's as guilty as Kaldani.'

'I guess so. Your "friends" gave you that recording?'

'They're very resourceful.'

'Yeah, nice to be able to bend the rules. But you're not thinking of using it as evidence, are you? It wouldn't be allowed in court.'

'Probably not, but that's not the idea, is it?'

'No, it's not.'

Donadze looked at Melua through the one-way glass. He sat motionless behind the table—his face now expressionless. 'I'd better get back in.'

He re-entered to room, placed two cups on the table and sat down. 'Coffee. I put some sugar in yours.'

'This is all down to you. You backed Dato into a corner. You made him do this,' Melua snarled.

'I made Kaldani order your murder? You don't really believe that, do you?'

'I'm part of the family. Dato's father was godfather to my son. We're close.'

'And now he wants you dead.'

'I can't betray him.'

'But that's not what's happening here, Petre. I heard

you at the Dream. You went to Kaldani after we'd talked, told him everything. You trusted him, put your life in his hands. You were loyal and *he* betrayed *you.*'

'So you say. But even if that was true, Dato is still my client and protected by rules of client confidentiality.'

Donadze shook his head. 'Up to a point, yes. But client confidentiality doesn't apply to criminal acts being planned—isn't that right?'

'What are you talking about?'

'You're an officer of the court and are obliged to tell the Police about any planned criminal activity that you become aware of—in this case Kaldani's orders to have you killed.'

'He'll definitely have me killed if I do that. And there's different ways of dying…'

'Kaldani wants you dead regardless of what you do or don't do, Petre. But this way you have a chance. Let's get him behind bars where he can't get to you.'

'And if I cooperate?'

'We'll keep you safe. You've not been directly involved with Kaldani's criminal activities—you only offered legal advice. The Prosecutor's Office might want to bring conspiracy charges, but I'll speak on your behalf. It'll be a light sentence and you can start again.'

'I'll start again with nothing.'

'You'll be alive. Do you really have a choice?'

'I would never do this if he hadn't made me. I was loyal…'

'Yes, you were. Are you ready to answer our questions?'

Melua looked at Donadze, his eyes red and puffy. 'Yes, let's get this over with.'

TWENTY-FIVE

The CCTV and voice recorders were running as Donadze formally opened the interview. Arziani and Donadze sat facing Melua across the table with Meskhi observing through the one-way glass. Melua had regained his composure; having decided to cooperate with the Police, he was now resigned to his fate, Donadze thought.

The first questions asked were factual, structured to build confidence and to make the lawyer less guarded as the interview progressed. 'Mr. Melua, please describe your relationship to Dato Kaldani,' Donadze said.

'I'm his attorney,' Melua replied briskly.

'Do you have any other clients?'

'No. I work exclusively for Mr. Kaldani. I sometimes offer legal advice to his associates, if instructed to do so.'

'How long have you worked for Kaldani?'

'For the family—twenty-five years. Zaza first and then

Dato after he took over the business.'

'Would you say that you and Kaldani are close?'

'Yes, at least I thought we were.'

Satisfied with the question and answer tempo which had been established, Donadze now made his questions more specific. 'Tell me why you are speaking to us today.'

'It has come to my attention that Mr. Kaldani has ordered a criminal act to be committed. As an officer of the court I am obliged to bring that to your attention.'

'He has in fact ordered your murder, is that correct?'

'Yes.'

Donadze paused as he made a show of consulting his notes. 'Are you aware of any other murders which Kaldani may have ordered?'

'I cannot answer that question as attorney-client privilege preserves the confidentiality of any prior communication between Mr. Kaldani and me.'

'Do you know why Kaldani ordered *your* murder?'

'I believe he is worried that I might divulge information about his affairs to the Police.'

'Do you mean divulge his criminal affairs?'

'No.'

Donadze consulted his notes again. 'Do you have names for the individuals who Kaldani has hired to kill you?'

'I don't, but I believe Mr. Kaldani may have hired professional assassins from Chechnya.'

'Why do you think that? Has he hired these assassins before?'

'Attorney-client privilege prevents me from answering that question.'

Donadze tried a different approach. 'Are these the same assassins who murdered Captain Bukia?'

'Please ask me questions which I am able to answer, Lieutenant.'

Donadze glanced at Arziani who shook his head slightly—time to change tack.

'Do you know Nikoloz Shengelia and Luca Mamedov?'

'Yes. Shengelia was killed—'

'And Mamedov has been arrested,' Donadze interrupted, trying to step up the tempo and give Melua less time to think. 'Did Kaldani order these individuals to kill Major Levan Gloveli at his home in Shindisi?'

'I can't answer that.'

Donadze abruptly changed direction again. 'Do you know two Russian nationals called Lobodin and Pilkin?'

'Yes,' he said.

'What is their relationship to Mr. Kaldani?'

'I can't answer that.'

'Has Kaldani been acting under instruction from Lobodin and Pilkin?'

'I can't answer that either.'

'Does Kaldani's relationship with Lobodin and Pilkin have a bearing on his order to have you killed?'

Melua paused, taking time to formulate his answer, Donadze thought. 'I believe it does, at least in part,' he said at last.

'Are Lobodin and Pilkin operatives in the Russian SVR?'

'Yes.'

'Are they conducting a covert operation in Georgia?'

'Yes.'

'Is Kaldani involved in that operation?'

'I can't answer—'

Arziani threw his arms in the air. 'Come on, Petre. This ties in with Kaldani's plan to have you murdered. You're allowed to answer.'

'That's not my interpretation, Sergeant.'

'Has Kaldani ordered your murder because he fears you'll divulge knowledge of that operation?' Donadze continued.

'I believe that is part of his concern.'

Donadze changed direction once more. 'Did you know a woman called Nino Adamia?'

'Yes.'

'What was the nature of your relationship with her?'

'She worked at the Dream Casino. I was friendly with her.'

'Did you have sexual relations with her?'

'No.'

'Are you aware of the circumstances of her death?'

'Only what was reported in the media.'

Donadze watched Melua closely as he asked, 'Did Kaldani have her killed?'

The lawyer held Donadze's gaze. 'I think that's unlikely,' he said.

'You didn't discuss her murder with Kaldani?'

'No, if I had, I wouldn't be able to tell you about it.'

'Was Nino involved in a blackmail scheme organised by Mr. Kaldani?'

'I can't answer that.'

'Who were the subjects of that blackmail scheme?'

'I can't answer that either.'

'What did the blackmailers hope to achieve?'

Melua shook his head, 'Again, I can't answer that,' he said.

'We're coming to an end now, Petre. Is there anything you would like to add?'

'No.'

Donadze looked at Arziani. 'Sergeant?' he said.

'That man wants you dead, Petre. Why let him hide behind that attorney-client privilege bullshit? Tell us everything you know, give us a chance to break him.'

'I'm still an attorney, Sergeant. I have obligations.'

'Let's wind it up at that for now,' Donadze said. 'Mr. Melua, thank you for your co-operation. Sergeant Arziani, take Mr. Melua back to his cell.'

'We're getting close to the truth,' Meskhi said.' He, Donadze and Arziani were in the interview room from which Melua had just been removed. 'What's your assessment, Sergeant?'

Donadze smiled to himself as Arziani straightened and puffed his chest before answering, eager to impress the senior officer. 'I agree, sir. We've driven a wedge between Kaldani and his lawyer. It's just a pity he wouldn't tell us what Kaldani's game is—who's being blackmailed and what's the objective?'

'Lieutenant?'

'Sergeant Arziani is correct. It's very positive that we are opening rifts in Kaldani's organisation. But I think we can draw some useful conclusions based on what Melua *wasn't* prepared to tell us.'

'Such as?'

'He didn't confirm that the SVR operation involves blackmail, but he didn't deny it either. I think we can be certain that the Russians used blackmail to achieve their objectives and that Kaldani was contracted to do their dirty work.'

'I agree. What else did you conclude?'

'Melua told us he knows Kaldani contracted the Chechens to kill him,' Donadze spoke hesitantly, weighing his words. 'They're the best Kaldani can find and that's why he used them to assassinate Bukia—we heard how he described his own men as "fucking amateurs." If they're that good then Melua isn't safe, even in our custody—and he knows it.'

'Yes, I agree. Where does that insight take us?'

'Misha?' Donadze said.

Arziani looked hesitantly at Donadze who nodded for him to continue. 'Melua's scared and wants Kaldani brought down, but he can't quite bring himself to do it—yet. He *will* tell us all he knows—he just needs a bit more time to think about it. But when he does speak, it won't be on the record.'

'Thank you, Sergeant, I believe your analysis is accurate,' Meskhi said, looking at his watch. 'Lieutenant, it's been a long day. I want you both to go home and rest. Come back here tomorrow morning and have another conversation with Mr. Melua.'

'Thank you, sir.'

'And after you've done that come and see me. I want to talk to you about these Chechens that Kaldani's been hiring.'

Donadze was grateful for the underground parking slot at his Kandelaki Street apartment. He left his car and made a short, weary walk to the elevator. Early Beatles music was playing quietly as he opened his front door. An appetising smell of cooking spices made his mouth water and he realised he hadn't eaten in more than twelve hours.

'You're home,' Avto said.

Donadze looked around his living area and kitchen. They had been cleaned and tidied, the surfaces wiped and free from the constant Tbilisi dust. Low flames were playing under two cooking pots. 'You've been busy,' he said.

'It's the least I could do, considering. Glass of wine?'

'Not sure I have any.'

'I've been to the market, got you favourite— *Mukuzani* right?'

'That sounds really good.'

'It's a nice evening. Why not take a seat on the balcony. I'll bring your wine. Food will be about fifteen minutes.'

'What's going on, Avto?'

'Nothing at all, just trying to be nice.'

Avto had put cushions on the cane chair and placed it and a small table on the balcony. 'Enjoy,' he said, putting a large glass of wine on the table and going back into the living area, sliding the balcony doors closed behind him.

Donadze sat down tiredly. Avto was right, it was a

beautiful evening. The air was warm and relatively fresh, the traffic in the streets below was thinning and the corresponding noise from car horns and blown exhausts was fading. He picked up his glass, swirled the contents and inhaled the vapour deep into his lungs. He could think of nothing more soothing—drinking the dry, oak-aged wine was almost unnecessary.

He thought about his case, sensing that events were coming to a head. Kaldani just had too many cracks in his organisation, some of which had been caused by his own misjudgement and carelessness. The information Melua had provided would do further damage and he was confident the lawyer had more to say. Licheli had twisted and turned, hating disloyalty but ultimately forced to trade Kaldani to save himself.

Donadze's instincts told him that Toreli and his counsel, Jibuti were somehow tied into the Russian's conspiracy. There couldn't be a legitimate reason for a secret meeting with the SVR.

He cradled the glass in the palm of his hand, the wine slowly warming, and felt his eyes grow heavy. He thought of his childhood in Abkhazia, his sister Ana—who his mother said couldn't be saved—and the life his family had made in Tbilisi. He thought of Tamuna and the child she was carrying—his child. Somehow, they completed him and made him feel protective in ways he couldn't understand.

He sniffed the wine again before taking a drink, retaining the liquid in his mouth before letting it run down his throat to warm his empty stomach. He thought of Nino Adamia, the lost girl from Rustavi, whose death someone hoped would go unexplained and unpunished. He thought of Nino's mother, living out a cheerless existence, the one light in her life, extinguished. He held the glass to his face and tilted it, admiring the wine's dense-red colour. He took another sip and silently renewed his promise to find the killer.

He felt the wine and the autumn warmth calming his thoughts, slowing his breathing, closing his eyes.

'Food's ready,' Avto said, knocking on the sliding doors, wakening Donadze before he dropped the wine onto his lap. 'Come in and sit down.'

'You know, Avto, this is very kind of you but I'm really too tired to eat now.'

'No, you have to eat something. You need to look after yourself better.'

'I told you before, you're not my mother,' Donadze said smiling.

'The things that poor woman has had to put up with,' Avto replied, a huge grin on his still-bruised face.

TWENTY-SIX

'What do you want to tell me?' Donadze said, stepping into Melua's cell. The lawyer was sitting reading a Russian novel, the door unlocked, free to leave should he naively feel safe in doing so.

'You have my statement, Lieutenant. I think I made my obligation to maintain client confidentiality clear.'

'You did and noted for the record. But I know you've got more to say.'

Melua smiled, put a marker in his novel and placed it on the small fold-down table beside his chair. 'This can't be attributed to me.'

'It won't be.'

'And I want nothing on tape or on paper. If you present any of this in court, I'll deny it'

'Understood.'

'Let me see your phone.'

Donadze unlocked his phone and showed it face-up to Melua before putting it on the table. 'I'm losing patience,' he said.

'Sit down.'

Donadze sat on the bunk, facing Melua across the width of the narrow cell.

'What do you want to know, Lieutenant?'

'Tell me how your blackmail scheme works.'

'Let me be clear. It is not my blackmail scheme. I'm an attorney—all I do is offer legal advice.'

'In that case tell me how Kaldani's blackmail scheme works.'

Melua smiled again. 'Well, Dato's a great businessman. He's always looking for ways to grow his business, to increase asset utilisation, to build profit.'

'If you say so. And in this case his assets are—'

'His girls—exactly!' Melua continued excitedly, his voice rising. 'He's got the best girls in the city. They're classy, dress well, smell good. They bring men into his casino, encourage them to part with their money at the tables and the bar. Sometimes these fools have a good night and want to celebrate. More often they're looking for consolation. The girls have places they can go—hotels probably. His best earners have their own apartments.'

'You probably want to keep your voice down, Petre. And the blackmail?'

Melua leaned forward and dropped his voice. 'It's obvious isn't it? Girls like that don't come cheap. The men who can afford them are prominent. Businessmen, politicians, sportsmen, judges—priests, would you believe?'

he said, grinning. 'Dato is very selective; he doesn't want the Dream to get a bad reputation. But every now and then someone will be targeted.'

'Targeted how?'

'Video of course. It's so easy, tiny devices planted in the hotel rooms and apartments. All angles, and I do mean all angles, covered. High quality footage—makes for great viewing.'

'I thought you only offered legal advice.'

Melua sat up primly. 'That's exactly right. I didn't say I had seen these videos personally.'

'How does Kaldani pick his victims?'

'He knows who they are, what they can offer.'

'And they pay, or the footage gets released?'

'They don't always pay cash. Sometimes it's a service Dato needs, now or in the future. It helps to have co-operative politicians and judges watching your back.'

'How often does he release footage?'

'Not too often. But he'll expose someone now and again, just to keep the rest in line. Lots of ways to do it: anonymous online posts, files sent to newspapers. Sometimes he just sends their wives a USB stick.'

'Tell me about Nino Adamia.'

Donadze watched the lawyer's expression soften. 'She was one of Dato's best. Beautiful girl, sweet nature. Something else which was unusual given how she earned her living—innocence. I know that doesn't make sense, but you could feel it. She would have changed though. It was inevitable. Maybe it's just as well she died when she did.'

'Be careful, Petre,' Donadze said evenly.

Melua looked up, surprised. 'Sorry, bad choice of words.'

'And to be clear, she didn't die—she was murdered. Was Nino involved in Kaldani's blackmailing scheme?'

'Very selectively, just a few times that I'm aware of.'

'How did Kaldani get tied-in with the Russians?'

'I'm not sure, they probably approached him, somehow. I know they played the tables now and then. Drank a lot of vodka.'

'Did Kaldani know they were SVR?'

'Of course he did. He's got good instincts and probably had them checked out. But they didn't look like typical businessmen anyway.'

'What did they want—not money?'

Melua shook his head. 'No, Mr. Putin doesn't need cash from his little neighbour in the south.'

'What then?' Donadze asked.

'Influence, probably. A service to be rendered. I don't know the details.'

'But the service or influence was achieved by blackmail?'

'Yes.'

'By videoing Nino having sex with someone?'

'More than one person I think.'

'Who were these people?'

'I don't know that detail either.'

'Did Kaldani have Nino killed?'

'As I said yesterday, I really don't think so. She was a good earner and he had no reason to kill her.'

'She was part of his blackmail scheme. She knew the victims. She could have gone to the Police.'

'Yes, she knew who they were, and that Dato wanted something from them. But she didn't know what that was. And why would she go to the Police? What did you ever do for her?'

Donadze paused, considering Melua's last comment. 'Let's move on,' he said. 'Did Kaldani have Captain Bukia killed?'

'I believe so.'

'Did he also attempt to kill Levan Gloveli?'

'Yes.'

'Why?'

Melua sat back on his chair. 'I know this is an off-the-record conversation, Lieutenant, but I want to stress that I am passing on information in good faith, things I have picked up or overheard. I most definitely was not involved in the murder or attempted murder of these two Police officers.'

Donadze smiled. 'So stated. Please answer the question.'

'Well, Bukia was on Dato's payroll, had been for years. He told Kaldani you had been sniffing around. He also knew about Dato's association with the SVR. He knew too much and was weak. He might have talked, I suppose…'

'And Gloveli?'

'Gloveli unfortunately raised his head above the parapet. At your request, I believe. Used his contacts in the old KGB to identify the Russians. That attracted attention in the wrong places. Dato was told to get rid of him.'

'Told by whom?' Donadze asked.

'Well, his instructions came from Lobodin and Pilkin but who knows where they got theirs from.'

'What is so important about the SVR's operation that they were prepared to murder two Georgian Police officers to keep it quiet?'

Melua sat back and looked at Donadze in contrived disbelief. 'That's rather naïve, Lieutenant. You should know that murdering Georgians means nothing to the SVR. We both live in this country. We know our neighbour well, know what he's capable of. These Russians—they subvert our politics, our church and our economy, turn Georgians against Georgians. When we defend ourselves, they invade our territory, support the break-away regions and harden their borders. We do our best to alert our friends in the West. But they don't want to confront reality and without proof they're happy to turn a blind eye.'

'That's quite a speech, Petre.'

'It wasn't a speech—I love my country.'

'We can debate that point another time. Let's talk about Kaldani. Didn't he realise how we would react to the murder of two of our own?'

'Of course he did. The last thing he wanted was war with the Police. But he thought killing Bukia would be okay when you guys realised he'd been on the take. That's why the money was left in his apartment.'

'Planted?' Donadze asked.

'No, left in place.'

'Why use the Chechens for Bukia and his own men for Gloveli?'

Melua looked disappointed. 'It was a miscalculation on Dato's part, I think. It doesn't happen often and it was understandable in the circumstances. Gloveli's an old man and was already injured from the beating he took previously. Maybe he also thought Shengelia and Mamedov wouldn't stand out in Gloveli's village as much as the Chechens would.'

'Why does Kaldani want you dead?'

'You know why. You came to my apartment, compromised my relationship with him and made him doubt me. We used to be close.'

'He only let you think that because it suited him. You should know that Kaldani isn't close to anyone. Tell me—what's keeping him alive?'

'What do you mean?'

'The Russians are cleaning house. Kaldani knows everything. What's keeping him alive?'

'Dato Kaldani isn't a man to be toyed with, even by the SVR.'

'Or maybe someone's holding his insurance policy.'

'You'll have to explain that to me, Lieutenant.'

Donadze leaned across the narrow cell and held Melua in his gaze. 'Kaldani has evidence that proves the SVR is running an operation in Georgia, something they would find embarrassing, or worse. He gave it to you for safekeeping. Where is it?

Melua shook his head. 'I think that will do for now. You got what you wanted.'

Donadze reached into his pocket and brought out a second phone, the memo app open and recording. 'Not quite. Where are you keeping his insurance?'

Melua stared at Donadze in disbelief. 'We had an agreement! You talk about Dato Kaldani, despise him—but you're not any better. I shouldn't have trusted you.'

'Probably not. Where is it?'

'We're done here,' Melua said, picking up his novel and sitting back in the chair.

TWENTY-SEVEN

'Where have you been? I've been calling you for hours.' Avto said, his voice small and frightened.

Donadze was returning the many calls Avto had made while he had been interviewing Melua. 'More like ninety minutes. Listen, I'm busy. I can't jump every time you call. What's the problem?' he said.

'It's your Mum. I'm at the hospital. I was visiting when—'

'What's wrong? Where is she?'

'We're at the International Hospital. She didn't look well, and I wanted to call you. But she said no, she was just a bit tired. She was in the kitchen and I heard her fall. I didn't know what to do so I called an ambulance. I couldn't get you, so I called Tamuna.'

'I'm on my way.'

Donadze ran to his car. He used the car's blue lights and

siren and muscled his way to the hospital in fifteen minutes. He abandoned the car in a loading area and ran into Casualty.

'Ramaz!'

He turned to see Tamuna and Avto sitting in the row of chairs he had just passed. Both stood and Tamuna took his hand and squeezed it. 'What's happening?' he said. 'Where is she?'

'She's in good hands. Sit down and I'll tell you what's happening.'

'Can I see her?'

'Not just now. Ramaz, your mother has had a heart attack.'

'No, she can't have. She's so fit, hardly ever ill.'

'Calm down and listen,' Tamuna said sharply. 'Your mother *has* had a heart attack. We should be grateful that Avto was with her and got help quickly. She's been taken to Coronary Care for assessment and, if we're lucky, there won't too much damage to her heart. That's all we know until we speak to the cardiologist.'

Avto put his hand on Donadze's arm. 'She'll be okay, Ramaz,' he said.

Donadze took a deep breath. 'Yes, I know she will, thanks to you. You did well, Avto.'

'Let's speak to the cardiologist,' Tamuna said, taking Donadze by the hand and leading the way through the interconnecting corridors to Coronary Care.

The cardiologist came out to meet them immediately. Donadze thought he looked worryingly young as he strode towards them in his surgical scrubs. He glanced at Tamuna

and she shook her head slightly—no, she didn't know him.
'Mrs. Donadze is stable and resting now,' the cardiologist
said in a reassuring tone. 'She was lucky that we got to her
in good time. But, unfortunately, she has had the most
serious form of myocardial infarction. We need to begin
immediate treatment to limit the damage.'

'Do it,' Donadze said.

'Will you be performing angioplasty and stenting,
Doctor?' Tamuna asked.

The cardiologist looked at her inquisitively. 'She's a
doctor,' Donadze said.

'An orthopaedic surgeon,' Tamuna clarified.

'Yes, it would be the best and safest procedure for her.'

'What about risks?' Tamuna said.

'You know as well as me that no surgical procedure is
completely risk free. Angioplasty and stenting requires very
fine control and damage to the blood vessels is always
possible. There are other risks, such as stroke or heart
attack—the more arteries affected, the greater the risk. But
this is a fairly routine approach now.'

'When would you expect to start?'

'Almost immediately. We have a theatre and surgical
team available.'

'And you'll be conducting the procedure?' Donadze
asked.

'Yes.'

'How many of these have you done? No offence meant
but—'

'I'm sure the doctor is suitably experienced, Ramaz,'
Tamuna said, looking embarrassed.

The cardiologist smiled. 'Thanks for the compliment, but I'm not as young as I look.'

'Sorry, I didn't mean to question your abilities. Can we see her?' Donadze said, observing Avto suppressing a smirk.

'Just give us a little more time. I'll ask a nurse to come and get you when she's ready.'

Donadze watched the cardiologist walk away. 'Are you happy with that?' he asked Tamuna.

'It's not my field, but yes. Your mother's strong and otherwise healthy. She'll be fine. But you need to be positive when you see her. The last thing she needs is to worry about us.'

'Tamuna's right,' Avto said.

'I know—you're both right.'

'Ramaz, you know she'll need several days to recover?' Tamuna said.

'That's okay, I'll take time off, make sure—'

'No, go in and see her. Then get back to work. It's what she would tell you herself.'

'I can't, what if—'

'I'll stay here until the operation is over, make sure she's okay. I'll call you if there are any problem. Avto?'

'I'm staying as well. We'll look after her, Ramaz.'

'Well, okay, thanks,' Donadze said, coughing to mask a catch in his voice. 'Let's see what's happened to that nurse.'

'Excellent work, Lieutenant,' Meskhi said as the recording finished playing. He and Donadze were sitting in the

Commander's office, facing each other across the desk.

'Thank you, sir. Melua has answered most of our questions, even though we can't use him as a source in court.'

Meskhi leaned towards Donadze and spoke quietly, 'Who else has heard this recording?'

'Sergeant Arziani heard some of it.'

'Do you trust him to keep it to himself?'

'Yes.'

Meskhi paused before speaking. 'So, as far as anyone else is concerned, we arrested Melua, tried to make him give us information about Kaldani and he refused, claiming client confidentiality.'

'That's correct,' Donadze said warily.

'I wasn't asking you to confirm my analysis, Lieutenant. So, if we're not bringing charges against Melua, we have to release him.'

'Release him? We can't—Kaldani will kill him. We can't let that happen. Besides, he's a valuable witness.'

'Let's come to that in a minute,' the Colonel said. 'If we release Melua, what will happen?'

'There's still a contract on him. The Chechens will kill him.'

'Or try to kill him. What if we get to them first?'

Donadze shook his head. 'It's too dangerous. They're the best Kaldani has—we can't keep Melua safe.'

'I think you should have a bit more faith in your colleagues, Lieutenant. Tell me, how beneficial would it be to catch these assassins?'

'Very beneficial. We could try to turn them against

Kaldani, although I think we'd have trouble getting them to talk.'

'They wouldn't talk—it goes against their supposed code of honour. But they would go to jail for a very long time. And that would send a strong message to others like them.'

'Yes, stay out of Georgia. I'd certainly like to see that happen. But I still think Melua's too valuable to risk.'

'I agree, that's why we'll use a decoy.'

Donadze was struggling to keep pace as the conversation changed direction. 'You mean someone disguised as Melua?' he said.

'That's generally what the term "decoy" means.'

'And the decoy would be bait. Like a goat tethered to a tree to kill a tiger.'

'Precisely.'

'But it's still too dangerous! We couldn't ask anyone to risk their lives in that way.'

'Please keep your voice down, Lieutenant. And it's not open to debate—we *are* going to do this. Tell me, what characteristics would our decoy need?'

Donadze shook his head, trying to focus his thoughts. 'Someone about the same build as Melua, someone who would understand the operation and Police communication protocols, someone with a strong nerve. He'll have to be able to defend himself if things go wrong—so firearms trained.'

'A police officer?'

'It's an obvious choice. You're asking me to be the decoy?'

'No, I think Sergeant Arziani would be a good

candidate. Do you think he'll agree?'

'Yes, of course he would. He'd do it to please you. He's young and ambitious, wouldn't worry about the risks involved. But I won't ask him.'

'You'll carry out the orders I give you—is that understood?'

'Yes, sir,' Donadze snapped out reflexively before continuing, 'But there's no need to ask Arziani. I'll do it.'

'No. Tell me about your mother, Lieutenant.'

'My mother?' Donadze said, confused. 'She's had a heart attack and is receiving treatment at the International Hospital right now. She's going to be okay.'

'Why aren't you with her?'

'I can't walk away from this investigation. Not at this stage. My mother would insist on it. Anyway, she's not on her own.'

'What if she's not okay? What if the treatment isn't a success? What if she dies?' Meskhi paused as Donadze struggled to respond. 'I'm sorry to be so blunt, Lieutenant, but there's too much at stake to worry about your sensitivity. We will run this operation, using a decoy for Melua—and with me in command.'

'So, I'm off the case? Is this because I said I wouldn't ask Arziani to be your decoy.'

'You should try to listen a bit better, Donadze. I didn't say you're off the case—I said that you're not running this operation. You can't be one hundred percent focused if you're worrying about your mother. And there's no need to ask Arziani, I'll do that myself. Tell him to come and see me. You're dismissed.'

Donadze stormed out of the station, brushing past Soso Chichua who was smoking with some uniformed officers outside the main entrance. 'Clean your mess up after you,' he snapped, scuffing the cigarette butts which were littering the area.

He continued to his car, got in and wound the window down, breathing deeply. He slammed his hands on the steering wheel and took out his phone. Tamuna had sent a text, '*Spoken to the cardiologist. Mother suitable for stenting procedure. Going ahead now. All looking good so far. T xxx*'

He took a deep breath and texted back, '*Thanks, really good of you. Let me know if you need me there*'

He shut his eyes tightly for a moment then dialled Levan Gloveli. 'Ramaz, we've not spoken for a while,' he said.

Donadze thought the Major's tone was a little cool. 'I know, sorry. Can you talk now?'

'I've got nothing but time, Donadze, you know that,' Gloveli said, his usual good humour restored.

Donadze felt his anger return as he brought Gloveli up to speed with the investigation and with Meskhi taking over the operation against the Chechens.

'I'm sorry to hear about your mother. But she's a tough lady, I'm sure she'll be okay.'

'I think she will as well. That's why Meskhi should have left me in charge.'

'Did you call to cry on my shoulder, Donadze? I thought better of you than that.'

Donadze had expected a sympathetic response. 'Why, what have I done wrong?'

'You're acting like a child, that's what's wrong. Meskhi was right and I would have done exactly the same thing. This isn't about you. It's about running a successful operation. It's especially about keeping everyone involved safe. Do you really think you could do a better job than Meskhi?'

'No, of course not.'

'Then be grateful for his support.'

Donadze looked out the side window of his car and observed one of the uniformed officers sweeping up the cigarette butts. 'You think I've lost perspective?'

'Don't be too hard on yourself, Ramaz. You're under more pressure than you realise. Let others help if they can. Meskhi will catch or kill these Chechens—you've got plenty of other things to concern yourself with. Go to the hospital now. Make sure your mother is okay then get back on the job.'

'Thanks, Major. I'll see you soon.'

'Make sure you do and bring your mother and Tamuna with you.'

'Yes, they'd like that,' he said, ending the call.

TWENTY-EIGHT

Tamuna and Avto were sitting by Donadze's mother's bed when he returned to the hospital. Both stood and he gratefully accepted a hug from Tamuna—Avto's attempt at a hug transforming into an awkward pat on the arm. He stood over the bed and watched his mother sleeping quietly after the stenting procedure, her breathing slow and shallow, her wrist and arm bandaged and bruised where the catheter had been inserted. He thought that she looked frail, the harsh hospital lighting accentuating lines around her eyes and mouth that he hadn't previously noticed. His mother had always been the main source of strength in their family and he realised that he had never thought of her as old before. He bent and kissed her forehead. 'How is she?' he said.

Tamuna stifled a yawn and he felt guilty about leaving her on her own. 'She's fine. The procedure went well, and she should get home tomorrow or the day after. How have you been?'

'Childish, apparently. I'll tell you about it later.'

'I'll leave you two to talk,' Avto said. 'See you back at your apartment, Ramaz.'

'Why not wait and I'll drive you there?'

'Thanks, but I'll get a taxi.'

Donadze watched Avto leave the hospital room. 'I'll have to help him find a job and a place to stay soon,' he said.

'I don't think you'll have to do that. He'll explain himself but you and I need to talk. Your mother will sleep for a while, let's go for a coffee.'

She led the way to a waiting room and Donadze bought two coffees from a vending machine and took them to the chairs she had chosen. 'Doesn't smell too appealing,' he said, sniffing the plastic cups. He looked at her closely. 'Should I be worried?'

'No, but there's something we need to discuss. Listen Ramaz, we should see this as a warning. Your mother needs to slow down. She needs time to recuperate and there will be check-ups she needs to attend. And you should know, the procedure she's had might not have completely cured the problem—it's possible that she'll need additional treatment.'

'The cardiologists said that?'

'Yes. He said that it's not unusual to have repeat stenting procedures and that sometimes bypass surgery becomes the better option. But that's further down the road. Your mother needs someone with her now and in the longer term.'

'You're already looking after her, aren't you?'

'Partly, she's probably been looking after me more. I think we need to make it a permanent arrangement.'

'You want her to stay with us permanently?'

'Well, to stay with me anyway.'

'I don't understand.'

'Don't read too much into this, Ramaz. I really do want us to be together, but we're not ready to commit to that yet.'

'But we've been much better recently.'

'Yes, much better, and I know how hard you're trying. But, although the timings not good, your mother needs help now. It's not all one-sided either. I'll be going back to work after the baby's born and who better to help look after her than your mother?'

'Don't shut me out, Tamuna.'

'I'm not, that'll never happen, you'll always be part of our lives.'

'We'll make this work, I promised you that.'

'Yes, I know—but let's give it some time' she said.

They left the hospital and Donadze dropped Tamuna at her apartment then returned to Mtatsminda Station. Meskhi was in the Commander's office and stared at Donadze through the glass panels as he made his way through the detective's bureau. 'Come in, Lieutenant,' he said, leaning back in the office chair.

Donadze stepped into the cramped space and stood awkwardly. 'I would like to apologise for my earlier behaviour and offer my support in the operation against the Chechens, sir.'

'You've been speaking to Major Gloveli.'

'Yes, but—'

'You're lucky to have him looking out for you. You could learn a lot from the Major—I know I did.'

'Yes, sir, thank you. How can I help?'

Meskhi motioned for Donadze to sit in the chair opposite. 'I've spoken to Arziani and he's agreed to act as Melua's decoy. The stakeout will be at his apartment. You've been there, it's a good location. When you come in tomorrow, spread the word that Melua isn't cooperating and that I've decided not to waste any more time on him. That will get back to Kaldani and he'll pass it on. I'm setting up a surveillance vehicle in the car park and I want you there with me.'

'We're waiting until tomorrow?'

'Yes, tomorrow evening. It'll take that long to get everything in position, and it ties in with our cover story of trying to get more out of Melua.'

'Have you selected your team?'

'Yes, from this station it's you and Arziani. The others are officers in my command, all good people.'

'No one else from this station? That won't go down well, these Chechens killed Bukia, our people—'

'Tell me, Lieutenant, do you think Bukia was the only corrupt officer at this station?'

'As far as I know, yes.'

'As far as you know. Are you willing to gamble success on your limited knowledge?'

Donadze held Meskhi's stare for a long moment then looked away. 'Will Arziani be on his own inside the apartment?'

'Yes, we need to keep this as realistic as possible. If these people are as good as we think, they'll sense an obvious trap.'

'I'm still concerned for his safety, sir.'

'And you think I'm not? He'll be in constant communication with the command post and if things go to plan these assassins won't even get into the apartment. There are two ways in—through the front door or the balcony door. Both will be covered but it's much more likely they'll come in the front. They could try to bluff their way in, possibly by saying Kaldani sent them or they could try picking the locks. Either way, we'll be ready for them.'

'We'll take them at the apartment door?'

'Yes, they'll be stopped outside Melua's apartment— one way or another. Understood?'

Donadze looked at Meskhi who stared back, unblinkingly. 'Completely, sir,' he said.

'Good. Anything else?'

'One further question. We're assuming the Chechens want to get close to Melua. So, no explosives, no poison...'

'Yes, remember, Kaldani wants to make Melua's death look like suicide and to blame you for it. That's still a credible scenario, at least as far as the outside world is concerned.' Meskhi looked at his watch. 'It's late, go home and get some rest. It'll be a long day tomorrow.'

Donadze returned to the hospital and sat with his mother as nurses readied their patients for the night ahead. Lights were turned low, beds and trolleys which had transported people, food, dressings and medicines now stood immobile. Doctors who had hurried importantly from bed to bed were now off-duty or on-call—slaves to the pagers which would haul them unpredictably out of fitful sleep. Staff and patients spoke in hushed voices, the peace intermittently disturbed by unfortunates moaning or shouting out in their pain or confusion.

Donadze had quickly run out of things to say to his mother who would, under normal circumstances, have easily carried their conversations. So, they sat together in comfortable silence watching television. TV1 was covering news that United Energy had decided not to build additional pipeline capacity in Georgia. Their General Manager, Robert Morton, was facing hostile interrogation from reporters attending the press conference. He sat behind an oval table, the UE company logo on the wall behind presenting the perfect corporate backdrop—a company conference room Donadze thought. He was flanked by two other men, Georgian functional managers, enlisted to support Morton and to blunt the perception of an American overlord being the sole bearer of bad news.

Morton had seemingly dressed down for the occasion. The sleeves of his open-necked white-cotton shirt were rolled over his flabby forearms and he wore company ID on a lanyard around his neck, the contrived picture of a kick-ass oil man. He gave his audience the benefit of his too-white smile sparingly and apologetically, the subject being too serious for joviality. 'UE is still fully committed to our operations in Georgia,' he said, his nasally English being simultaneously translated into Georgian. 'We are, and will continue to be, one of the biggest employer and investor in this beautiful country.'

A reporter asked a question which Donadze couldn't clearly hear and Morton shook his head sadly before replying. 'As a company, we must look at the full business justification and protect our shareholders' interests. Unfortunately, we couldn't develop a strong case to invest in Georgia at this time.'

There was a pause as another question was asked. 'A significant decision of this type is made by our main board in the States but, yes, I of course provided input,' Morton replied.

He pointed to another reporter then answered his question. 'I can't go into the details, but I can assure you that this decision was not taken lightly. As someone who has come to love this country, I am as disappointed as you are.'

The manager on Morton's right said, 'Rob will take one more question.'

Morton listened attentively, a half-smile playing on his lips. 'No, at this stage I can't say where we will invest. We have a number of options, but we haven't committed to any of them yet.'

He closed a folder, a visual signal that the conference was over. 'Thank you for your questions. You will find briefing packs by the doors as you leave.' He stood and a technician removed his radio mike as reporters continued shouting questions.

The coverage shifted to the TV1 newsroom where a presenter used graphics to show the volume of gas currently being transported by pipeline through Georgia and the additional volume which would now be routed elsewhere, probably through a Russian system, it was thought.

'Do you find this interesting, *Ramazi?*' his mother asked.

'Yes, *Deda,* I do, it's very interesting' Donadze replied, standing to kiss her goodbye.

TWENTY-NINE

It was late in the evening when Donadze returned to his apartment. Avto was waiting and, without asking, poured him a large glass of *Mukuzani* and laid out cheese and bread on the breakfast bar. 'Thanks,' he said flatly, sitting on a stool and taking a sip of the wine.

'You're welcome,' Avto said, ignoring Donadze's tone. 'Listen Ramaz, I wanted to talk to you.'

'You as well? What about?'

'I'll be moving on in a couple of days and I want to say thanks for everything you've done for me.'

'Moving on? Where to? Have you got a place to live?'

'Yes, a friend got me a job at the Casino International in Batumi. I'm going to live with him, at least for a while.'

'Are you sure? There's no rush to leave. What about your mother?'

'You've been very kind to me but it's a good opportunity. And, to be honest, I could do with getting out of Tbilisi for a while. Mum can visit me, it's only five hours by train.'

'Well, living in Batumi will be great. You'll be able to swim in the Black Sea.'

'I'll have to learn how to swim first... But there's something else.' Avto opened a drawer, took out a small zipped case and placed it in front of Donadze. 'Open it,' he said.

The case contained six USB flash drives in individual compartments, each compartment labelled with initials and dates. 'What's this?' Donadze snapped.

'It'll be obvious when you've looked at them.' He tapped one of the drives. 'These are videos of Nino...'

'Nino—when did you get these?'

'I got them today. I didn't know if I could trust you when we first met—but I'm sure now. You do your best to hide it, but I know you're a good man. You'll respect Nino's memory as much as you're able.'

'How did you get them?'

'From Gio, I asked him to get them for you. He stole them from the Dream.'

'Why didn't he give them to me himself?'

'Why would he? He did it for me.'

'Wait, you're not going to Batumi to be with—'

'What? No, of course not. He's not who you think he is, but we could never be together in that way.'

Donadze took a large sip of wine. 'Let me get my laptop,' he said, standing up.

'I'll leave you to it, I don't like to think of Nino that way,' he said, walking to his room.

Donadze glanced at his watch while his laptop booted up. It was nearly midnight and he was very tired—but he knew he couldn't sleep without viewing the files first.

He inserted a drive and clicked an icon to run the first video. He recognised Nino's apartment in Vake. She was sitting on a couch, flicking through a magazine when a buzzer sounded. She stood, straightened her short skirt, put her feet into heeled shoes and walked to a wall mounted intercom. She pressed a button and spoke accented English in a voice which Donadze thought was almost comically sexy, 'Rob, how lovely to see you, I'll let you in.'

She walked out of camera range and Donadze heard muffled voices as she opened her apartment door. She walked back into range with Robert Morton following close behind.

'Nice apartment,' he said, flashing a nervous smile.

'Thank you,' she said, smiling back. 'Let me get you a drink. Wine, vodka?'

'Scotch on the rocks. That means with ice.'

Nino smiled again and walked sexily on her heels to a drinks cabinet where she made a show of putting ice into a glass and adding a large measure of single-malt whisky. She carried the glass back to Morton and presented it to him with another smile. 'Please have a seat,' she said, pointing to the couch.

Morton took a large gulp from the glass. 'How does this work?' he said in a tight voice.

She sat on the couch, leaving room beside her. 'What do you mean? I like you, you're a very attractive man. There's no reason we can't be friends.'

'But how much should I give you?'

'You don't have to give me anything. Come and sit here,' she said, patting the couch.

Morton took another large swallow from his glass and sat beside her. She kicked off her shoes, curled her legs on the couch and leaned into him, placing an arm around his neck and kissing his ear. 'What would you like me to do?' she said in the same faux-sexy voice.

Morton squirmed on the couch and awkwardly manoeuvred her head onto his lap. She was trying to unzip him when his face contorted. 'Oh God,' he groaned.

Nino straightened and kissed him on the cheek. 'Don't worry, it'll be better next time,' she said, 'I'll get you a towel.'

'No, it's okay, where's your bathroom?'

She sat back on the couch and wiped away a tear as Morton went out of camera range to clean himself.

He came back into shot with a swagger. 'How much did you say?'

She fixed her smile. 'Absolutely nothing. Dato wanted me to look after you. He said you are a very important man.'

'Dato?'

'Dato Kaldani, he's a businessman, my boss.'

He offered her his best smile. 'Well, tell Dato thanks from me. When can I see you again?'

'You have my number, give me a call. Don't leave it too long,' she said suggestively.

'I won't be doing that, honey,' he said, finishing his drink.

Nino accompanied him to the door, kissed him on the cheek then closed the door behind him. She stood for a moment, face in hands, then walked to a table, lifted her phone and dialled a number. 'It's done,' she said.

There were two other videos. Morton visited Nino two more times and they had sex in her bedroom on both occasions, the camera and microphone capturing his predilections and lack of stamina. Donadze noted that she was careful to stress on each occasion that the sex came courtesy of Dato Kaldani—a notion Morton seemed more than comfortable with.

Donadze rolled his shoulder and yawned, it was now after one in the morning. He took out his phone and dialled Colonel Meskhi. He answered after two rings, 'Lieutenant?'

He told Meskhi about the flash drives and described the videos he had just viewed. 'There are six drives in total and I would guess each is about an hour long. I thought we could watch the rest together.'

'That makes sense. Be at Mtatsminda for six, that should give you about four hours sleep.'

Not quite, Donadze thought, reaching for the second flash drive.

Meskhi and Donadze sat together in one of the station's interview room, Donadze's laptop and the case containing the USB flash drives on the table in front of them.

They had watched the videos on all six drives. Each was of a prominent man having sex with one or more girls or boys in hotel rooms and apartments. The video was high definition, the sound quality good and all parties would be easily identified.

It had taken more than six hours to view the videos and Donadze was exhausted. He glanced at Meskhi who was, as always, dressed and groomed immaculately. He rubbed his own unshaved face, knowing how dishevelled he must look in comparison.

Meskhi had made little comment while watching the videos and was now leaning back in his chair, his eyes closed. Donadze remembered that was his habit while thinking and he didn't interrupt.

After a few moments he opened his eyes and sat up in his chair. 'So, Lieutenant, this is the material Kaldani uses for his blackmailing scheme?'

'Yes. It's as Melua described. A classic approach, obtain compromising video and then threaten to disclose it.'

'We have six flash drives, six sets of video and six victims. Do you think there are more?'

'Yes, these are recent, I would guess Kaldani's been running this scheme for some time. Melua also mentioned the type of person targeted and they're not all represented here.'

'But we have to work with what we've got. And Melua said Kaldani isn't always looking for money.'

'Yes, it's sometimes for influence or a favour.'

'Let's discuss Russian involvement. Mr Putin or one of his acolytes wants to influence a certain outcome. He dispatches the SVR to this country and they contact Kaldani. They know or become aware of his blackmail scheme and they buy into it, telling him who to target. Agreed?'

'Completely, sir.'

'Of the six victims on the drives, who are the Russians interested in?

'It's obvious, Morton and Toreli.'

'Why is it obvious?'

'United Energy isn't going to put its gas through Georgia now and that means it'll go through Russia instead. It's what the Russians want more than anything. They can shut down supply at any time—they've done it before. They'll have a free hand to do virtually anything—invade Georgia again, rebuild their empire in Putin's image. Europe won't do a thing to interfere. Didn't you watch the news yesterday?'

'Watch your tone, Donadze. And try to keep emotion out of your thinking. Our information isn't complete and we're trying to develop logic-based scenarios.'

Meskhi tapped the laptop's screen and continued. 'It's logical that Morton has been targeted and the reason for that was to have the UE gas project moved away from Georgia. I did watch the news yesterday and I heard him say he had input into that decision. I think his input would have carried weight. And he would certainly have a lot to lose if these videos were ever released, his marriage possibly, his career, his reputation. But tell me why you're convinced that Toreli is involved.'

'The Russians would want some back-up and who better than the Economy Minister, especially as Toreli will probably be our next Prime Minister. If Morton couldn't stop the project, then *he* certainly could. It wouldn't be popular but he's a politician, he'd find a way to dress it up. And, even if the Russians didn't need him to stop the UE project, it'd still be useful to have him in their pocket going forward.'

'True, but we both watched the video of Minister Toreli with Nino Adamia. Apart from cheating on his wife, which isn't unusual, there wasn't anything too compromising. Red-blooded sex with a beautiful young girl. There are many voters who would be jealous or even admire him for it. It might harm his career, but I don't think it would derail it. Think about what you saw *and* heard for a moment.'

Donadze sat up straight in his chair. 'Of course! It's not what he did, it's what he said!'

'Yes, Lieutenant. Minister Toreli made the classic male mistake of letting his tongue run off in the bedroom. His comments to Adamia about the American President, our President, the Germans, the Church, not to mention his true opinion of his mentor—the current Prime Minister, would destroy him politically. That's the compromising material Kaldani and the Russians have on Toreli and that's why he succumbed to their blackmail.'

'So, you agree he is their backstop?'

'Of course he is.'

'What will we do about it?'

'Right now, nothing. Events are moving very quickly but our priority is this evening's stakeout.' He looked closely at Donadze. 'I suggest you do something about your appearance. Remember, you're in a leadership role and your people expect high standards. It might not seem important to you, but they need to have confidence in you and your abilities.'

'Yes, sir,' Donadze said, tight-lipped as he zipped the USB drive case closed.

'Make sure you've backed these up,' Meskhi said,

leaning back in his chair and closing his eyes again.

Donadze went to the station's locker room and used his electric shaver to remove two day's growth. Looking closely at himself in the mirror, he wetted and combed his hair into a form of temporary control but concluded he could do nothing about his skin pallor or the bags which had developed beneath his blood-shot eyes. He took a clean shirt and a tie out of his locker, put them on then used a paper towel to polish his shoes, the paper disintegrating on the leather as he rubbed.

He tried not to think of how little sleep he had had or how long it would be until he could sleep again. Some of his colleagues took caffeine tablets to stay awake and focussed but he had always resisted doing the same, fearing side effects and long-term dependency. He briskly rubbed his cheeks but saw no colour return. He sighed as he walked out of the station and into the car park, breathing deeply to oxygenate his blood.

Tamuna had taken time off work to be with his mother and he had listened for resentment or reproach in her voice when he had called—but had heard neither. She told him that, although his mother was doing well, she would not be discharged until the following day and he felt relief over the timing, which was convenient for him, then guilt for wishing her an extra night in hospital. He told Tamuna that he would be working overnight but would visit the next day. 'Be careful, Ramaz,' she said.

He wondered if her words carried a deeper warning, but he chose to hear them at face value and replied appropriately, 'Always, you too.'

The stakeout team was established discreetly during the late afternoon. Donadze was not familiar with the surveillance vehicle, a converted Ford van, painted white and externally branded to represent a company offering heating and air conditioning services. The interior was heavily insulated to contain sound. A workstation controlled the communication and recording equipment which was fitted into a rack in the forward bulkhead. Blackout curtains prevented leakage of internal light and the air was kept fresh and cool by a silently running air conditioning unit.

Donadze sat alongside the technician who was operating the equipment, with Meskhi in a temporarily installed chair placed, disconcertingly, behind them.

Communication with the team had been tested and everyone, other than Arziani was in place. As previously arranged, he was brought to the apartment block in the early evening by a car disguised as a yellow taxi and made his way to the elevators, his head down, walking at a pace consistent with Melua's age and fitness. An external pinhole camera located on the van displayed the lights going on in Melua's apartment and Arziani's voice was heard clearly over the speaker, 'In location, all good.'

'And now we wait,' Meskhi said, stretching his legs along the van's restricted floor space.

Although the stakeout had been established early, a move by the Chechens wasn't expected until the early hours of the morning, the quietest time of the night and a time when most people's defences were at their lowest.

It had been agreed that Arziani would simulate Melua's return home. He would have some food and a hot drink and sit in the lounge watching television before going to bed. He followed that plan, moving around the apartment, turning lights on and off and running water.

The stakeout team was well rehearsed and followed all communication protocols precisely. As the evening deepened, the car park filled and more lights came on in the apartment block, families moved onto their balconies to eat and drink wine in the pleasant autumn warmth and television soap operas flickered against windows and glass doors.

At around ten, Arziani called to say he was going to the bedroom and Donadze watched the CCTV screen as the bedroom blinds were closed and the lights turned off. *Stay alert*, Donadze thought, imagining Arziani sitting in a chair to the side of the bed, the doorway in his line of sight, pistol to hand.

Donadze had been on several stakeouts before and knew this one would be like all the others—excruciatingly tedious. He fought sleep every second, substituting caffeine tablets for several cups of strong coffee supplied by the technician who seemed to have no trouble staying awake. It didn't help that Meskhi dominated the space behind him, an intimidating presence, eyes closed, his breathing even, very much awake but saying little.

The night dragged on and by four in the morning, the apartment block was quiet, most of the lights extinguished, the residents asleep.

'The flash drives, Lieutenant. You said they came from the Dream Casino?' Meskhi said abruptly.

'Yes, sir. Indirectly. Licheli obtained them and passed them on to Avto Sabauri.'

'You mean Licheli stole them. Do you know who or where they were stolen from?'

'No, I haven't asked Licheli. I assumed it was from Kaldani.'

'You remember, we questioned what was keeping Kaldani alive. We speculated that he had insurance of sorts, something to incriminate the SVR and expose their operation in Georgia—should they start to see him as a liability?'

'Yes, we thought he might have given it to Melua, but we couldn't get him to give it to us or even confirm it existed.'

'Does Melua have an office at the casino?'

'I think so, he works exclusively for Kaldani.'

'In that case, unless I'm mistaken, Licheli has stolen Kaldani's insurance policy from Melua's office and we won't be seeing the Chechens here tonight.'

THIRTY

Metreveli was the duty medical examiner and he stood up from the corpse as Donadze stepped into Kaldani's office. 'Live by the sword, die by the sword, eh, Lieutenant?' he said.

Kaldani was lying face down, his head turned to the side, staring at Donadze in vacant greeting. His hands were trussed behind his back and a rag stuffed into his mouth. Blood, grey matter and fragmented bone had exploded from his shattered skull and were sprayed in an ugly arc over the deep-pile carpet and the closest walls.

'I've not had the benefit of your education or experience, Doctor, but I suspect this man was shot,' Donadze said.

'Yes, very droll. I'm glad you've not lost your famous sense of humour, Lieutenant.'

'What can you tell me?'

'It looks like a straight-forward execution. The victim

was clearly overcome and silenced, most likely forced to his knees before two rounds were fired into the back of the head, doing the damage you see here,' Metreveli said, gesturing with the thermometer he had extracted from Kaldani's rectum.

'Time of death?' Donadze asked, pointing to the thermometer.

Metreveli seemed surprised to see the instrument still in his hand. 'Yes, judging by the drop in his core temperature, about eight the previous evening.'

Donadze approached the corpse carefully to avoid contaminating the crime scene. The office air conditioning had slowed decomposition, but the familiar sickly-sweet stench of autolytic cell destruction was pervasive. He gazed at the broken body and tried to find compassion for a boy raised by his father to follow a life of brutal crime, a man who had enthusiastically embraced that destiny, a killer who was himself now slain—his nemesis for many years. 'Goodbye Dato,' he said, feeling nothing. He turned to Metreveli. 'Let me know when the autopsy gets scheduled.'

He stepped into the privacy of the office reception area and called Colonel Meskhi. 'Lieutenant?' he said.

'Kaldani's dead—shot yesterday evening at about eight.'

'Professional?'

'Yes, but possibly not by who we first thought.'

'What do you mean?' Meskhi said.

'Kaldani wouldn't have been easy to get close to—I think he must have known and trusted his killer.'

'Killer or killers? Weren't the Chechens diverted away from Melua and onto Kaldani?'

'Possibly. We're looking for DNA, dusting for prints, there might be useful CCTV footage...'

'But you have a theory.'

'I don't think Kaldani would have invited the Chechens into his office. But he would probably have agreed to see Licheli.'

Meskhi paused. 'Yes, that might make sense. Let's think it through. Means—he would have had no problem finding a weapon. Opportunity—Kaldani provided that by letting him get close. And his motive was?'

'Saving himself and Avto. Kaldani would have discovered very quickly that Licheli had taken the videos and would have guessed where they had ended up. Licheli had to kill Kaldani before Kaldani got to them.'

'And the Chechens?'

'Kaldani was their client and he's dead. They will want to get out of Georgia as soon as possible.'

'That certainly seems plausible. Let's bring Licheli in and discuss this with him. Put out an alert, he may be on the run.'

'There's no need, I know where he is,' Donadze said.

Donadze parked on the road and took the stairs to the fourth level. He stood outside his apartment, listening for sounds through the heavy steel door. He unholstered his pistol and, holding it by his side, unlocked the door, pushed it open with his foot and stepped slowly inside, passing Avto's packed luggage bag which had been placed close by.

'You won't need that,' Licheli said. He and Avto were sitting at either end of the sofa, a small kitchen plate containing a smouldering cigarette butt on the space between them.

Donadze slowly holstered the pistol. 'Where are you going, Avto?' he said.

'I told you, Batumi.'

'He can't go with you.'

'I'm not going anywhere, Donadze,' Licheli said. 'I told you I wanted to see him.'

'You killed Kaldani.'

'No choice, he'd be dead if I hadn't,' he said, nodding in Avto's direction.

'And you as well.'

'Yes, and me. But that doesn't matter, I'm a dead man anyway.'

'I told you I'd protect you as best I could. You didn't have to do it.'

'I think I did. But what do you care, it's what you wanted, isn't it?'

'No, it wasn't... You know I have to take you in?' Donadze said, watching Licheli closely as he reached for his handcuffs. Licheli stood and turned his back, allowing himself to be cuffed without resistance. 'You can still testify—I'll speak to the Prosecutor's Office.'

'No, I told you, I'm dead. Kaldani's family will come after me, there's no place to hide. Anyway, I deserve it—I should have stayed loyal, shouldn't have taken these drives. And it's all because of that little queer!' he spat, glaring at Avto, his face contorted.

Avto stood and put his arms around Licheli who dropped his head onto his shoulder and wept. After a moment Avto released Licheli and stepped back. 'Could you please take him away,' he said.

Donadze took out his phone, called Mtatsminda Station and requested a car to take Licheli into custody. It arrived within twenty minutes. Donadze followed the uniformed officers and their prisoner as he was led out of the apartment and into the elevator.

Avto was standing in the passageway as Donadze returned to his apartment. 'I'm sorry, Ramaz,' he said.

'Don't be. Could you look in on my mother before you leave? I can't think why, but she seems to like you.'

Donadze phoned the hospital ward and was told his mother was continuing to recover well and that she would probably be discharged later that day. He made sure that the nurse in charge had his phone number and asked to be contacted when a firm time for her discharge was known.

He texted Tamuna. '*Mum doing well, probably get home later today. Going for a sleep now. D xxx*' It was just after 10:00 a.m. and he set the alarm on his phone to give himself three hours sleep.

He walked into his bedroom, stripped down to his underpants and lay on top of the bed. His mind was racing but sleep must have come at some point as he was woken by his phone buzzing on the bedside cabinet. 'Yes?' he said.

'Hey, Ramaz,' Rokva replied. 'Can I see you?'

Donadze held his phone away from his ear—12:20 p.m. 'If it's important. But I really don't want a burger.'

'You never do. Anyway, that's not an option. I'm at your door.'

'One minute.' He stood, pulled on some clothes and opened the apartment door. 'Come in,' he said.

She walked past him as he held the door open, the faint trail of her perfume reminding him how unkempt and grubby he felt. 'Sorry for the short notice,' she said.

'No notice would be more accurate. Have a seat.' He went into the bathroom and brushed his teeth, washed his face in cold water and wet and combed his hair into approximate shape.

Rokva smiled as he came back into the lounge then dropped into a shooting position and extended her hand to imitate a pistol. 'What have you done with Ramaz Donadze?' she said sternly.

'Funny. Is humour part of your GIS training? And what have *you* done with Pataraia?'

'He's been busy. As have you, I think.'

'You know about Kaldani.'

'Yes, it's been on the news.'

'But you knew anyway.'

'Intelligence – it's what we do.'

'What do you want?'

'An agreement. Your Chechens are still in Georgia, probably waiting to slip back over the border. I can tell you where they are.'

'OK, where?'

'I told you, we're looking for an agreement. We want

Lobodin and Pilkin and we want you to keep quiet about Kaldani's blackmail scheme until we have them. We particularly want you to keep a lid on their attempt to stop the pipeline project coming through Georgia. That means you don't confront Morton or Toreli—yet.'

'You *are* well informed. Why does it matter?'

'It's important to the GIS, for Pataraia and me. Our job is to protect this country from outside threats. But it's also about politics of course. Exposing Lobodin and Pilkin will force the EU, America and NATO to publicly acknowledge the games Russia plays in this part of the world. And some of our own people might not be so nostalgic for the Soviet period when they know what's been going on.'

'How long do you need?'

'Twenty-four hours probably, thirty-six at the most.'

'I don't have the authority to agree that.'

'I know, but speak to Meskhi, he respects your opinion.'

'Does he? I'm not so sure.'

'Call him. I'll make us a coffee.'

Donadze stepped onto the balcony and called Colonel Meskhi. They talked for a few minutes and Donadze stepped back into the lounge. Two mugs of coffee and a plate with bread and cheese were on the breakfast bar. 'Well?' Rokva asked.

'So, tell me where they are,' he said.

THIRTY-ONE

The Chechens were hiding in a ramshackle low-rise apartment over an auto parts store on Kutaisi Street, chosen for its location close to Tsereteli Metro Station, Donadze thought. Meskhi decided to use the same team which had been staking out Melua's apartment to make the arrests but agreed with Donadze's request to include Soso Chichua as well as Misha Arziani.

No one doubted how dangerous it would be. The apartment was put under observation by officers in unmarked cars. The intention had been to keep it under watch and to make the arrests in the early hours of the morning when it was hoped both assassins would be sleeping.

That plan had to be abruptly changed when one of the Chechens left the apartment shortly after nine, carrying a small bag and walking in the direction of the metro station.

Meskhi ordered his officers in. A car was driven at speed

and pulled in front of the hit man, blocking his escape route. Two officers, with automatic rifles held at shoulder height and sighted on their target, approached quickly and ordered him to the ground. Resistance would have been suicidal, and the arrest was made with no shots being fired. At the same time, another group smashed the apartment door open and stormed in. This take down wasn't as clean and an officer was hit in the shoulder with a round from the Chechen's pistol before he himself was shot dead.

The arrest team spent ten minutes securing the apartment before declaring it safe. Donadze and Meskhi walked through the broken door into the shattered apartment—the pungent stench of nitro-glycerine from the many rounds fired lying heavy in the air.

The Chechen was sprawled on a brown leather couch, his arms and legs splayed, blood and bodily fluids oozing from multiple holes in his chest and head. Only one eye remained, open and dilated, staring out into the devastated room.

Meskhi walked to the couch and stood over the dead man. 'Pity,' he said, turning his back and walking out.

Chichua had been put on the team storming the apartment. He was standing on his own in a corner of the room, florid, with sweat flowing freely down his face and neck and staining his shirt collar, breathing hard. One hand was on his chest, the other held his pistol by his side.

Donadze touched him on the shoulder. 'Are you okay, Soso?' he said.

Chichua startled, seemingly surprised to see Donadze, but smiled broadly, 'I'm too fat for this type of thing, but yes, I'm okay.'

'Did you discharge your weapon?'

Chichua looked down at his pistol and returned it to its holder. He took a large white handkerchief from a trouser pocket and wiped his face and head. 'Yes, two rounds, both into his chest, I think. I didn't have a choice—he fired first.'

'Good for you, Soso, you saved lives.'

'We got them Lieutenant, we got them for Bukia.'

'Yes, we did,' Donadze said.

The media had gathered quickly outside the apartment on Kutaisi Street, more evidence of Meskhi's approach to news management, Donadze thought. He skirted the throng, staying in the shadows produced by the on-camera lights illuminating the Colonel's tall, slim frame as he responded to the reporters' questions.

He had missed several calls from Tamuna, and he called her back whilst walking to his car.

'Hello, Ramaz,' she said coolly.

'Sorry, I missed your calls, I was—'

'Your mother is waiting to go home.'

'Is she? I didn't hear from the hospital.'

'And they didn't hear from you either. Anyway, we're waiting to go. Can you pick us up now?'

'Yes, sorry. I'll be there in twenty—.'

'Fine,' she interrupted and abruptly hung up.

Feeling that he had been unfairly chastised, Donadze walked unhappily to his car. He told himself that Tamuna was being unreasonable—that crime doesn't keep office hours. But then he put himself in her shoes. He had been thoughtless, made no allowance for her pregnancy or her recent health scare. He knew that she worried about his safety and he should have called sooner to let her know he was okay. He arrived at the hospital having decided a course of action and, feeling more positive, hurried to his mother's ward.

'Ramaz,' Tamuna called.

He turned to see her and his mother, sitting in a waiting area, a small bag at their feet. He bent and kissed his mother, 'You're looking great,' he said as she smiled at him.

Tamuna stood and he put his arms around her, kissed her on the lips then whispered in her ear. 'I'm really sorry. Let's talk when we get back to your apartment.'

'Fine,' she said, her tone flat.

A nurse helped his mother into a wheelchair, pushed her out of the hospital and waited until she had transferred to the car. Donadze put her bag in the boot, got in the car and started the engine. 'Will you be okay on Tamuna's stairs?' he asked.

'I've already asked the doctor about that. I just need to take it easy,' she said.

Tamuna was quiet on the drive to her apartment. Donadze dropped her and his mother off, parked illegally a short distance away and raced to catch up with them as they walked slowly up the stairs.

'I'm tired, I think I'll go straight to bed,' his mother said, flashing Donadze a warning look.

Tamuna helped her into bed then came back into the living area. 'Is she okay?' Donadze said, standing and holding his hands out to her.

Tamuna folded her arms across her chest and made no move to close the distance. 'Yes, she's fine. And she wasn't all that tired. Listen, Ramaz,' she continued briskly. 'I know your job—'

'Tamuna, please let me say something.'

'Okay,' she said, eyes flashing. 'What do you want to say?'

'I know you're mad at me and you've got every right. You've been wonderful— looking after my mother and putting up with me. But this case has been like nothing I've known before. I've got to see it through. It's important in ways I can't even tell you about. But I'm asking you to be patient a little longer. I said before that nothing is more important to me than you and our baby. I'll prove that to you. Give me a few more days to close the case—then I'll resign. I'll leave the Police and get a job with regular hours.'

Tamuna unfolded her arms and put her hands on her hips. 'Is this a ploy, Ramaz? Something you've dreamt-up? Do you expect me to say, "No, carry on, stay in the Police, everything will be fine?"'

Donadze took two short steps to close the distance between them but Tamuna took one step back, her hands going up to warn him to come no closer. 'No, I mean it. I'm being totally honest with you,' he said. 'Being a detective means a lot to me, but you and the baby mean everything. I *am* going to leave.'

Tamuna shook her head. 'No! You're not leaving the Police because of me. It wouldn't work anyway—you'd come to resent me and the baby. You'll have to figure this out yourself, Ramaz—but don't make us your excuse.'

'There *is* no excuse. I want to be with you and if that means I have to leave the Police then I'll happily do that. But that's down to me, it's something *I've* got to do, not something you're forcing on me.'

'You're saying that now, but you might not always see it that way.' She paused and took a deep breath before continuing in an even tone, 'Okay, let's do it this way. You asked me to be patient—I'll try. Close your case, then we'll talk.'

Donadze thought that Mrs. Adamia had made a special effort with her appearance for her bus trip from Rustavi to Tbilisi. He watched her sipping water from the plastic cup he had given her and thought he could see traces of her daughter's beauty in her tired and prematurely worn face. She had arrived unannounced at Mtatsminda Station and he had taken her to one of the station interview rooms.

'You promised you'd find Nino's killer,' she said.

'Yes, and I will.'

'I've been watching the news. That terrible man, Dato Kaldani. Nino talked about him—was it him?'

'We don't think so, not directly anyway.'

'What do you mean—not directly?'

'Nino worked for Kaldani. He was an extremely dangerous man and she was forced to do things that put her at risk. But we don't think he was Nino's killer.'

'Then what's going to happen now? That man's dead.

And the foreigners who killed your boss, Captain Bukia? One arrested and the other one dead. I saw that tall policeman on television bragging to reporters. He won't be interested in my Nino now, will he?'

'His name's Colonel Meskhi and he wants justice for Nino as much as I do. He has an unusual manner, but I think he cares.'

'He should do. People like him, like you—you have to care,' she said, taking a small white handkerchief from her jacket pocket and dabbing her eyes. She reached across the table and took one of his hands in both of hers, squeezing hard. 'Do you really still believe you'll find the man who killed my Nino?'

'Yes, I do. I wouldn't tell you that if I didn't believe it.'

She searched his face. 'Don't let me down,' she said.

THIRTY-TWO

'Let's recap, Lieutenant,' Meskhi said.

Donadze had been surprised to be invited to join the Colonel for coffee in the station canteen. The two men sat in a corner, attracting curious looks from the uniformed officers and detectives at neighbouring tables. 'Sir?' he said.

'I'm pleased with what's been achieved so far but events have moved on and we now need to re-prioritise and re-allocate resources. What stage are we at and what do you suggest our next steps should be?'

Donadze took a moment to gather his thoughts. 'Well, Kaldani's death will be a serious blow to the family business, of course. We've got Licheli's confession for that and he'll have plenty more to tell us. The family will regroup, and someone will take over—eventually. Or maybe they'll be squeezed out by another gang. Time will tell and there will always be plenty to keep us busy. As for Bukia, we have a good result on that—one of the Chechens dead and the other going to court. But they were acting under orders from Kaldani and ultimately the Russians—and the Russians are still out there.'

Meskhi slowly stirred sugar into his cup. 'Are you regretting the deal we made with your GIS colleagues?'

'No, we wouldn't have got the Chechens without them and finding Bukia's killers was a priority. We've done that now and I'd like to stand the investigation team down.'

'Yes, agreed, but I'll speak to them first.'

'They'd appreciate that. Some of them feel they weren't given all the information available.'

'They weren't—but that was just the nature of this case. I'll discuss that issue with them. What else?'

Donadze shook his head slightly. 'I'm frustrated that we can't move forward with Morton and Toreli yet.'

'As am I, but don't take any action on them without my authorisation—understood?'

'Yes, sir.'

Meskhi took a sip of his coffee and grimaced. 'What else?'

'Nino Adamia—we've still to find her killer.'

'Yes, of course. And you still think her murder is connected.'

'It must be, she worked for Kaldani, he used her to blackmail Morton and Toreli, it's too co-incidental.'

'But perhaps her line of work was just inherently dangerous? Maybe she just met the wrong man?'

'I don't think so.'

'No, I don't either. I said we should re-prioritise. That's where I want your focus to be now.'

'Yes, sir, that's what I'd hoped. You also said we need to reallocate resources?'

'I was referring to myself. I've done all I have to do here and am returning to HQ. I've other matters to attend to. Bukia's replacement will be appointed in due course. In the meantime, you will be in temporary charge. I want you to keep me fully appraised of developments.'

'Thank you for your confidence, sir.'

'Make sure I don't regret it. Thanks for the coffee,' he said, leaving his cup full and pushing back his chair to leave.

Donadze returned to the detectives' bureau and sat in the Commander's office. Meskhi had taken his few paper documents and the cables for his laptop and mobile phone and the space somehow felt bigger without his domineering presence. He looked at his watch: 2:20 p.m., more than twenty-four hours since he had spoken to Rokva. He took out his phone and called her. 'Hey, Ramaz,' she said.

'You asked me to give you some time to catch up with your Russian friends."

'Catch up with my Russian friends? Oh right, I see what you did there—very subtle, I must say. Are you looking for a new job?' she teased.

'You'd be surprised. Anyway, what's happening?'

'We should discuss that. Probably best to meet up, say at six?'

'Okay, where?'

'Well, I'm going to be hungry. Why don't you buy me dinner?'

'No burgers.'

'Right, in that case, what about a *shawarma*. There's a great booth on Kvernadze Street, opposite the Holiday Inn—nine *lari* including a Coke! Do you know it?'

'I don't even know what a *shawarma* is, but I'm sure it'll be delicious,' he said, hanging up.

Donadze had let his admin slip over the last few days and he returned to his own desk to update his files. He was about to log on to the system but paused, checked his watch again and quickly left the station.

Tamuna opened the door to her apartment. 'Ramaz,' she said. 'We weren't expecting you.'

He stepped forward and hugged her, holding her a bit longer than was necessary but pleased when she seemed to respond. 'About yesterday...' he said.

'Don't, we said all we had to say. Close your case, then we'll talk.'

'Can I come in?'

'Of course you can,' she said, stepping to the side.

'How are you, *Deda*?' he said.

His mother was sitting on the couch watching television, the volume turned low. 'Me? I'm perfectly fine. I'm sorry to have made such a fuss. Anyway, let me get you something to eat,' she said, starting to rise.

'No, definitely not. I'm not hungry anyway,' he said, omitting to add that he would be eating later with Rokva.

'She's under doctor's orders to take it easy,' Tamuna smiled.

'Would that be Doctor Tamuna?' his mother replied in a mock-stern voice.

Donadze looked at Tamuna, failing to see a baby-bump yet. 'How are *you* feeling?' he said. 'You're meant to be taking it easy as well.'

'And, I am,' she said, placing both hands over her stomach 'We both feel fine.'

'And you still think it's a girl?'

'Yes, you'll see,' his mother said.

'How long are you staying?' Tamuna asked.

'I'll have to leave here about five thirty. I've someone to meet—Police business.'

'Well, in that case, I'm going to slip out for a couple of hours and catch Lela for a coffee.'

'Lela? There's nothing wrong is there?'

'No, Lela was my friend before she was my obstetrician. It's just for a coffee.'

Donadze surprised himself by being able to forget about the investigation while he sat with his mother, drinking tea and listening to her stories of their early family life, all of which he had heard many times before.

Tamuna called shortly before five. 'I'm downstairs, can you help me with my bags?'

'One minute.'

She had been shopping and was carrying two plastic bags with groceries. 'I could have driven you to the supermarket,' Donadze said.

'It's just a few things for the meal tonight. Why don't you join us?'

'That would be great, I should be back about seven. Is that okay?'

'It's up to you. Your mother and I are to take it easy—

that means you're cooking.'

'I knew I should have stayed at the station.'

'Just do your best, Lieutenant,' she said.

Kvernadze Street and the adjoining roads were thick with near-stationary cars and darting scooters and the sooty stench of their unregulated exhausts. Their drivers and riders viewed road markings with disdain and threw up their hands in theatrical exasperation at the incompetence of every other road user.

Donadze parked his car in the Holiday Inn car park, waited an age for the pedestrian lights to turn green then crossed Kvernadze Street and walked the short distance to the food outlet Rokva had specified. She was in a queue waiting to order her *shawarma* and talking to a man in his mid-forties. He was tall with an athletic build and dressed in suit trousers, a pale blue shirt and polished black shoes, his eyes protected from the low autumn sun by tortoise shell sunglasses.

'Hi Ramaz, this is Shota.' Rokva said.

'Shota Gelashvili,' he said, taking his glasses off and extending his hand.

'Donadze.'

'Let's have a seat while Tanya orders our food.'

Gelashvili led Donadze to a nearby concrete bench, looked at it suspiciously, then sat down in the middle, indicating for Donadze to join him.

'You work with Rokva?' Donadze asked.

'Yes, and Pataraia—they're both in my team.'

'So, you're aware of our agreement—thirty-six hours before we move on Toreli and Morton—your time's nearly up.'

'Yes, and we are ready to move.' He paused and watched as Rokva approached with a large brown paper bag and three plastic bottles of Diet Coke cradled awkwardly in both hands.

Donadze stood and took the bottles from her. She sat on the bench leaving a space for him to sit between herself and Gelashvili. He sat on her other side, declining to be sandwiched between the two.

Gelashvili smiled easily. 'I was telling Ramaz that we're ready to move.'

'Yes, thanks for giving us the extra time, Ramaz,' she said, dipping into the bag and distributing three large foil-covered tubes. She uncovered hers, revealing pitta bread wrapped around sliced meat, onions and chilies, the bread folded at the bottom to prevent sauce and other juices dripping out as she held it to her mouth.

Donadze placed his *shawarma* on the bench beside him. 'You didn't come here to tell me that.'

'You're right. We wanted to meet you and let you know how we'll be doing this,' Gelashvili said. He stood and indicated to Rokva that he wanted to change places with her.

Gelashvili sat close to Donadze, unwrapped some of the foil from his *shawarma* and took a bite. 'Pretty good,' he said, swallowing. 'Yes, we're ready to move,' he continued quietly. 'But we want our actions coordinated.'

'Coordinated? What does that mean?'

'This thing is huge: a conspiracy against our country, senior people in government and industry coerced into taking measures to hurt our economy, a Police officer murdered—and strong evidence that Russia is behind it all. You don't need me to tell you how important that is to our political masters.'

'I'm a detective, not a politician. Why should I care?' Donadze asked.

'We both know you could be made to care,' Gelashvili smiled. 'I'm only here as a courtesy and because Tanya asked me to meet you and explain the big picture. She said you could be trusted.'

Donadze looked at Rokva who nodded in agreement. 'What do you want from me?' he said.

'You'll help us get most benefit from this. Lobodin and Pilkin are on their way home—tomorrow's Belavia flight— 13:25 to Moscow via Minsk. They won't be allowed to board. We want you to arrest Toreli at the same time.'

'Toreli? That's going to make waves.'

'Exactly, it's what we want—maximum publicity and maximum impact. Don't worry about him though, he's got no friends left in government, especially not after his comments about the Prime Minister.'

'How about Morton?'

'He's not to be touched. Toreli's successor will speak to United Energy, the Prime Minister is confident their decision will be reversed.'

'You mean we let Morton walk and Georgia gets a pipeline?'

Gelashvili looked at Rokva who said, 'You need to put

that in perspective, Ramaz. What happens to Morton isn't important.'

'Speak to Colonel Meskhi,' Gelashvili said. 'He'll help you understand your priorities.'

Donadze stood and held out his hand. 'Thanks for the advice,' he said evenly.

Gelashvili also stood, took Donadze's hand and pulled him close, searching his face. 'Big picture, Ramaz,' he said, smiling.

Rokva stood, kissed him on the cheek and spoke quietly into his ear, 'Don't get hurt because of this, Ramaz.' She pulled away and pointed at the *shawarma* which was still sitting on the bench. 'I'll give that to Gia if you don't want it,' she said, brightly.

THIRTY-THREE

The co-ordinated Police and GIS arrest operations dominated national and international news. The timing was impeccable. Pilkin and Lobodin had been intercepted at the Belavia check in desk and led out of Tbilisi Airport with maximum flourish. Toreli was being interviewed by a TV1 news crew when Meskhi, Arziani and two uniformed officers interrupted and arrested him on conspiracy charges. He was spared the ignominy of hand cuffs but was sandwiched between the two uniformed officers and led out of his ministerial office to cars which were waiting to take him to Mtatsminda Station where another news crew was on hand to see him being led inside. The arrest was captured on video, the footage being shown repeatedly during excitable news reports.

Speculation about Toreli's arrest and the arrests at the airport had built during the afternoon and President Zoidze's promised statement was eagerly anticipated.

The station canteen was full when Donadze entered, the television turned to maximum volume. Soso Chichua was standing at the back, watching the screen, as Donadze joined him. 'You know what this is about,' Chichua stated.

'I think so,' Donadze replied. 'Let's see what Zoidze says.'

The television coverage switched to the presidential office. Zoidze sat behind a desk, two Georgian flags on poles, crossed behind him. He looked sombre as he saluted his fellow citizens. 'This afternoon at Tbilisi Airport, brave men and women of our security services intercepted and arrested two Russian spies who have been foiled in their attempt to destabilise and damage our country. They had masterminded a conspiracy involving leading criminal elements and, I'm very sad to inform you, a Georgian government minister, who has, himself, been arrested. All parties have been appropriately charged and will be afforded the opportunity to defend themselves in our courts of law.

In fairness to them and with due respect to our judicial system, I cannot go into details about the alleged conspiracy at this stage. Needless to say, I am shocked, but not surprised, by this latest example of aggression shown to our country by the Russian Federation. This is yet another instance of Russia meddling in the affairs of independent nations in pursuit of its expansionist aspirations.

We have, for some time now, been warning world leaders of the threat to global security posed by Russian actions of this kind and I will be discussing this particular case with our allies and friends in Europe and the United States.'

Zoidze paused while he waited for his television

audience to absorb his words. 'In concluding, I want to offer my gratitude to the men and women of our security services who identified and foiled this criminal action. Be assured that your safety and security is our top priority and we will remain constantly alert to threats of this kind.'

The president wound up his statement and there was an excited buzz in the canteen as station personnel indignantly reflected on his words and his revelation about Russian spies operating in Georgia.

Chichua shook his head. 'Gratitude to the security services? Didn't we have something to do with this?'

'Doesn't look that way, Soso,' Donadze said.

Donadze and Arziani faced Irakli Toreli across the interview room table. He was looking reasonably fresh, despite having spent a night in a Mtatsminda Station cell and sat, drumming his fingers on the table while he waited for his legal counsel, Alex Jibuti, to arrive and the formal interview to commence.

'You must be feeling very proud of yourself, Donadze,' he said.

'How so, Minister?'

'It's got to be a good career move. It's *Lieutenant* Donadze isn't it? Not too high in the pecking order and yet you've brought down a government minister.'

'Not particularly proud, you're just another criminal as far as I'm concerned, although maybe a bit more conceited than most.'

'Listen, I've not been convicted yet. I've still got friends and you—'

'I'll sit in on this one, Lieutenant,' Colonel Meskhi said as he entered the room. 'Minister,' he added, nodding to Toreli. Arziani stood and gave up his seat. 'Thank you, Sergeant. Mr. Jibuti is in Reception, please bring him here.'

'Yes, sir,' Arziani said and left the room.

Jibuti arrived a few minutes later, his briefcase under his arm. He didn't acknowledge the Police officers or apologise for being late. 'How have you been treated, Minister?' he asked.

'Let's get started,' Toreli said.

Donadze placed a folder on the table, switched on the recording equipment and formally opened the interview, noting for the record the people present. 'Let's begin with your association with Danya Pilkin and Pavel Lobodin, now under arrest and identified as agents of the Russian Foreign Intelligence—the SVR.' He opened his folder and placed images of both men on the table in front of Toreli.

'My association? As I told you when you accosted me outside my office, I was told they were traders and I had a courtesy meeting with them—all part of my job.'

'And you only met them that one time?'

'As far as I can remember, I meet lots of people.'

Donadze opened his folder again and arranged six of the images the GIS had provided on the table. 'These images show Pilkin and Lobodin entering an apartment in Kazbegi Avenue which had been rented by Lobodin. Can you confirm that these other men are you and Mr. Jibuti?'

Toreli picked up the prints, scanned through them and

tossed them back on the table. 'Could be. Could also be photo-shopped, I suppose. It's difficult to be sure these days.'

'Is it usual for government ministers to meet foreign businessmen, alone and in clandestine locations?'

'Well, if it was me, and I'm not agreeing that it was, I obviously wasn't alone. Jibuti was with me. Anyway, what makes a location "clandestine?"'

'Do you recollect being at this location with these men?'

'Possibly. As I said, I meet lots of people and I can't remember them all.'

'How about you, Mr. Jibuti?' Donadze said.

'Let's confine our discussion to Minister Toreli for now, Lieutenant,' Meskhi said. He remained impassive as Donadze flashed him an inquisitive look.

'Let's move on then. How would you describe your relationship with Dato Kaldani?' Donadze said.

'I like to gamble, and he owned the Dream Casino.'

'Did Kaldani ever ask you, in your official capacity as Economy Minister, to take any specific actions?'

'No.'

Donadze reached to the floor, picked up his laptop and placed it, lid open, in front of Toreli. He clicked an icon and a video played. Donadze had deliberately set the volume high and the uncomfortable sounds playing through the speaker filled the room.

'This is a compilation showing you and Nino Adamia having sex—at her apartment, and on four separate occasions,' Donadze said.

The video ran for a few moments before Toreli pushed the laptop away.

'What's this about? I told you our relationship was sexual. So someone filmed us...'

'Is this the first time you've seen these videos?'

'Yes.'

'You weren't shown them by Kaldani or one of his associates.'

'The Minister has answered your question, Lieutenant,' Jibuti said.

'Did you discuss United Energy's pipeline project with either Kaldani, Pilkin or Lobodin?'

'I—'

'Before you answer, Minister,' Meskhi interrupted, 'Let me give you my interpretation of events.'

Toreli sat back in his chair and looked at Meskhi quizzically. 'Go ahead,' he said.

The Colonel nodded and spoke in a reassuring tone. 'You are essentially a patriot who wants the best for his country. You have an excellent reputation in government and could quote many examples of how your efforts have attracted inward investment to Georgia. This country has a stronger economy and more people are in work because of you.'

'Well, that's certainly true.'

'But, like everyone else, you have weaknesses,' Meskhi continued. 'You are attracted to beautiful women and you foolishly fell into a trap created by Dato Kaldani at the behest of two Russian businessmen, who you now know to be spies. You obviously recognise that it was wrong to cheat on your wife and you are disappointed in yourself for failing her and your family.'

'Go on,' Toreli said.

'You *were* approached by Dato Kaldani and you *did* meet secretly with Pilkin and Lobodin. They wanted you to use the powers of your office to stop the United Energy project from proceeding and they threatened you with disclosure of these videos if you refused. You certainly didn't agree to their demands and, in any case, your intervention wasn't required as United Energy stopped the project for its own reasons.'

Meskhi paused and looked expectantly at Toreli. 'Yes, that's absolutely correct,' Toreli said.

'And, as for the content of these videos,' Meskhi resumed, 'you are embarrassed and certainly regret the indiscreet conversations you had with Nino Adamia. Like many men, you have a foolish tendency to brag to beautiful women and you do not truly believe the adverse comments you made about the Prime Minister and others. You understand that your political career is over but you want to cooperate fully with the Police, as you know that is the right thing to do, and you hope that doing so will be recognised when your case goes to court.'

'You're offering a deal?' Jibuti asked.

'No, but I think Minister Toreli might understand where his country's priorities lie. Testimony from a government minister, albeit one fallen from grace, would provide compelling proof of Russian complicity in this conspiracy.'

'And you think the Prosecutor would recognise my cooperation?' Toreli said.

'I think that's likely.'

'No!' Donadze snapped. 'It's too easy. I won't go along with it.'

'Well, whether you go along with it or not doesn't really matter, wouldn't you agree, Colonel?' Jibuti said, smiling.

Donadze turned to Meskhi. 'We can prove he sold his country out. We'll get a conviction. If he wants a deal, he'll have to give us more.'

'Colonel Meskhi, would you please ask your Lieutenant to control his emotions,' Jibuti said, no longer smiling.

'I don't think I can do that,' Meskhi said evenly. 'Lieutenant Donadze is my lead investigator. He clearly feels your client is being shown too much generosity and, on reflection, I believe that he is right.'

Jibuti threw his pen on the table. 'What kind of game are you two playing? Minister Toreli has—'

'Would you like to know who killed Nino Adamia, Lieutenant? Would that be enough for you?' Toreli interrupted.

'Colonel, I want to consult privately with my—'

'He did it, he killed Nino!' Toreli said, turning in his chair and jabbing Jibuti hard in the upper arm.

'Irakli, what are you saying? You know that's not true. Why would you—'

'He killed her, and I can prove it! He came to my office and told me, said he'd done it to protect me, to protect my career, that I would never be Prime Minister if she had talked. He said she was just a whore, no one would miss her, and no one would care. But it was more than that, wasn't it, Alex? Were you jealous? Thought you could have a piece of what I had? Then what happened—did she turn you down?

And her just a whore? No wonder you got angry.'

Jibuti stood and faced Toreli. 'Irakli, don't do this, this is what they want—'

'Of course, the truth is, he's been riding my coat tails for years now,' Toreli continued. 'You enjoy working for me, don't you, Alex? Everyone knows that you're important—that they've got to go through you to get to me. It makes you feel good about yourself doesn't it? It gives you power. And how much more power would you have if I became Prime Minister?'

'Colonel, this is a complete fabrication! I don't know why the Minister would make such a dreadful accusation but it's not true. There is no proof because it didn't happen.'

'But it did happen, Alex. You think you know everything about me. But you didn't know that everything that's said in my office gets recorded. I have you on tape.'

Donadze stared at Jibuti as he stood, open-mouthed, his shoulders slumped, his hand reaching out in despair to Toreli—realising the awful truth that the world he had known was lost forever.

There was silence for a long moment before Meskhi spoke. 'Lieutenant, terminate our interview with the Minister. Have someone take him back to his cell then make sure Mr. Jibuti understands his rights.' He got out of his chair and bent low into Donadze's ear, 'Don't ever do that to me again,' he whispered.

THIRTY-FOUR

'Would you come to Rustavi with me?' Donadze said when Tamuna opened her apartment door.

'Rustavi, why?'

'There's someone I'd like you to meet, she lives there.'

'Sounds very mysterious, who is it?

'I'll explain on the way.'

'You want us to go now?'

'Yes, if that's okay. We'll be back in about three hours.'

'That's fine, I could do with getting out. Your mother's sleeping, just give me a minute to write her a note.'

He stood by the door and waited until she came out. They walked down the stairs together, Donadze watching nervously as she negotiated the worn steps. The mid-afternoon city traffic was reasonably light, and they picked up the Rustavi Highway after about twenty minutes.

'So, tell me who I'm meeting.' Tamuna said.

'Mrs. Adamia, the mother of the girl whose murder I've been investigating. We have her killer.'

'That's wonderful. And you're going to Rustavi to tell her?'

'Yes. I had to tell her that her daughter had died. It's a kind of balance.'

'I hope that'll bring her peace. But why do you want me to come?'

'I know you think I'm obsessive about my work, and you're right, I am. About some of my cases anyway. But I'm hoping that meeting Mrs. Adamia will help you understand why I behave that way.'

'I think I already understand why, it's because you care.'

Donadze pulled off the highway and drove into Rustavi. The soft autumn sun was bathing the rows of apartment blocks in a flattering light, partly excusing the audacity of the Soviet planners who had deemed that people should be made to live this way.

He parked outside Mrs. Adamia's block and offered Tamuna his hand as they made their way over a cracked and crumbling concrete pathway to reach the entrance. They climbed the stairs to the second level, passing doors which were unable to contain the commotion of televisions playing at near-maximum volume or the smell of meat and vegetables cooking in cramped and poorly ventilated kitchens.

Mrs. Adamia cracked her door open when Donadze knocked then opened it wide. 'You've found him,' she said.

'Yes.'

She shut her eyes and put her hand on the door to

steady herself. 'Thank God,' she whispered. 'Thank God, thank God.' She opened her eyes, smiled widely then looked inquisitively at Tamuna.

'Mrs. Adamia, this is Tamuna.' Donadze said.

'Your wife?'

'Not yet.'

'Please come in. Let me get you something to eat and drink.'

'There's no need—' Tamuna started to say.

'Thank you,' Donadze interrupted.

They followed her into the living area and sat in mismatched chairs. Mrs. Adamia bent to pull plates and glasses from the dresser which dominated the small space then straightened. 'Who was it?' she asked.

'His name is Alex Jibuti, a lawyer.'

'Why, what made him do such a—'

'He was powerful. He thought he was entitled, that he could take whatever he wanted, that Nino didn't matter and that no one would care.'

Mrs. Adamia nodded sadly then lifted a framed picture from the top of her dresser and handed it to Tamuna. 'My Nino,' she said.

'She's beautiful.'

'Yes. When's your baby due?'

Tamuna involuntarily moved her hands to her stomach. 'My baby? How did you know?'

Mrs. Adamia smiled, 'It's obvious—to me anyway. I wish Nino could have had children.'

'I'm so sorry… My baby's due in April.'

'You're blessed. Please keep her safe.'

'Thank you, I will.'

'Mrs. Adamia, there will be a lot of media interest in Jibuti's arrest,' Donadze said. 'You might hear some uncomfortable things said about Nino.'

'I don't care, they won't be true. I know who she was.'

'Yes, so do I.'

She turned to where Donadze sat and took his face in both her hands. 'You promised me you would find that man.'

'Yes.'

'And you did, thank you.' she said.

Levan Gloveli was snipping bunches of grapes from his vines as Donadze pulled up outside his house. He got out his car and walked through the garden. '*Gamarjoba*, Major,' he said. 'Good harvest?'

'Yes, should get about three hundred litres this year.'

'Well, save a bottle for me.'

'Of course. Let's go in. Do me a favour and carry that for me,' Gloveli said, pointing to a straw basket which had been overfilled with bunches of cut grapes.

Gloveli led the way inside, walking quite stiffly, Donadze thought. 'How are you feeling, Major?'

'Never better, take a seat,' he said as he set about opening a plastic bottle of white wine and putting plates of cold food on the table. He poured the wine into two glass tumblers, held one to the light then sniffed it. '*Gaumarjos*,' he said, taking a deep drink.

'*Gaumarjos.*' Donadze held up his glass in salute and took a sip. The wine was cool and pleasant.

'You must be happy with how your investigation turned out,' Gloveli said.

'Yes, thanks again for your help.'

'It keeps my brain active... But this isn't a social call is it?'

'There's certainly nothing wrong with your brain, Major... And no, it's not social. I wanted to discuss something with you.'

Gloveli reached for the bottle and refilled both glasses. 'Something about the investigation bothering you?'

Donadze put bread and cheese on his plate while he considered his response. 'We talk about the law and about justice—but what do they really mean?'

Gloveli fixed Donadze with a puzzled look. 'You're here for a philosophical discussion about law and justice?' Donadze didn't respond and Gloveli continued. 'Justice isn't the same as the law. The law's a set of rules, justice is a bit more abstract, a bit more subjective. Why do you ask?'

'Robert Morton. He's as corrupt as Toreli. He used his position to try to stop United Energy investing in Georgia. And it almost worked. Toreli's been held to account but Morton's not to be touched because we need his company's pipeline.'

'Yes, but you have to accept reality. You can't bring charges against Morton if it's not supported by the Prosecutor's Office.'

'So, we only apply the law when it suits us?

'Come on, Donadze, you know better than that—you

know how these things work.'

'I certainly do know how these things work, we have to see the big picture, isn't that right? So how about Nino Adamia—did she get justice?'

'You have Jibuti. Kaldani's dead. What's missing?'

'How about all the men who exploited her. How have they been punished?'

'She was a prostitute, lots of men exploited her, but buying sex isn't illegal in this country.'

'That's the law, I asked you about justice.'

'What are you talking about? You're a *law* officer, not a vigilante. You uphold the *law*, that's your job.'

Donadze shook his head slightly and took a sip from his glass.

'What's really bothering you, Ramaz?' Gloveli asked.

'I've just visited Nino's mother—told her we'd caught Jibuti. She was pleased of course, grateful that I'd kept my promise. But Jibuti's only part of the picture. What about Morton? He accepted her as a gift from Kaldani—treated her like a commodity to be traded.'

'Let it go, Ramaz. You're fixated with Morton. He isn't being charged and there's nothing you can do about it.'

'There are other ways he could be punished.'

'What are you saying, Donadze?'

'Licheli told me that Kaldani used to expose a few of his blackmail targets to keep the rest in line. What if Morton was exposed in that way?'

'You'd release the video! No, don't do it! Be satisfied that at least Jibuti's going to jail. Morton isn't important. Make that video public and you'll lose your job, possibly be on a charge yourself. Think of yourself. Think of Tamuna and the baby. I'm telling you as strongly as I can—let it go.'

'Would you have let it go, Major?'

Gloveli took a quick sip from his glass before replying. 'Yes, of course I would.'

Donadze smiled and raised his glass. '*Gaumarjos,*' he said. He sipped the wine and returned the glass to the table. 'I'd better get back to the city. Thank you, Major,' he said, standing to leave.

Donadze left Shindisi and returned to his apartment. It was late in the evening and it felt a little cool on his balcony as a light breeze whispered a promise of rain to come. He cradled his mug of hot tea in both hands and held it below his chin, the steam rising and condensing warmly on his face. He felt at peace.

Gloveli was right of course, the investigation was over, and he needed to concentrate on his personal life. He felt a pulse of excitement when he remembered that he would become a father in April. He was glad that he had taken Tamuna to Rustavi and thought that she understood his work better now, why it had been so important to him. But he had also promised her that he would resign when the investigation was over, and he intended keeping that promise. They were going out for dinner the following evening, her friend Lela sitting in with his mother. He was sure she knew that he would propose during the meal and he believed that she would accept this time.

He thought about his conversation with Gloveli and felt guilty about alarming the old man. He would call him tomorrow and put his mind at ease. Morton really wasn't important.

The breeze blowing across Donadze's balcony had freshened. He stood, pushed his chair under cover against the coming rain, stepped through the balcony's sliding door to the living area and turned on the television.

TV1 was broadcasting an earlier news conference. There had been wide coverage by the media and mild euphoria amongst politicians after United Energy had confirmed that it would route its pipeline through Georgia. Toreli's successor as Economy Minister was sharing a platform with Morton and both were fielding questions from reporters.

'As soon as I was appointed, I contacted United Energy's regional management and suggested that they reconsider their position,' the Minister was saying. 'Our discussions were frank and business-like and I'm very pleased with the outcome. This project secures Georgia's unique role in connecting East to West along a modern-day silk road. Marco Polo would be very happy,' he added to good natured laughter amongst the reporters.

A question was put to the Minister about his predecessor's involvement with a conspiracy to stop the project coming to Georgia.

'Well, these are matters of national security,' he replied, 'and I can't go into details at this stage. More information will be made available when corroborated but, suffice to say, it is clear that attempts were made by Russian agents to impede United Energy from investing in Georgia—but their efforts were thwarted, thankfully.'

Morton had been sitting looking relaxed and smiling thoughtfully as he listened to the questions and answers being translated into his earpiece.

A reporter stood, identified himself and said, 'Mr. Morton, there has been speculation that your company is transferring you back to the United States because you had threatened to resign if this pipeline project didn't come to Georgia.'

Morton turned his smile to full. 'Well, it's no secret that my wife, Erin, and I have come to love this country and we will both be extremely sad to leave. But, as for the reason for my transfer, let's just say that I was fully involved in the decision-making process and that has resulted in a great outcome for both Georgia and United Energy—and that's all that matters to me.'

'But wasn't this all an unnecessary and confusing waste of time and energy?' the reporter persisted.

Morton graced the room with a benign smile as he appeared to consider his response. 'Well, possibly but, as I said, we've had a great outcome and really, there's been no harm done.'

Donadze grabbed the remote control, used it to stab the television off then threw it across the room where it burst against the wall, its batteries springing from their compartment. He continued staring at the blank television for a moment, then stood and crossed to the breakfast bar where his laptop was charging. He started it and opened the search engine. It took a few minutes to find the site he was looking for. He typed in some text then crossed the room and opened a drawer, retrieving a USB flash drive. He put the drive in a USB slot and browsed its location on his laptop. He identified the relevant file, paused, and looked at the screen, his finger hovering over the mouse. *No harm done?* he thought as he clicked to begin the upload.

Donadze was unenthusiastically eating breakfast and flicking between news channels when his phone buzzed the expected text from Colonel Meskhi, '*Come see me at HQ*' A second text buzzed almost immediately, '*Now*'

He took a last mouthful of coffee and left his apartment. He was in no rush to meet Meskhi and drove carefully through the heavy traffic, strictly maintaining speed limits and slowing more than was necessary when cars in front cut in.

The video upload had reached national and international news. Television reports had not broadcast the graphic content but Donadze knew it was available to anyone with Internet access—now and forever.

Footage from the previous day's media conference had been re-run with Morton's slick replies to the questions put by reporters now considered to be deceitful and absurd. News crews were camped outside his apartment block, elevator access to his penthouse being denied by company security guards. Donadze had flinched when video was broadcast of Erin Morton carrying a small bag and forcing her way through the media scrum to a waiting car, grim faced and refusing to answer all questions.

Television analysis concluded that there had indeed been a Russian inspired plot to stop United Energy's pipeline being routed through Georgia and that Morton, as well as Toreli, had been blackmailed to influence that decision. The commentary which followed indignantly stressed Morton's eagerness to accept the services of a prostitute provided by Dato Kaldani, a known criminal.

There had been no comment from United Energy or the government. A Russian spokesman had laughed and said the notion of his country's involvement in such a conspiracy was far-fetched and ridiculous. Speculation as to who had posted the video online was rife.

Donadze parked outside Ministry of Internal Affairs' HQ and walked to Meskhi's office. The door was closed, and he knocked once then entered. Meskhi was sitting behind his two monitors, touch typing at speed. He paused and looked up. 'Take a seat, Lieutenant' he said, indicating the small conference table in the corner of his office.

Donadze crossed the office and sat straight-backed on one of the chairs. Meskhi finished typing, then joined him, sitting at the opposite side of the table. He leaned back in his chair and looked at Donadze closely. 'You look tired, Lieutenant. Didn't you sleep well?'

'Quite well, sir,'

'And your mother?'

'Making a good recovery, thank you for asking.'

'Do you know why I instructed you to come here?'

'I think so, sir.'

Meskhi leaned forward and stared at Donadze for a long

moment. 'We have some items to discuss,' he said, briskly.

'Sir?'

'Let's start with personnel.'

'Yes, of course.'

'I'm appointing Bukia's replacement, Lieutenant Bagrat Nakani, do you know him?'

'Yes, we were at Police Academy together.'

'This appointment will be a promotion for him.'

'I'm sure it's well deserved.'

'It is. I've also been impressed with Sergeant Arziani and think he deserves promotion—do you agree?'

'Definitely, sir.'

'And Detective Chichua. I intend putting a commendation in his file for his contribution during the Chechens' arrest.'

'Good, he'll appreciate that.'

Meskhi paused. 'Anyone else deserving recognition?'

'I don't think so.'

'Neither do I.' Meskhi leaned back in his chair and cupped his chin in his hand.

Donadze shifted in his seat. 'Will that be all, sir?'

'The video of Morton and Adamia. If I were to ask if you knew who put it on the Internet.' He paused again. 'Would you tell me the truth?'

'Yes, sir.'

Meskhi stared at Donadze for a long moment. 'I thought so... But there's no way you could possibly know— so there's no point in me asking. I suspect we will never know for sure. Don't you agree?'

Donadze returned Meskhi's gaze before looking away.

'Completely, sir.'

'You have the makings of a good detective, Lieutenant. But you also have some significant flaws to overcome.' Meskhi paused, watching Donadze a moment longer. 'You're dismissed,' he said

'Yes, sir. Thank you, sir,' Donadze said, as he stood to leave.

End

ACKNOWLEDGMENTS

My gratitude goes to the following people for their generous and constructive support:

Jacqui Liddle, my wife, who read every scene I wrote, several times, who advised me when to pare back extraneous or confusing text and who guided me on the likely perspectives of my female characters.

My beta reviewers: *Annette Rose, Fiona Macdonald, Mary Puttock, John Woodley, Kate Langley, Neil Aitkenhead, Alex Baldwin* (not the actor), *Douglas King*, my daughter, *Kirsty McMillan* and my mother, *May Liddle*—a very decent writer herself. All keen readers, their feedback was of an incredibly high standard.

I was especially grateful to receive encouragement and expert advice from author, *G.R. Halliday*. Gareth's support was particularly generous as he was preparing his second DI Monica Kennedy novel for publication at the same time.

Special thanks to my Georgian friends, *Sandro Chitadze*

and *Doctor Sasha Antelava*. In addition to reviewing my draft manuscript (no mean feat when English is your third language), Sasha provided expert medical advice and Sandro advised on security, crime and police matters, all within a Georgian context. Both also offered invaluable insights on aspects of Georgian culture which helped to ensure the novel's authenticity and, hopefully, enhance the reading experience.

ABOUT THE AUTHOR

Alistair Liddle is a former ships' captain, business advisor and operations manager in the oil and gas industry. No Harm Done, featuring Lieutenant Ramaz Donadze, is his debut novel. Alistair is married with two grown children and a granddaughter. His interests, when not writing, include travel, walking, cooking, self-defence and playing guitar badly with the not-so supergroup, The Grumps. After a lifetime of travel, Alistair has settled in Stirling, Scotland.

ajliddlebooks.com

AUTHOR'S NOTE

I was privileged to have worked and lived in the Republic of Georgia for fifteen years. The county has a unique culture which I attempted to describe faithfully in this novel. There are however a couple of deliberate inconsistencies which I included to make the story more understandable for non-Georgian readers e.g. it would be usual to address a man as Batono Ramaz rather than Mr. Donadze.

Georgia is a fascinating country with a proud and sometimes tragic history. The people are wonderful and you should visit when you can.

Printed in Great Britain
by Amazon

66594149R00203